Vengeance in Cedar Creek

Other books by Jim Willi:

The Frogman of Cedar Creek

Vanishing in Cedar Creek

The Firebug of Cedar Creek

VENGEANCE
in
CEDAR CREEK

Jim Willi

2023

Acknowledgements

This is the fourth book in the Cedar Creek Series. I'd only planned on publishing my first book—The Frogman Of Cedar Creek—but then Facebook came alive with my wonderful readers asking when the sequel was going to be published.

That interest in my first book, has resulted in me writing three more books in three years. I have had such a great time meeting the hundreds of people who bought my books at various book clubs, club meetings, and other events. I want to thank everyone who has supported my late-life writing career. I look forward to meeting more of you as I do signings for this book.

A big shout out to Sue and Dan Van Sistine. Their excellent editing skills, along with some great plot suggestions have improved my original drafts of my books.

I also want to thank the talented Vivian Freeman Chaffin who designed the cover for my last two books. Her expertise in formatting, editing, and publishing the book made it possible.

Happy reading!

One

THE RAPIDLY SETTING sun cast long shadows like fingers of darkness jutting out from the shoreline of Cedar Creek Lake. Twenty-year-old Cory Rhodes flipped his topwater lure toward the shade, knowing that it concealed a big largemouth bass. The lure plopped near the bank and splashed water as he reeled it back in, hoping to catch the attention of a monster fish.

He sat astride his Seadoo FishPro Scout, a specially outfitted personal watercraft for fisherman. It had a Garmin Echomap fish finder, and a special trolling mode, along with rod holders and a large cooler. Rhodes had purchased the $15,000 Seadoo three weeks ago. It was a hot night, so he shed his life preserver, draping it over the handlebars, despite floating in about fifteen feet of water.

Rhodes, concentrating on his casting, didn't notice the sun was almost out of sight on the opposite side of the lake, as the sky seemed like a painting of various shades of bright red. Within minutes the sun would disappear and so would the daylight. Seadoo's are not fitted with running lights and must be off the lake by dark.

At that moment, the young fisherman felt a huge tug on his lure, and a magnificent largemouth bass leaped two feet out of the water. Rhodes battled the monster for ten minutes before he landed him. By now, darkness enveloped the lake, and Rhodes knew he had to quickly head to his dock, about ten minutes away around the next bend in the lake. He didn't want a $300 fine for breaking the state law.

As Rhodes proudly put his fish in the cooler, he didn't notice the small water bubbles popping on the surface a few feet away. Suddenly, there was a big splash as a SCUBA diver erupted out of the water and grabbed the young man. Rhodes was too stunned to immediately fight back, as he felt steely arms envelop his body and drag him under the murky water. He thrashed his feet but was quickly immobilized as the diver in black wrapped their own legs around him. Rhodes felt like he was encased in cement. The air whooshed out of him, his lungs filled with water as he gasped for a breath, and his body went limp.

The mysterious assassin pulled the young man back onto the Seadoo, started it up, and slowly headed out to the deepest part of Cedar Creek Lake. When the fish finder showed the water was fifty-eight feet deep, the diver dumped the body and drove another mile away before abandoning the Seadoo and silently swimming the three hundred yards to shore underwater and unseen.

⁂

Fifteen miles away, festive red, white, and blue balloons and patriotic bunting decorated a large meeting room at Beacon Hill on Cedar Creek Lake. The master-planned community is just off Highway 175 on the northwest end of the lake. The 140-acre gated enclave is in a beautiful, wooded setting with a big, protected marina, nature trails and other amenities. It was election night in East Texas.

The party was being held for Henderson County Sheriff's candidate Crystal Dinsmore-King. The vivacious wife of former sheriff Buddy King was well known around Cedar Creek Lake for her work with pet adoptions and owning a successful detective agency with her husband. King also gained notoriety some years ago when, with Buddy's help, she'd escaped an abduction. Then wrestled a knife away from her captor, plunging it into his neck and killing him.

Her victim was a serial killer, and former SEAL team member named Cody Martin, who drowned nine people, making their deaths seem accidental. The newspaper dubbed the killer, "The Frogman Of Cedar Creek."

Tonight, Dinsmore-King was running to become the first female sheriff in Henderson County. She was attempting to join a select group. There is currently only half a dozen female sheriffs in the entire state of Texas. The first elected female sheriff in Texas was Edna Reed Clayton in1945. Policing is still a man's world here in Texas.

The special elite law enforcement unit, the Texas Rangers was born in 1823. The first female Ranger joined the force in 1993, 170 years after the unit organized. Today ninety-five percent of all licensed police officers in the state of Texas are men.

Crystal had the endorsement of outgoing sheriff, and valued friend, Billy Richardson, who was retiring after two terms. Richardson had succeeded popular sheriff Buddy King. Crystal's husband had worked hard to get her elected using his contacts and tirelessly hitting the campaign trail.

But she faced an uphill battle. Women enthusiastically supported her, but most men seemed against a woman being elected Henderson County's top cop. Her opponent was a popular deputy in the sheriff's department and the community. Sergeant Lonny Shields was a gregarious guy who was ready to retire after twenty-eight years in the Henderson County Sheriff's Department. He was well known and well liked. Shields seemed to know everyone.

The longtime sergeant was one of the founders of the Cedar Creek Lake Parrot Head Club. The non-profit was formed in 2000 when the founders attended a Jimmy Buffet event and were inspired to bring good into the world. Their main fundraiser is the annual Poker Run which raises tens of thousands of dollars each year. Parrot Head's motor around the lake in their boats collecting poker cards for prizes at various locations.

At Beacon Hill, a crowd of several hundred enjoyed snacks and drinks as they awaited the first returns of the night. Crystal worked the room, trying to quell her nervousness by talking to friends and supporters.

✿

Some thirty miles away in Tool, Martha Rhodes kept looking out of the window of her small home. It had been dark for over two hours, but her son Cory still had not returned from his fishing trip on Cedar Creek Lake. This was most unusual for him. Even on nights when he would join friends in the evening, Cory always backed his precious Seadoo under a tin-covered shed first to protect it from the elements. Martha sat back down in her well-worn rocking chair, and returned to the sweater she was knitting, trying to keep her nerves in check.

Martha had sent a text and left a voicemail message for Cory to please call her. So far, those attempts had been met by silence. Martha concentrated on her knitting, trying to take her mind off her son. He was a reliable young man, so she knew he was okay.

✿

At Beacon Hill, Crystal King checked her Apple watch. It glowed 10:10. She was sure election returns would be coming in soon. Standing alone outside the meeting room, Crystal took a deep breath and tried to relax.

✿

In Tool, Martha Rhodes nervously paced back in forth in her tiny living room. It had been dark for hours, but she still hadn't heard from her son. She tried calling his phone five more times, but it kept going immediately to voicemail.

✿

The SCUBA diver swam to shore, stripped out of the wet suit, and used a hammer from a white Chevy Trailblazer to smash Cory Rhode's cellphone to little pieces. The pieces were scattered at the edge of the water. The mysterious figure took a notepad out of the vehicle's center console and checked off the first item on the list.

✿

Back at the Beacon Hill festivities, the crowd quieted down as the announcer on KCKL radio said they'd have Henderson County election results in about ten minutes. Buddy King gave his wife a big hug and a confident smile, although he was far from sure she'd win a tough race for sheriff.

Martha Rhodes dialed the Henderson County Sheriff's Department. In a shaky voice, she explained how her son didn't return from an early evening fishing trip, and how unusual it was for him not to check in with her if his plans changed. The dispatcher took down the information, and promised they'd send a boat out to look for him at sunup.

Two

A HUSH FELL over the crowd at Beacon Hill as the radio announcer said, "...and in the race for Henderson County Sheriff, we have an historic result, Crystal Dinsmore-King has won by over 300 votes to become the first female sheriff in county history." The crowd erupted in hoots and applause, the balloons were released and floated down adding to the suddenly festive scene. Buddy King gave his wife a big hug and kiss. Outgoing sheriff Billy Richardson lifted her off the ground and spun her around.

Crystal's phone rang. It was her opponent, Lonny Shields, offering his congratulations. The crowd began to shout, "Speech! Speech!"

King hopped up on the stage, and the crowd quieted down. She smiled as she took in the view of all her supporters. Crystal took a deep breath and began, "We did it!" Again, pandemonium reigned with applause, shouts and wolf whistles filling the room.

Crystal held up her hands to quiet the revelers, "I want to thank every one of you for making this a historic day in Henderson County. Hopefully, one day soon, a woman sheriff will be commonplace here. In the meantime, I promise to do my best to uphold the law and make this a safe place for all of us. That also means attacking our meth problem. It will be a priority."

Applause echoed throughout the large meeting room. Crystal

continued, "But tonight is a night to celebrate. You've all earned it. Thank you again. Now, let's party!" The band started playing and people hit the dance floor.

Henderson County's new sheriff began to work the room with hugs and handshakes all around. Soon she was face to face with newspaper reporter Dwayne Murphy. He offered his congratulations and asked her for a few quotes. Crystal obliged, and then asked her sometime antagonist how he was holding up

Sadly, like many small-town newspapers across America, the *Cedar Creek Gazette* had folded three months ago. Murphy, longtime reporter at the *Gazette*, had been willed the newspaper when the old owner died, but despite his best efforts, Murphy could not keep it afloat.

Murphy had taken a job with the *Athens Courier*. His beat was the Gun Barrel City and Cedar Creek Lake areas, so he basically was doing the same job without the headaches that came with also being the editor/owner. Murphy said, "Thanks for asking, Crystal. It still bothers me that I let the newspaper fail. But I'm enjoying having no other duties than reporting."

Crystal was interrupted by two of her largest donors, and the conversation with Murphy ended. She spent the next hour working the room while her proud husband watched from a distance. This was her night, and he was determined to let her enjoy the spotlight on her own.

The mood was gloomier at the small house in Tool, as Cory Rhode's mother tossed and turned, her mind filled with fear over her missing son. She prayed everything would turn out okay the next morning.

Three

AS THE SUN came up the next morning, so did a gusty wind from the west, churning the lake and causing large white caps to foam as the waves crested. The forecast called for winds of twenty-five to thirty miles as hour, with gusts as high as forty. Two sheriff's deputies parked at the boat ramp near Tool and shook their heads as they scanned the ocean-like waters of the lake. It was too dangerous to take the boat out today. The search would have to wait until tomorrow when the winds were forecast to calm down.

The deputies drove over to Martha Rhodes tidy little home in Tool. She ran out the front door to greet them, shouting, "Have you found him?" The deputies shook their heads, informing her that the dangerous winds would not allow them to search on the lake today. They did promise to do an extensive shoreline search, hoping the Seadoo had floated to a nearby dock.

The deputies didn't tell Mrs. Rhodes, but they were sure it would be a futile effort. The strong west winds most likely had blown the small watercraft back across the lake to the east side. But they headed out anyway, hoping for a break as they scoured the shoreline.

The Cedar Creek Reservoir is built on Cedar Creek, which flows into the Trinity River. The popular getaway is about an hour Southeast of Dallas alongside Highway 175. The lake is about eighteen-and-a-half miles long, and a little over two miles wide. It was built in the mid-1960s to send water all the way to Fort Worth.

The Cedar Creek area has experienced a big growth spurt, much of it driven by Covid, which caused many companies to allow employees to work from home. Folks figured if I'm going to work from home, why not have a place with a view of a tranquil lake. That doubled the home values for those lucky enough to have lakeside property around Cedar Creek Lake.

Deputies, and volunteers from the Coast Guard Auxiliary spent all day trudging along the shore on the west side of the lake. There was no sign of Cory Rhodes or his Seadoo. They decided to spend tomorrow on the east side of the lake, thinking those strong west winds had blown the watercraft across the water. The winds were also supposed to be light tomorrow, so boats could aid in the search.

While the search continued, Billy Richardson ate breakfast at Mc-Duff's restaurant in Seven Points with Crystal King. They discussed plans for the new sheriff's swearing-in ceremony and outlined plans for a smooth transition of office.

Despite becoming the first female sheriff in Henderson County, Crystal was not happy this morning. She'd campaigned on her experience in aiding law enforcement, and on plans to move the department solidly into the computer age. Crystal avoided any reference to being a woman. But since her historic election, it seemed that's all anyone wanted to talk about.

She took a swig of orange juice, staring off in the distance. Richardson asked, "Hey, what's the matter? You just won a big election and I get to retire!" But the outgoing sheriff's attempt at humor fell on deaf ears.

Crystal looked up, "It makes me angry, Billy. No one wants to talk about my ideas to make law enforcement even better. All they see is a blond with a badge." She let out a long sigh.

Crystal went on, "I mean everyone from CNN to MSNBC, the Dallas TV stations, the Tyler TV stations, the local newspapers and the *Dallas Morning News* all want to do interviews about the new woman sheriff."

Richardson couldn't help but give her a big grin, "Be happy. Hell, I was sheriff for six years, and most people had no idea who I was despite my stellar work and obvious superior crime-solving skills."

This time Crystal broke into a laugh, "Thanks," she said. "I needed that, Billy."

It was quiet at McDuff's this morning, as Melinda Sue had a rare day off. The wise-cracking waitress always worked hard to rile up Richardson, and his pal, Crystal's husband, Buddy King. King had been sheriff before talking his pal Richardson into taking over, and now the torch would be passed to Crystal

In a nice change of pace for Crystal and Billy, Shelly, Mc-Duff's gracious and kind owner, stopped by their booth to ensure they enjoyed the meal. They told her it was tasty as usual. Shelly congratulated Crystal on her election win, and Billy on his pending retirement.

Then Shelly said, "I've got a treat for y'all coming here soon." Billy and Crystal looked at her, as Shelly grinned wide and said, "Well, maybe not everybody will think she's a treat." Now, Shelly had their full attention. She went on, "I just hired Melinda Sue's cousin from Jackson, Mississippi, to waitress for us."

Crystal and Billy groaned as he said, "I hope you're going to tell me that she's quiet, doesn't have crazy-colored hair and lipstick, and is shy and reserved?"

Shelly burst out laughing, "Ah, not exactly. Instead, think of a younger, sassier, more outrageous Melinda Sue."

Billy just shook his head, "Uh oh. You're going to have to sell tickets here." Shelly moved to another table, still laughing to herself.

Four

IT WAS A MORE somber scene across the Highway 334 bridge from Seven Points. The Gun Barrel City Fire Department boat had joined in the search on the choppy waters of Cedar Creek Lake. As the rescue boat rounded a point on the lake, one of the firemen trained his binoculars on a dock about a quarter mile away. He shouted, "There is a Seadoo bobbing up and down under that dock in front of the white brick house." The boat sped to the dock, before slowing thirty yards away.

Sure enough, a battered Seadoo was stuck under the dock near the seawall. The fiberglass watercraft had been shredded by yesterday's rolling waves as they smashed it against the walkway on the dock. The firemen pulled alongside. The key was still hanging in place. There was no life jacket in sight. The seat had been torn up by the dock and waves with long gashes, allowing the insulation to come out. There was no sign of Cory Rhodes.

Sheriff Richardson was sopping up the last little river of gravy with one of McDuff's famous steaming biscuits, when his phone rang. Crystal watched as he shook his head and then said into the phone, "Okay, I'm on my way. I'll be there in a few minutes." Breakfast was over.

After visiting the scene, and helping the firemen secure the Seadoo, Sheriff Richardson headed to Martha Rhodes' house. He hated this part of the job, and hoped this would be the last time he had to tell a loved one terrible news before he retired. He parked his cruiser in the driveway and walked toward the house. Martha Rhodes nearly shot out of the front door when she spotted the sheriff.

Richardson saw the hopeful expression on her face, knowing he would soon shatter that façade. Martha Rhodes noticed his grim look. She stopped in her tracks, and tears filled her already blood-shot eyes. He grabbed her to stop her from collapsing to the ground and led her to a rocking chair on the tiny porch of her home.

Sheriff Richardson took her hand and gently explained they found the wrecked Seadoo on the east side of the lake, most likely driven that way by the high west winds yesterday. He tried to explain not finding her son didn't necessarily mean he had drowned. Richardson said he was still hopeful they'd find Cory some place safe.

Martha Rhodes raised her tearful eyes, and said, "Thanks for saying that, Sheriff, but we both know the odds are he drowned somehow." Then she added, "But he was such a strong swimmer."

Sheriff Richardson put out a short news release, explaining that Cory Rhodes was missing after disappearing while fishing from his personal watercraft. The story was carried on the third page of the *Athens Courier*, written by Dwayne Murphy. Each year close to three hundred people drown in lakes and rivers across Texas. A recent article put Cedar Creek Lake on a list of the seven most dangerous lakes in the state. The writer determined what makes the lake dangerous is that it can become blindingly dark at night, keeping boaters from seeing tree stumps and other submerged things like bridge pilings.

Five

A WEEK LATER, Crystal King was sworn in as sheriff in a small ceremony at the Henderson County Courthouse. Despite her protestations, the national TV and cable networks attended, along with local media from all over East Texas. The *Dallas Morning News* did a Sunday profile on King. Her first appearance in uniform would be at the Annual Fiddle Fest in Athens over the upcoming Memorial Day Weekend

A gorgeous, cloud-free Saturday morning, led to an unseasonably warm afternoon on Memorial Day Weekend. The TV weather folks said the thermometer could nudge its way to near one hundred today. That didn't deter the hundreds of fans of the Athens Fiddle Fest from gathering in lawn chairs under the shade trees on Courthouse Square. This was always a big way to kick off the summer season around Cedar Creek Lake.

After a day of fancy fiddlin', too much food and drink, and an overabundance of sun, the younger couples, children in tow, left for home. As the brutal sun disappeared over the horizon, a country band set up their gear for the street dance to end the weekend festivities in Athens.

The crowd flocked to the closed-off street between the courthouse, and the First Texas Bank. Adult beverages were consumed, the music was loud, and the dancing was Texas style. It was a great party with lots of old friends getting together, and new friendships being made. Little did the revelers know that death was stalking one of them.

***

Nineteen-year-old Luna Ortiz and her family ran one of the most popular food trucks in East Texas. The neon orange and green paint stood out and their homemade Mexican food was mouth-wateringly delicious. The Ortiz Family food truck had done a booming business all day, and into the evening hours. Even as the crowd died down, there was a line at the Ortiz' truck.

Luna Ortiz had beautiful olive skin, long black hair, and a lovely figure. She was quite the party girl, and a big hit at gatherings around the lake. Ortiz had a long list of boyfriends, with most of her romantic escapades lasting less than a month before she moved on to the next.

Her promiscuousness had driven her strict, Catholic father crazy since Luna was a teenager. Back in the old days they'd have called her "boy crazy." These days they called it "sleeping around." Luna's gorgeous eyes always grabbed handsome guys' attention, including today during the Fiddle Fest.

Luna's father noticed his daughter spending time talking to a good-looking guy during the event. He noticed the dude disappearing with his daughter as the night wound down. He called her name and came around the corner of the food truck just as they finished a long, lingering kiss.

***

No one noticed the person standing off to the side of the brightly colored food truck, in the shadows. A closer look would have revealed an angry face, with cold, steely eyes wearing denim jeans, and a tight black t-shirt devoid of logos. The shadowy figure had an impressive set of guns, their biceps bulging out of the t-shirt.

***

People in line shouted out their orders and left with steaming hot plates of tacos and enchiladas. The lovely aroma of grilled onions and peppers filled the night air. Inside the stuffy food truck, Luna's parents quickly and expertly filled the orders. Luna's father handed her a blue five-gallon pail and told her to head to the ice truck for a refill.

Luna grabbed the pail and quickly headed down the street. She was in a hurry and distracted as she talked to the young man and failed to notice the figure walking behind her in the shadows under the downtown streetlights.

Luna arrived at Billy's Ice Service truck and handed him the pail. He expertly scooped the pail into a big freezer filled with frozen water in the form of long ice cubes. The guy she'd been talking to headed for his car, promising to meet Luna at the Athens Park in an hour.

Billy hefted the heavy pail to the ground, as Luna handed him $10 for the ice. Luna grunted as she grabbed the plastic handles on the pail and headed back toward the food truck. Concentrating on the heavy pail, the young woman still did not notice the person following a few steps behind her.

Luna was a half-block from the food truck, as she stepped over a thick power cord supplying electricity to a carnival ride. The ride, filled with giggling children an hour ago, was now silent and shut down for the night. It was also in darkest part of the courthouse square.

The shadowy figure suddenly stepped out in front her, startling Luna as she gasped and dropped the five-gallon pail of ice. Cubes scattered in all directions. She felt a gun pushed forcibly into her side, as a voice said, "Shut up and say nothing or I'll blow you away right where you stand."

Luna's eyes were filled with terror as she pleaded, "Don't hurt me. I won't say a word. Just don't shoot me please."

Without a word, she was led away from the darkened ride, and down the street, away from the crowd of line dancers. Luna struggled against the powerful arm holding her but it was futile. She felt the gun dig deeper into her side as the killer said, "Knock it off or you will be shot dead right here, right now." The gunman's chilling actions and words nearly paralyzed her in fear. They stopped at a black Cadillac. It was Van Cleave's old Cadillac that had been left in the garage at the funeral home. Luna was told to get into the trunk.

Luna hesitated, quickly calculating her chances to run away, but the attacker's grip was far too strong, and the large gun jabbed hard in her side. Reluctantly, the young woman laid down on what appeared to be a thick piece of plastic, and then felt a syringe plunge into her arm. Within seconds the liquid worked its way into her veins, and she stopped breathing.

Six

LUNA'S DAD, JOSÉ, glanced at his watch for the third time in the last couple of minutes. He was a real taskmaster, believed in hard work, and had a short temper when it came to Luna and her work ethic. He was always pushing her to work harder and faster. And now she'd been gone for nearly a half hour for what should have been a five-minute trip for ice.

José flipped the tortilla shells on the grill and glanced at his watch once again. He shouted to his wife, asking her if she knew where Luna was. She just shook her head. José's impatience with Luna seemed to get shorter every day.

An hour had passed since Luna went on the ice run. It was nearing midnight, and the band was playing their last tune. Everything was shutting down, as the crowd headed home. José turned off the grill and cleaned it. He was furious with Luna. This wasn't the first time she'd wandered off during an event. It never crossed his mind that someone would take her right in the middle of the square and snuff out her young life.

Soon the courthouse square was nearly deserted. The country band, and various food trucks were packing up. The bright lights of the vendors blinked off, as darkness descended on the square. José closed up his food truck, locked it, and set out in search of his wandering daughter.

Luna Ortiz had, on a number of occasions, met a handsome young man at the various festivals and disappeared for a day or two. She kept reminding her strict father that she was almost twenty years old and could look out for herself. Unfortunately, someone else had other ideas.

José walked the entire courthouse grounds. He stumbled onto the blue pail, but found no sign of his daughter. That's because Luna lay lifeless on a plastic sheet in the trunk of a black Cadillac. Her abductor had used a syringe with a combination of embalming fluid and morphine to quickly snuff out her life at the age of nineteen. Her assailant found the deadly chemicals left at the funeral home. The same combination Van Cleave had used on his victims.

As he glumly walked back to his food truck, José ran into Henderson County Sheriff's Sergeant Lonny Shields. The veteran lawman noticed the disturbed look on Ortiz' face and asked, "What's up, José?" Ortiz explained that his lovely daughter Luna went for a bucket of ice over an hour ago and did not return.

Shields looked at the distraught father, as he gently said, "Well, José, we both know this isn't the first time Luna has gone off with some young dude." Sergeant Shields had been on a number of searches for the young woman over the last couple years.

José glumly nodded, his eyes showing both concern and flashing anger at the same time, "I know, Lonny, but I worry every time it happens. All it takes is for her to meet one bad dude and she could lose her life."

Shields put his arm around Ortiz' shoulder, trying to comfort him. The sergeant said, "We've been through this before, José. Hopefully Luna will be home by the time you get there. Give me a call in the morning and give me an update." José promised he would as he climbed aboard his food truck and headed home after a long day and night.

But Luna wouldn't be coming home. She was already dead as the black Cadillac drove down a dusty, pot-filled dirt road along the east side of Cedar Creek Lake. As the dust settled, the black luxury

18

car pulled into the gravel driveway that led to an abandoned funeral home and crematorium. Tall weeds grew around the building. The lawn had not seen a mower in several years.

The killer pulled around to the rear of the building, and quickly removed the lifeless woman's body from the trunk, placed it on a plastic covered gurney, and wheeled it into the musty-smelling building.

As José Ortiz drove home to Payne Springs, he had no idea his only daughter's body was being turned into ashes. Ortiz got home, pulled off his cowboy boots and massaged his tired feet. He'd been standing behind the hot grill all day and his feet were on fire. He cracked open an ice-cold bottle of beer and took a long pull. The cool brew soothed his parched throat, as he put his feet up on the tattered ottoman.

Fifteen miles away in Kemp, The Rest In Peace Funeral Home had an eerie history. Six years ago, it was owned by a troubled loner named Thaddeus Van Cleave. Seeking revenge for his daughter who was killed by a drunk driver coming from the Malakoff Cornbread Festival he allegedly snatched young women from local celebrations, killing them with a mixture of morphine and embalming fluid. He'd then used the funeral home's crematorium to reduce the victims to ashes, which he would dump into Cedar Creek Lake, destroying any evidence of the murder.

Van Cleave was tried for murder. He was represented by Dallas hotshot defense attorney, Harold "Double Down" Haines and found not guilty. Following the contentious trial, Van Cleave had dinner with his attorney to celebrate the acquittal. The funeral home director was never seen again after returning home from dinner. He was never reported missing, apparently had no relatives who cared about him and the funeral home was left vacant all this time. Since no one reported him missing, there never was an investigation by local police. Most everyone felt he had left quickly in shame, as his funeral home was suddenly out of business.

19

If police had looked into Van Cleave's disappearance, it might have led them to Mabank rancher Shane Malaby. Malaby's daughter was the Mabank Rodeo Queen when she vanished. Van Cleave was charged with murdering her, and two other women after their DNA was found in the crematorium. It's believed that Van Cleave killed seven women before being arrested.

Unknown to anyone except Van Cleave, Malaby was waiting in the dark inside the killer's home. He held a gun on Van Cleave, gave him a shot of the morphine and embalming fluid mixture, and then turned his body into ashes using the crematorium. The next morning, Van Cleave's ashes were dumped into Cedar Creek Lake.

Since then, Malaby was seldom seen around town. He became a recluse, spending all his time on his sprawling ranch and avoiding most everyone. His wife never recovered from the death of her young daughter and became hooked on alcohol and pain pills. She spent her days sitting in a chair in the ranch home, basically staring into space. She hardly spoke to her husband.

Now, a new serial killer had arrived in town, determined to get vengeance for the death of the man they called the Frogman Of Cedar Creek while baffling the authorities by sending people to their death either from drowning (as the Frogman had used to kill ten people) or by using the crematorium after making young women disappear as Van Cleave had done.

The two-pronged murder scheme would eventually become something local police would have to investigate. It would scare local lake residents, and most importantly draw out new sheriff Crystal King, the real target of the serial killer.

⁂

Henderson County Sheriff's Sergeant Lonny Shields' phone rang the next morning as he patrolled along Highway 198 near Payne Springs. It was José Ortiz whose voice shook as he said, "Lonny, there still is no sign of Luna. I've called her phone six times, and it always goes to voicemail. She isn't answering texts either."

Lonny, who could recall four or five times the promiscuous

daughter had shacked up with a young man really didn't want to go through all the paperwork to report her missing, figuring it was a waste of time. He said, "José, it's only been one day. We can't file a missing person's report until she's gone forty-eight hours. I'm thinking by then she'll be back home from this little escapade."

Her father didn't share the sergeant's feeling. "Lonny, I hope you're right but this feels different. I mean she just vanished after getting the bucket of ice. That's not like her."

Lonny, in a soothing voice told the distraught father, "It'll be okay, José. Give me a call tomorrow, if she isn't back home." He hung up.

Seven

IN ATHENS, NEWLY elected sheriff Crystal King was settling into her new office. She hung a few pictures on the wall and set up her prized Breville the Barista Express espresso machine. The nearly $400 device allowed Crystal to make her own espresso each morning. It was an expensive machine but allowed the sheriff to indulge in the guilty pleasure to start each day.

There was a knock on the door. It was Henderson County Fire Marshal Fate Hamilton. He stuck his head into Crystal's office. "Hey, Sheriff, how's your new digs?"

Crystal gave her friend a hug, "Thanks for stopping by, Fate. I'm getting things organized."

Fate replied, "I'm really proud of you, Crystal. Everyone said there's no way we'd elect a woman sheriff. Welcome to the Brave New World."

Crystal smiled, "Yeah, pretty amazing, right?" Then she turned serious, "Fate, how's the rebuilding of your house coming along?" The fire marshal's brother had turned into a serial arsonist that the media dubbed "The Firebug Of Cedar Creek." His hatred of his more popular brother had driven him to torch a number of homes and businesses. One of the fires resulted in the death of a fireworks stand operator in Log Cabin.

He used Molotov cocktails to set his brother Fate's home on fire, before swallowing a cyanide pill and taking his own life, while handcuffed in a police cruiser after being caught in the act by his retired fire chief father. Their father had been keeping an eye on Fate's house while he was on a European vacation. The father was shocked to see that his estranged son was the arsonist.

Fate replied, "It's a slow process, Crystal. At least the fire only damaged about a third of the house, and we didn't lose any valuables thanks to the quick work by firemen."

Crystal gave him a wry smile, "Well, I guess that's fortunate. I still can't believe your brother was the arsonist, especially coming from a family where his father was the fire chief in Rockwall, and his brother is the county fire marshal."

Fate sadly shrugged, "He obviously had some mental issues. I still can't believe someone who grew up in our loving family could turn into such a monster."

"There's been a definite pattern in the serial killers and your brother who have preyed on Cedar Creek Lake residents in recent years. Both the guy they called the 'Frogman' and the funeral home director plus your brother, all were out for revenge. All three were loners and tormented by some nasty demons."

Fate nodded in agreement. "Hopefully things will be quieter on your watch." Both Hamilton and the new sheriff had no idea a new, equally crazed serial killer had already taken the lives of two people, with much more mayhem planned.

A few minutes later, Sheriff King's phone rang. It was Dwayne Murphy calling from his new gig with the *Athens Courier*. Crystal answered, "Hey, Murph, what's going on?"

Murphy congratulated the new sheriff on her historic election, and then said, "Crystal, I'm calling about the guy who apparently drowned in Cedar Creek Lake. His name was Cory Rhodes, and I guess he disappeared while on one of those tricked out Seadoos used for fishing. I just need some info for the story I'm writing."

The sheriff replied, "Well, we don't know much more than that, Murph. We think he may have drowned while fishing, but so far, we have not found his body. We've been unable to drag the lake because we have no idea where he might have drowned."

Murphy said, "Yeah, that much I knew. His mother called me asking for help in finding her son, so we're putting a story together for the paper. Anything else you can tell me?"

Crystal sighed and said, "That's all we've got, Murphy." Murphy, thanked her for the information and the phone call ended.

A few minutes later, Sergeant Lonny Shields knocked on the sheriff's door, "Crystal, do you have a moment?"

Crystal pointed him to a chair at a side table and joined him, "What's up, Lonny?"

Shields told her about the missing young woman, Luna Ortiz. He ended by saying, "Sheriff, this is not the first time she's gone silent. She has a reputation for hooking up with guys for a few days and basically goes off the grid. I know her father, José, quite well and I've been basically putting off filing a missing person's report because of her past indiscretions. But it's been a couple days now and José just called me. He still hasn't heard from her, which is a bit unusual, even for her."

Crystal steepled her fingers in front of her, obviously weighing options in her head. She finally leaned forward and said, "Well, Lonny, technically it has been forty-eight hours now since she went missing, so we can fill out the paperwork. Let's do that, and send a message to all the deputies to keep an eye out for her."

Shields nodded, "Yes ma'am, will do." The sergeant rose from the table.

Crystal said, "Maybe you suggest to José that he put a "Life 360" app on her phone so he knows where the hell she is when she heads off on her adventures." Shields smiled and went on his way.

Eight

MEANWHILE THE SERIAL killer was going through a sweat-inducing workout, lifting weights and topping it off with a five-mile run. All the while, mulling options for the next victims. The Mabank Rodeo was coming up next week. The rodeo is where Van Cleave grabbed the rodeo queen and killed her. To follow his pattern, the serial killer needed to take a victim from the rodeo.

There was also the matter of drowning a second person to continue following in the deadly footsteps of the Frogman Of Cedar Creek. The top of the list was a young woman named Melody Highsmith. She lived on the lake and swam early every morning with hopes of making the U.S. Team for the next Olympics. While most competitors preferred to do laps in a pool, Highsmith liked to train in the sometimes-choppy water of the lake, making for a more difficult workout.

As the serial killer took a shower and gulped down a big glass of orange juice following the strenuous workout, Melody Highsmith was also winding down after a brisk swim in the lake. She, too, took a shower, and then created a specially-designed smoothie to give her protein, and help her recover from the workout.

Highsmith was about five-foot-seven with close cropped hair that fit snugly under her swimming cap. She was thin with well-defined muscles, the perfect build for a competitive swimmer. She had chiseled facial features, but no one would describe her as being attractive. Her face was plain, and despite the fact she was almost twenty-one years old, still suffered from acne that had plagued her for years.

She lived with her mother and father in their well-kept home in the Indian Harbor subdivision. Melody was a senior at Trinity Valley Community College in Athens, pursuing a degree in nursing.

Early the next morning, the serial killer sat in a car off to the side of the boat ramp in the Indian Harbor subdivision, peering through a powerful set of binoculars. The magnified image of Melody Highsmith climbed down the ladder on the dock of her parents' home and plunged into the lake. The sun was just peeking over the horizon, and the lake was unusually calm, almost like glass starting to shimmer in the growing light.

The killer watched as Highsmith, propelled by strong arm strokes, and a powerful kick, headed along the shoreline. She was wearing a powder blue swim cap, and a black Speedo swimsuit. The young woman seemed oblivious to the world around her, concentrating on her rhythmic strokes, head turning from side to side to grab breaths along the way.

The killer used the binoculars to scan the lake homes nearby. It appeared that every place was vacant on this Tuesday morning. Most every home must be owned by weekenders—the ones who live in bustling Dallas during the week, before retreating to their escape homes each Friday afternoon and head back to the city on Sunday night.

Once again expertly using the binoculars, the killer watched as Highsmith churned her way along the vacant docks filled with various water toys. The seventh dock from Highsmith's seemed to be the ideal place to lie in wait for her to swim by. Satisfied, the killer put the car in gear and left the boat ramp area.

Highsmith did a U-turn and headed back toward her house, finishing with a flourish. The young swimmer climbed up the ladder and toweled off, resting on a metal bench bolted to the dock. The bolts prevented it from being dislodged during the sometimes-powerful storms that cross Cedar Creek Lake.

After a few minutes to catch her breath, Highsmith headed into the house. Her mother was off today and had prepared a hearty breakfast of pancakes with plenty of fruit. The swimmer was extra careful with her diet.

She gave her mother a hug and a hearty "good morning" as she sat at the kitchen table. Her mother put a plate of pancakes with sugar free syrup along with a banana, an orange and a bunch of blackberries in front of her. Highsmith eagerly dug into the food, which was also accompanied by a special high-protein smoothie.

Her mother joined her at the table, and said, "How was the workout, honey?"

Melody said, "It was awesome, nice calm day so I could work on some new strokes and kicks. You know the first qualifying meet for the Olympics is just a month away."

Her mother gave her another hug, "And I know you'll be ready to make the team, honey. It's very exciting." Unfortunately, neither of them could know that a date with a serial killer would snuff out her life before that very important competition that she'd been working toward for three years.

Nine

AS NIGHTFALL DESCENDED on Cedar Creek Lake, the sun disappeared into the horizon along the west shore sending shards of red, purple and blue light into the partly cloudy sky. In the abandoned funeral home, the serial killer prepared to cremate the body of Luna Ortiz. As crickets chirped and the moon was obscured by thickening clouds, the crematorium was fired up, just as the old grandfather clock bonged a dozen times with the sound reverberating through the old home connected to the crematorium.

The killer wheeled the lifeless body of Luna Ortiz from the cooler to the Crematorium Room. Once inside, the casket was positioned next to the heavy door of the cremator, the steel door was opened, and the casket was quickly slid inside. It has to be inserted as rapidly as possible to avoid heat loss. The eighteen-hundred-degree flames would consume the wooden casket and body in about ninety minutes. During the cremation process the majority of the body, especially the organs and other soft tissues are vaporized and oxidized by the intense heat. Gases are released and discharged through the exhaust system.

When the incineration is complete, the dry bone fragments are swept into a machine called a cremulator and pulverized, processing them into ashes. This leaves the bone with a fine sand like texture and color. The average weight of the ash remains is about five pounds.

In the darkness outside the crematorium, a small puff of smoke exits a pipe in the roof. It was all but undetectable in the darkness of night unless you were standing right next to the pipe. When the process was completed, the cremains of Luna Ortiz were placed in a nondescript urn and set on a shelf filled with another dozen or so urns. Satisfied the process was complete, the serial killer headed home, climbed into bed just before 1 a.m. and slept like a baby.

The next morning in Athens, reporter Dwayne Murphy finished his article about the missing fisherman and submitted it to his editor. It had been a difficult transition for Murphy from the free rein of running his own newspaper, to once again having a boss. But he was grateful that the *Athens Courier* had acknowledged his expertise and numerous contacts to pay him above what most reporters receive at a small twice-weekly newspaper in East Texas.

As Murphy returned to his desk, his phone rang. On the other end of the line was a very distraught José Ortiz. The two men knew each other from meeting at various festivals and events around Cedar Creek Lake. Murphy couldn't get enough of José's tacos with his special, homemade hot sauce.

Murphy said, "Hello, José. How ya been?" Ortiz, usually an affable man, was terse and his voice was shaking. He explained to Murphy how his daughter hadn't been seen or heard from since the Athens Old Fiddler's Reunion six days ago. He felt the cops weren't doing much to attempt to locate her, since she had a bit of a reputation of disappearing for days with a new man. They just assumed she was off on another of her secret adventures.

Murphy had received dozens of similar calls during his reporting days, and he was well aware of José's daughter's reputation. Despite that, he tried to be sympathetic, "I'm sorry to hear that, José. Tell me exactly what happened."

José explained how Luna had gone to get a bucket of ice, and

29

never returned. Murphy said, "Did you see her getting cozy with anybody before that?"

The father said, "Well, there was this young stud who spent a lot of time talking to her at the food truck, and I did see them sneaking a kiss behind the truck."

Murphy thought to himself, *that sounds like her*, but instead he said aloud, "What did he look like, José?"

After a pause, José said, "Close to six feet, long brown hair, kinda stringy, strong build, and a white guy with a good tan. He had a close-cropped beard, and was wearing a blue T-shirt, very tight with no logo, and jean shorts." Murphy was impressed with how specific José's description was.

Murphy said, "That's a very clear description, José. Tell ya what, let's give it another couple of days, we don't publish until the weekend. If you still haven't heard from Luna, I'll see if my editor will let me write a story for the paper. It might help find her." José, obviously hoping for instant help reluctantly agreed to the idea, thanked Murphy and hung up.

After Murphy cradled the phone, he sat gazing out the window of the newspaper building. As usual his overactive brain was already churning with conspiracy ideas. *Right now, we have a missing fisherman, with all indications pointing to a drowning, and a missing, admittedly promiscuous, woman from the Athens fiddle event. Could they be connected?* After pondering for a few minutes, he heard his editor call his name, and moved on to his next project.

The serial killer had risen hours earlier and trailered a twenty-four-foot pontoon boat to the Big Chief boat launch in Gun Barrel City. The boat headed out onto Cedar Creek Lake just as the sun was beginning to come to life as a warm glow on the horizon. Big grey clouds were blowing past high above the lake, with a slight chop on the water.

The boat passed a couple of early rising fisherman on its journey toward the home many lake residents referred to as "The Lighthouse." It was actually designed to be a replica of a real lighthouse. The pontoon boat stopped about two hundred yards out from the

30

lighthouse in about twenty-five feet of murky lake water. The killer checked the surroundings. Not a boat in sight along this section of the lake so early in the morning.

The urn was opened, and grey ashes poured into the lake and disappeared. That was the last anyone would see of Luna Ortiz. The killer returned to the boat ramp, trailered the boat and headed to a peaceful breakfast.

About fifteen miles away, the Mabank Rodeo committee was also at a breakfast meeting. The potential rodeo queens had been selected, and their photos were being taken for the local newspapers. The young women excitedly posed for the snapshots in their finest western wear. They had no idea a serial killer planned to end one of their lives in a little over a week.

Meanwhile, the serial killer sipped on an herbal smoothie while pondering just how to snatch a member of the Mabank Rodeo queen candidates. It would be a tricky job because of the thousands of people crammed into a small, mostly well-lit venue. Van Cleave kidnapped the rodeo queen, mainly because he got lucky and found her under a dimly lit area near the livestock corral after a sneaky rendezvous with her boyfriend.

The killer considered someone else, other than a member of the rodeo queen's court. It would be easy to grab a young woman from the crowded concession area, by sticking a gun in her ribs and quietly ordering her to shut up and walk. No one would notice.

But that idea was quickly rejected by the serial killer's sick mind. The mission was two-fold to scare the residents and kill that woman sheriff. As Van Cleave had experienced, grabbing the most high-profile person there would cause a much bigger splash.

Ten

DAWN BROKE UNDER cloudless blue skies that promised a sunny and warm day in East Texas. The TV weather guy said it would be in the low nineties. Sheriff King was up early to run a few miles with her husband, Buddy. It was a beautiful morning, birds chirping, squirrels scurrying all around, accented with the occasional roar of a boat motor.

Crystal took a quick shower and hurried out the door. She had an 8 a.m. breakfast meeting with the Seven Points police chief, as she continued the style of her predecessor of keeping in close touch with other law enforcement in the county. It allowed them to discuss any issues or threats that may be coming their way.

Crystal walked into McDuff's Restaurant, waved at the owner, Shelly, and then spotted Seven Points Police Chief Calista Gomez. Like the new sheriff, she'd been in her new position only for a short time. Gomez was in her nineteenth year with the department and had slowly risen through the ranks.

She stood as King approached. They shook hands, and both slid into the plastic-covered booth seat. Before they even had a chance to settle in, Melinda Sue bounded their way, with another waitress in tow. Today, Melinda Sue's hair was deep purple, her lipstick was thick and bright red, and she was smacking her ever-present wad of gum.

The other waitress was barely five feet, she had a pretty face and was quite thin. Her hair was puffed up Texas-style, and was a slightly different shade of purple than her cousin's. She also sported iridescent red lipstick and was working a wad of gum hard. She was truly a mini-me of Melinda Sue.

The waitress said, "Hey y'all, this is my cousin Lucinda Sue. She's from Jackson, Mississippi."

Lucinda Sue said, "So happy to meet y'all. Now, what the hell ya want for breakfast? Time's a wastin'." Not only did she look, and sound just like Melinda Sue, but they shared the same rude qualities.

Crystal and Calista laughed out loud at the outburst. Crystal said, "Well, Melinda Sue, it appears you've taught her well."

Melinda Sue said, with a big grin, "Yup and now ya can count on both of us for great service."

Crystal couldn't help but ask, "Melinda Sue, have you introduced her to that reporter Murphy you spy for?"

The waitress' expression didn't change, as she turned to walk away, mumbling over her shoulder, "I ain't no spy, Sheriff." She stomped her way toward the kitchen after taking their order.

The sheriff and police chief got down to business. They talked about various open cases, the continuing drug problem with Meth, and other issues. Sheriff King said, "It's pretty quiet in Henderson County right now as far as ongoing concerns. A guy is still missing in Cedar Creek Lake, apparently drowned while fishing on a Seadoo, and a woman has been missing since the Athens Fiddler's Reunion."

Gomez asked for more information on the missing woman. Crystal explained how she had a rather troubling reputation of hooking up with guys she just met. The sheriff said, "She's done this quite a few times before."

Gomez said, "I know of her and I've met her father, José, a few times when I visited their food truck. They've got the best tacos on the lake."

The two women were wrapping up their conversation when a gum-chomping Lucinda Sue sauntered over, "Everything alright, ladies?"

Gomez said, "Excellent as usual, thanks for checking on us." Lucinda Sue slapped down their bill and waved as she hurried away.

As King paid the bill, Shelly asked what she thought of the new waitress. The sheriff grinned, "You've now got bonker twins on your hands, Shelly. Good luck!"

Thirty miles away at the *Athens Courier*, Dwayne Murphy's phone rang. He glanced at the caller ID. It was José Ortiz. It had now been six days since his daughter had vanished. Ortiz' voice sounded like any father who had no idea where their child had disappeared, although at age nineteen, Luna was hardly in that category. Murphy answered, "Hello, José. Anything new on Luna?"

José Ortiz' voice quivered as he said, "Nada. Her phone is still off. I haven't heard from her. She's never done something like this before."

Murphy replied, "Well, she has wandered off with guys before, José."

Ortiz' voice turned indignant, "Damn it, Murphy. She's not some whore, and she always lets me know where she is by now. I'm afraid something happened to her this time."

Murphy was apologetic, "I'm sorry, José. You're right. I promised you a story that she's missing, and I will go talk to my editor about it right now. He makes the final decision, but I'm sure I can convince him."

Ortiz let out a long sigh, "Thanks, Dwayne. Hopefully it'll make a difference." Murphy said he'd let him know the verdict on the article as soon as possible. They hung up.

Eleven

THE MID-AFTERNOON temperature reached ninety-six degrees, with light winds out of the south, under endless blue skies. When someone drowns and sinks underwater, the decay of flesh creates gases, mainly in the chest and gut, that eventually inflate a corpse like a balloon. It then floats to the surface, usually in three days or more, depending on the depth of the body and the water temperature.

Kyle, one of the many fishing guides on Cedar Creek Lake, was midway through a trip guiding a dad and his twelve-year-old son in search of the tasty crappie. They'd almost reached their limit of twenty-five fish each, as the boat slowed over a brush pile. The father said, "Kyle, you are the crappie guru. I've never caught so many in one trip and I've been with many guides on Cedar Creek over the years."

Kyle said, "Thanks man. Y'all are making it happen."

Just then, the youngster who was sitting on a chair at the bow, let out a yell, "Stop the boat. Stop the boat, right now."

Kyle killed the engine, "What's up?"

The kid pointed in the water about ten yards in front of them, "Is that a body?"

Kyle took a close look, "You're right." The fishing guide dropped his trolling motor into the water and slowly moved toward the floating mass in the murky lake.

He put the trolling motor in Spot Lock so it held them steady about five feet from the body. Kyle called the Henderson County Sheriff's Office. They arrived quickly in their boat and recovered the body. It was the missing fisherman, Cory Rhodes. They used a cellphone to inform the sheriff. They didn't use their two-way radio because too many ears were listening in.

Sheriff King hung up the phone and drove to the Rhodes' house. She informed Martha Rhodes that her son's body had been found in Cedar Creek Lake. King explained there would be a mandatory autopsy to determine if he indeed drowned or if there was foul play involved.

The next morning dawned dreary and rainy with a thick grey fog shrouding Cedar Creek Lake. Melody Highsmith walked out on the deck of her parents' lake home. It was difficult to see more than twenty or thirty yards in the thick fog. It was also a bit chilly. But she was super dedicated to maintaining her training regime for the Olympics, so she went back inside, and shrugged into a neoprene wet suit to help repel the cold during her two-mile swim.

The super athlete climbed down the dock ladder and slipped into the water. She would stay as close as possible to the dock along her path to avoid any boats roaring up on her without being able to see her in the thick pea soup fog.

With powerful strokes, Highsmith worked her way along the shoreline. At least the water was pretty calm this morning. As she approached the seventh dock from her home base, suddenly someone in a wet suit with a SCUBA tank grabbed her wrists and pulled her toward them with incredible strength.

After a quick, rather loud splash the attacker quickly pinned Highsmith's arms to her sides, and pulled her to the bottom of the lake, about seven feet below the waterline. As the young swimmer gasped for air, her assailant used strong leg kicks to carry her away from the docks into much deeper water.

Highsmith, eyes wide open in the murky water caught a

glimpse of her assaulter through the face mask for a brief instant before her lungs filled with water and another promising life ended. The SCUBA attacker continued using strong leg kicks to move farther and farther away from the shoreline. After about five minutes, they reached a depth of thirty feet. At this point Highsmith was released and her limp body settled on the sandy lake bottom.

Back on shore, ninety-one-year-old Charles Scott sat on a wooden rocking chair, wrapped in a blanket against the foggy, brisk morning. His face had that splotchy look that occurs as the lucky ones reach his age. His fingers were brown from holding three packs a day of unfiltered cigarettes for eight decades. His white hair was thinning and combed to one side in an attempt to cover a bald spot. He was a bit frail and used a walker to move through his home.

Scott's daughter had moved in with him several months ago when early onset Alzheimer's began to attack her father's mental capacity and memory. She fed and bathed him and took care of his every need. Suddenly, she heard him loudly calling her name.

She hurried out to the deck that had a wide clear view of the lake and anxiously asked, "Dad, what's wrong?"

Scott turned to her and slowly said, "I just saw the biggest fish ever splash in the water in front of the Peterson's dock."

His daughter smiled, "Really, how big was it, Daddy?"

The old man turned his light blue eyes toward her, peering through his thick glasses, "Big as a damn shark! That's how big."

He became a bit indignant, reacting to her smile, "It's true. I saw it. You don't believe me, do you?"

The daughter gave her father a big hug and a kiss on the cheek and said, "Of course, I believe you. I just wish I had seen it." She held his hand, silently praying her father's dementia wasn't getting worse.

❀

Back in Athens, Sheriff King had her assistant write a short news release about the discovery of Cory Rhodes body. It explained how he was fishing on his Seadoo when he disappeared, and the watercraft was found a few days ago, and the young man's body was found in the lake today by a fishing guide. The sheriff had no idea another drowning victim was laying on the lake bottom under a cloud of fog.

At Cedar Creek Lake, the SCUBA attacker swam a good mile underwater, before surfacing in a small cove that contained only a few homes. On this midweek day they all seemed to be deserted, probably all owned by weekenders. The attacker stripped off the SCUBA gear, secured it in the car trunk and drove away, satisfied the plan was moving forward.

Twelve

AT 5:15 THAT afternoon, Melody Highsmith's parents arrived home from work. Her mother was concerned because she had not heard from her daughter all day, which was most unusual. There were usually several texts but today she received none, and Melody hadn't replied to the texts her mother sent. She'd tried calling Melody's phone a few times too, but it kept going to voicemail.

Melody's mother, Alice, followed her husband into the house and threw her purse on a nearby table as she shouted Melody's name. Her voice echoed throughout the house with no response. Now she was worried. Alice rushed into Melody's bedroom.

It was there she found her iPhone, car keys and purse. She ran back into the living room, where she found her husband gazing out the window at the lake. The sun had broken through right after lunch, and the lake was placid with sparkles reflecting the bright sunshine on a now clear day.

Alice Highsmith was a realtor, one of the top producers in East Texas, dealing mainly in high-priced lake homes. Her husband, Terrence, owned a successful pawn shop. Alice was known for straight talk when dealing with clients, and she was a tough negotiator. But you'd never guess by looking at the short, petite woman with a friendly face, jeweled glasses, and a nice figure. Her husband was a burly guy. He played defensive line on a division three college football team. He was about thirty pounds overweight, had large biceps, and a rapidly receding hairline. Terence was much more laid back than his wife of twenty-six years.

Alice came up to him with a worried look on her face, "Terrence, her phone, car keys and purse are all upstairs. Her car is in the garage. But there is no sign of Melody, and I haven't heard from her all day."

Her husband replied, "Maybe she went somewhere with friends, and forgot her phone and purse?"

Alice gave him a sharp look, "Really? And when have you ever known that to happen?"

Melody's mother hurried out the patio door and headed to the dock, thinking maybe she decided to go for an afternoon training swim. She found a large fluffy beach towel on a bench on the dock, but no sign of Melody. Terrence followed her outside, and they both searched the lake with their eyes, hoping to see Melody swimming along the shoreline.

After a few minutes, Alice plopped down in a deck chair, her face was a pained mask of fear for her daughter. She said, "Oh my God, Terrence. You don't suppose something happened to her during the swim, do you?"

Melody's father was also becoming concerned, "I honestly have no idea, honey, and I'm not sure what we should do?"

Alice grabbed her phone and called the Henderson County Sheriff's Office. She described the situation to the dispatcher. The voice on the other end of the line was calm and terse, "Mrs. Highsmith maybe she just took off with friends. Since she's an adult, you really need to wait forty-eight hours before we can file a missing person's report."

Alice was indignant, "Please put me through to Sheriff King right now." The dispatcher explained that Mrs. King had left for the day and would be back in the office first thing tomorrow. The worried mother was getting more irritated, "Look, whatever your name is, Crystal and I are friends, so please give her this number to call right away."

The dispatcher said, "Yes ma'am, I'll give her the message but it's up to her whether she calls you back. I can't control that." Alice hung up the phone, swearing under her breath.

She instructed her husband to head to the neighbors to the left of their property, while she'd check with neighbors on their right. Terrence dutifully did what she asked. Alice walked along the shoreline. No one was home next-door, so she kept going. Few neighbors were home, since for most of them, their lake home was a weekend getaway.

The couple of neighbors she talked to said they had not seen Melody all day. Eventually she knocked on the door of Charles Scott's house. His daughter answered and Alice introduced herself. When asked if she'd seen Melody swimming past their place this morning. The daughter shook her head, "No, I've seen her swim by several times, she is really fast and strong."

Alice anxiously asked again, "But you didn't see her today, right?"

Scott's daughter shook her head, "No, I didn't. Sorry."

Alice persisted, "How about Charles, did he happen to see her, can we ask him?"

The daughter replied, "Unfortunately he is taking a nap right now. And you may be aware he is suffering from early dementia, so his recollections are not very reliable."

Alice gave her a sympathetic look, "I'd heard that. I'm so sorry. He has been a wonderful neighbor for years."

The daughter said, "Thanks. That's why I've moved in to help him out." She seemed to drift off in thought. Alice caught the look and was curious.

Alice asked, "Is there anything else?"

The daughter sighed, "Well, it's probably nothing, as I've said his mind is rapidly leaving him. It's a terrible disease. But he did call me out to the deck this morning, claiming he just saw a splash in the water that could only have been made by a huge fish, like a shark. Of course, there are no sharks in Cedar Creek Lake."

Alice replied, "That's odd. There have been rumors for years of

41

an alligator somewhere in the lake, but most everyone thinks it's a myth. Did you see it as well?"

The daughter said, "No. I hurried out to the deck but the water was calm, and it was extremely foggy as well. I saw no one or no huge fish splash the water. Unfortunately, I believe his mind was playing tricks on him again. It's so sad."

Alice needed to check with more neighbors. She thanked the daughter and moved on down the way. Just then her phone rang. It was Sheriff King. Alice answered, "Oh, Crystal, thanks so much for calling me back, and congratulations again on winning the election." Crystal thanked her, and then Alice filled her in on her concerns about the missing Melody.

Sheriff King said, "I understand what you're going through, Alice. But let's monitor the situation tonight. She may be home again very soon. If you don't hear from her by tomorrow morning. Give me a call and I'll have our deputies look into it."

Reluctantly, Alice said, "Okay, Crystal. I understand the rules. I'll let you know if I hear anything, and please call me if you find out something." The sheriff promised she would.

Thirteen

CRYSTAL MET HER private eye husband, Buddy, for an early dinner at the Hot Jalapeno restaurant in Gun Barrel City. They ordered margaritas and munched on chips and a very tasty salsa as their food was being prepped in the busy kitchen. It was only five o'clock, but the restaurant was pretty crowded for a weekday. The former sheriff and his wife sat in a brightly colored booth in a quiet corner.

Buddy was on an interesting case of potential theft by an employee at the biggest department store in Athens. Crystal listened to the story of his day, but her mind had obviously drifted off somewhere else. After a few minutes, Buddy noticed and asked her what was wrong.

The current sheriff said, "We just had a young man drown while fishing off his watercraft, and today I got a call from a friend saying her daughter apparently disappeared while going for her daily swim in the lake. You've heard of her, Melody Highsmith. She's training for the Olympic tryouts in a few weeks."

Buddy leaned forward, taking Crystal's hand, "Sure, I know the name. She seemingly has a great future ahead of her in international swimming competitions. What happened?"

Crystal sighed, "No idea. Her parents were at work, and they believe she did her daily two-mile swim, but they're afraid something happened to her. They returned from work and found her unused towel on the dock. Her phone, car keys, purse and vehicle are still at the house, but there's no sign of her."

Crystal dipped a tortilla chip in the salsa, and took a bite, "Her mother called me, very distraught. I told her we'd keep our eyes open, but would have to wait forty-eight hours before she could file an official Missing Person Report. Cedar Creek Lake averages about one drowning a year, and now there appears to be two in less than a month."

Buddy replied, "Ya know, honey, I was just reading an article that listed the seven most dangerous lakes in Texas. It surprised me." He pulled up the Google article on his iPhone. Buddy continued, "Cedar Creek made the list along with Lake Conroe, Lake Travis, Lake Lewisville, Canyon Lake, Joe Pool Lake, and Lake Livingston." Buddy read aloud, "One of the largest lakes in Texas, the 32,000-acre Cedar Creek reservoir is about an hour east of Dallas. What makes Cedar Creek so dangerous is that the lake can be blinding dark at night. The water becomes deceptively shallow and conceals hidden objects like tree stumps, causing deadly boating accidents."

Crystal said nothing as the waitress arrived with two steaming plates of tacos and chimichangas, with the obligatory side dishes of rice and beans. As the waitress walked away, Crystal said, "I understand all that, Buddy, but neither of these were boating accidents. I'm concerned to have two potential drowning deaths in such a short space of time, and I'm worried about Melody, she is an amazing young woman."

While the Kings were having dinner, the killer was slowly cruising around the grounds of the Andrew Gibbs Memorial Arena, site of the annual Mabank Rodeo.

Mabank's past is an interesting Texas tale. The area was originally settled by Lorenzo Stover in 1846. It was named Lawndale, after a popular cotton dress material sold in Stover's store. But in 1890, the Southern Pacific Railroad bypassed Lawndale by less than a mile. G.W. Mason and Thomas Eubank owned nearby acreage called the Mason-Eubank Ranch.

Like many others in the old West, they realized the potential benefit of having a railroad pass through your town, so they set aside a tract of land and named it Mabank (a combination of their last names). They were right. With the nearby railroad, and especially due to the fertile soil, great for growing the top cash crop at the time—cotton—Mabank, Texas, grew rapidly. Lawndale merchants angered by being bypassed by the railroad moved their businesses to Mabank as well. Mabank's population grew steadily and received a big boost in 1966 when the Cedar Creek Reservoir became a reality.

Today, Mabank's Annual Rodeo and Western Week is a fun, family affair. One lucky high school lady is crowned Rodeo Queen, with other contestants riding in her court. There is also a Bed Race through downtown that creates some hysterical moments. It is simply a great week of events for the entire family set in a small, safe town. The crowds are always large, especially for the rodeo shows at the Andrew Gibbs Memorial Arena. It's all for a great cause, too, with proceeds benefitting the Mabank Fire Department.

The killer's reconnaissance showed the rodeo grounds were packed into a small space with aluminum grandstands on either side. The horse corral was on one side, chutes for bucking broncos and bulls on the other. A concession stand was also on that end of the grounds.

A partial fence funneled customers through the ticket office. The lights shined mainly onto the dirt of the rodeo arena, so it would be quite dark in certain areas behind the bleachers. After one more trip around the site, the killer headed home.

Fourteen

SHERIFF KING STROLLED into her office promptly at eight o'clock, sat behind her antique desk, and started reading reports from the night before. Her phone rang. It was Alice Highsmith, mother of the missing Melody Highsmith. She was known in the real estate world as a tough negotiator, and this morning she was in true form. Without so much as a greeting, Alice said, "Crystal, it's been two days, and there is still no sign of my daughter. I want to know what the hell you're going to do about that right now!"

The sheriff was a little taken aback by her aggressive behavior. After a pause, Crystal said, "First of all Alice you need to dial it down. I understand your concern, but shouting at me will do you no good."

In a contrite voice, Highsmith answered, "I apologize, Crystal. But you can't imagine how frightened I am that something has happened to her."

In a more conciliatory tone, the sheriff replied, "I'm going to send a dive team over your way this afternoon, and also a boat to drag the bottom. Let's just pray she is not in the lake." Highsmith was crying as she thanked Crystal, and clicked off the phone.

Meanwhile, the killer was having lunch at McDuff's Restaurant. Seemingly mesmerized by the phone, head down, trying to be as inconspicuous as possible. Lucinda Sue brought the order, a veggie omelet, "Here ya go. Everything look alright? Are you new around here, haven't seen you in here before. Of course, I've only been in town a few weeks from Jackson, Mississippi."

The killer never looked up from the article on the iPhone, and grunted, "Nope. Thank you." The diner was clearly dismissing the chatterbox waitress.

Lucinda Sue gave a semi-nasty look, "Well, okay then. Enjoy your meal." She turned on her heel and stomped away, miffed at the rude reception from the new customer.

In truth, the killer was trying to find articles regarding the Mabank Rodeo. There weren't many, but one story was especially interesting about the queen candidates for this year's event. Most were in high school. The mysterious murderer was a bit concerned about trying to snatch the rodeo queen like Van Cleave had done during his murder spree. It seemed a bit reckless and dangerous. If there was one thing being a SEAL had instilled during training it was try to eliminate potential problems and to get in and out without being seen.

As the killer dug into the tasty egg dish at McDuff's, the sheriff's search for Melody Highsmith was in full gear. Following rules for these searches, the boat with the drag hooks establishes a boundary to cover, assuring they are not anywhere near the divers also searching for the body. That's because the boat is dragging heavy metal anchors. Dragging hooks are designed to dig into the flesh and clothing of the victim. Imagine the horror of parents seeing their daughter recovered this way. There is no doubt using divers is a more humane way to recover a body. But, using both divers and hooks is the most efficient way to find a drowning victim.

Terrence and Alice Highsmith walked along the shoreline of Cedar Creek Lake, watching as the recovery teams searched for their missing daughter. Neither the Highsmiths nor the sheriff's deputies knew the killer had taken the body out into the middle of the lake, far away from the shore before releasing Melody to fall to the bottom in forty feet of water.

While this somber scene played out, the eleven queen candidates for the Mabank Rodeo donned their most festive western attire as they prepared for the queen nominees' banquet to begin at 7 p.m. It was at the banquet that this year's Mabank Rodeo Queen would be crowned. It was one of the biggest nights of their young lives.

The killer was most interested in the results of the queen contest but knew it would be dangerous to attend the banquet. That did not jive with keeping a low profile and out of sight. If one of the queen candidates vanished, police were sure to obtain as many cell phone pictures and video as possible to help identify a suspect.

The crowd let out a big cheer as the announcer said, "This year's Mabank Rodeo Queen is Trinity Reed." It was a popular choice. Trinity, only seventeen years old, was a state champion in barrel racing, a straight A student, class president and one of the most admired people in her large circle of friends.

Trinity, a junior at Mabank High School, was average height with way above average looks. She had a pretty face, framed by blonde hair that made her radiant. Most every boy in school wanted to date her, but Trinity preferred to concentrate on her studies. She was set on becoming a surgeon someday.

Her father, Bart, was Justice of the Peace in Precinct 3, a position he'd held for twenty-four years. Trinity's mother, Mary, blessed with the same beauty as her daughter, ran a boutique that sold lake merchandise. Mary had also been a state champion barrel racer and had even traveled the pro circuit for a couple years before she met Bart and traded her glittering western wear for a wedding dress.

As they crowned the new rodeo queen, runner-up Addison Crow sadly watched with the other candidates. The native American belonged to the Cherokee Tribe from Oklahoma. Her father, an engineer, had relocated the family to Cedar Creek Lake when he accepted a job working for the Tarrant Regional Water District at their pump station on the lake. Her mother was a third-grade teacher at Mabank Elementary.

Addison had long black hair, and ebony eyes. She was nearly five-feet-ten, and an outstanding member of the Mabank High volleyball team. Addison had scholarship offers from three large universities, including Oklahoma to play volleyball.

A few days later, the killer read the newspaper article on the queen and her court in the *Athens Courier*. The next target for the Van Cleave copycat killer would be the queen, or the runner up. The big question was how to grab one of them without being seen by the hundreds of people attending the rodeo.

There was another interesting story in the *Courier*. It seems that two young women were reported missing. Murphy wrote the story detailing how Luna Ortiz had vanished at the Athens Fiddler's Reunion, and a well-known Olympic hopeful was also reported as a missing person by her parents. The usually flamboyant, conspiracy-obsessed writer had played it straight with the story at the insistence of the paper's editor, a conservative, old-line journalist.

Murphy, his conspiracy machine already questioning how this could happen, had been reined in by his editor who threatened him with his job. The longtime *Courier* leader, Adler Huxley, had printer's ink running through his veins after over three decades at the helm in Athens. Huxley was old school, believing in "only the facts" without speculation or wild theories.

Huxley was a large man, punishing the scale at close to three hundred pounds on a short frame. He had a doughy face, narrow eyes, and wore coke-bottle lenses on his large black frames. He was constantly disheveled, finding it difficult to buy clothes that fit his girth. He was a true chain smoker, unfiltered Camels, and had the brown stained fingertips to prove it. His hair always seemed to be in search of a comb.

His demeanor was gruff and frankly unlikable, but he could care less. Huxley's life was dedicated to grinding out the best newspaper, with admittedly limited resources. He would read a reporter's copy, and reject it with a scowl, telling them to go back to their desk and write something that was readable.

While Murphy wasn't allowed to write a story possibly connecting the two missing women, Huxley couldn't control his thoughts, or what he did in his off time. Murphy tapped into all his many contacts around Cedar Creek Lake looking for any snippet of info that could lead him in that direction. He came up empty-handed, even his most reliable spy, Melinda Sue, had heard nothing.

Fifteen

SATURDAY NIGHT WAS one of those great early summer evenings in Texas with clear, star-studded skies, a slight warm breeze and no rain. The temperature hovered around seventy-five degrees as the sun set and darkness settled over the Mabank rodeo grounds. The crowd swarmed onto the grounds, with parents towing small children, and many of the women dolled up in sparkling western wear, hoping to hook up with one of the handsome rodeo cowboys.

Just as the rodeo grand entry got underway the killer pulled onto a grassy spot outside the fence that kept non-paying customers from sneaking in. The dress for tonight was black jeans, a tight-fitting black t-shirt, and a black ball cap, pulled snugly down to make it difficult to see the face under the cap.

The killer was a bit uneasy, having no clear plan for grabbing one of the two targets. It flew in the face of the SEAL training, which called for everything to be carefully planned and executed. But there seemed to be no option. It all depended on when one of the young women offered an opportunity to quickly snatch them, and escape before being noticed. It all came down to patience and opportunity.

The killer stood unobtrusively by a corner of the grandstand near the concession stand and restrooms. It was a busy spot with dozens of people returning with arms full of cheeseburgers, fries and drinks, others headed to the restroom, others just stood near the killer, watching the calf ropers head out of the nearby chutes. No one seemed to notice the lonely figure mingling among them.

After about twenty minutes, Trinity Reed walked by wearing a heavily sequined red, white and blue outfit, with a white hat, and a sash that declared her the queen of the rodeo. Reed was with three girlfriends as they headed to the restroom where she wanted to check her makeup and outfit for the umpteenth time.

Chattering and laughing, the four of them walked within a few feet of the killer without so much as a glance. The steely eyes of the attacker watched them disappear into the cinderblock building, slowly moving in their direction. The SEAL was hopeful the queen would come out alone. That wasn't to be.

Reed happily walked out of the women's restroom, trailed closely by her three friends, and was greeted by another bevy of classmates. They were giggling and having fun. Other people were also heading in and out of the restroom, with quite a few stopping to congratulate Reed. With a disgusting look, the serial killer realized it would be impossible to grab her in this environment. The SEAL slowly walked to the concession stand, bought a bag of popcorn, and returned to the side of the bleachers as the bronc riders started their competition.

After another half hour, darkness enveloped the rodeo grounds beyond the glaring lights pointed on the dirt-filled arena. It was time to claim a victim. The final event, bull riding, was beginning. The killer was frustrated and anxious.

After a few riders were rudely and painfully tossed in the air, the bull riding ended, and the announcer thanked everyone for coming to the annual Mabank Rodeo. The crowd rose from their seats and headed for the single exit. The killer remained next to the bleachers, intently scanning the crowd.

It was pure serendipity that runner-up rodeo queen, Addison Crow, brushed right past. The killer was elated when her father said, "Addison head to the car, we'll be there in a minute." Both parents stopped to talk to a couple of friends they hadn't seen in months. As they accepted congratulations on their daughter's success, Addison dutifully kept walking toward the exit. The killer followed a few feet away, blending in with the other customers heading to the parking lot.

Once outside the gate, Addison headed to the left, away from any light, as she walked toward her parent's car. The parking area was reserved for officials and the queen's court, so the majority of the crowd headed in the other direction. To the amazement of the stalker, Crow was all alone, with no one else within fifty yards of her. She walked on in the darkness, before stopping at her parent's car.

As she hit the key fob, and the car chirped unlocking the doors, Addison Crow suddenly was confronted with someone clad in black from head to toe. Her first instinct was to run. But before she could move a strong hand grabbed her by the bicep sending pain up to her shoulder. She turned toward her attacker and said, "Who are you? What do you want?" She tried to wrest her arm from the steely grip with no success and saw the fire and hatred in her attacker's eyes.

"Shut up or I will shoot you dead right where you stand."

Addison's fear grew stronger as the killer pulled out a large handgun, rudely and painfully sticking it into the teenager's rib cage. The young athlete tried mightily to break loose, but her attacker's grip was impossible to escape.

Suddenly, she was half-dragged farther into the darkness, away from the rodeo grounds and the thinning crowd. When they arrived at a black Cadillac, the attacker popped the trunk and rudely shoved her inside. Crow tried to get up and run but the killer cracked her in the head with the pistol. She fell backward into the trunk as blood rolled down her face from a gash in her forehead.

Moving quickly, the killer grabbed the syringe, plunged it into her arm, and soon the lethal dose of morphine and embalming fluid ended Addison's life. With a quick look around, the killer closed the trunk. The black-clad assailant saw Crow's parents heading through the gate on the way to their car. The killer jumped into the Cadillac and drove away in a hurry.

By the time the Crow's reached their car, the Cadillac was on its way to Kemp. Her father stood with his hands on his hips, "Where is Addison? I told her to head right to the car." They walked around the few vehicles remaining in the VIP parking area, most likely owned by rodeo officials who were finishing up their evening and paying the winning cowboys. There was no sign of Addison.

Her father said, "Okay, I'm going to head back inside to see if she's still there hanging out with her friends. You check around here to see if you can find her." Addison's mother, fearful of what might have happened to her daughter, silently nodded. Her husband ambled off, grumbling under his breath.

After twenty minutes of futile searching Addison Crow's parents once again met at their car. They were worried and frustrated. Her mother had called her iPhone several times. It went straight to voicemail. Crow's father said, "We have no way to get home. Addison has my car keys. Let's take one more look around.

The couple crossed the gravel parking lot. Crow's father held a flashlight to help illuminate the extremely dark area of the park. Addison's mother called her iPhone again. Suddenly she noticed a light shining about twenty feet away. They both hurried over and found Addison's phone lying on the ground. The flashlight shone on something shiny. It was the car keys. There was no sign of Addison.

Her mother gasped, and hung onto her husband, "Oh my God, honey. What do you think happened to her?"

Addison's father tried to put on a brave façade, "I don't know. Maybe she went off with some girlfriends and didn't realize she'd dropped her phone and keys?"

Her mother scoffed at that idea, "Are you kidding? That phone never leaves her sight. She sleeps with it under her pillow." She gave her husband a frightful look, "Do you suppose someone kidnapped her?"

Addison's father, trying to hide how frightened he was by that possibility, dialed 9-1-1. He explained the situation to the Henderson County Sheriff's Department dispatcher, who put out the call over the radio. Sheriff King picked up the call on her radio, and instantly dialed the dispatcher from her cell phone, "What's going on, Jeff? I also do not want a transmission like that going out over the air. There are too many scanner freaks around here listening in."

Sixteen

WHILE THE SHERIFF sped toward the rodeo arena, Chester Roman was already on the phone calling Dwayne Murphy. Roman, a disabled Vietnam Veteran, was one of those scanner freaks. He had difficulty sleeping and would spend hours and hours each day monitoring the area police frequencies. He fed Murphy information all the time. In turn, Murphy would bring him his favorite meal on occasion, fried catfish from McDuff's Restaurant.

Murphy answered on the second ring, "Hey, Chester, what's up?" Roman explained a member of the rodeo queen's court had apparently vanished from the Gibbs Arena. Two police cruisers were on the way. Her father made the call and was also at the rodeo grounds. Murphy was already out the door as he thanked Roman and headed to the scene.

The darkness was pierced by flashing police lights as the deputies and sheriff arrived almost simultaneously. Addison Crow's father hurried toward them, waving his arms. He explained how Addison walked to the car by herself as they talked to some friends for about five minutes, and when they got to their car, she had vanished. They pointed to the ground, shining a flashlight on her phone and the car keys.

Sheriff King asked a number of questions as a deputy took notes. They put out a BOLO for Addison Crow, hoping someone knew something or had seen something. The deputies on scene spent an hour walking the grounds in search of Crow to no avail. Addison's mother and father aided in the search, growing more concerned by the minute.

While the search went on, reporter Murphy drove into the parking lot, and was immediately stopped by a deputy who recognized him, "Hey, Murphy. I guess your scanner head heard the call, huh?"

Murphy nodded, "I need to talk to Sheriff King. Please let me through." The deputy called King on his radio.

She said, "Yeah, send him this way."

Murphy parked next to the sheriff's cruiser and hopped out of his car. King stopped him in his tracks, "Whoa, Murphy. This is a potential crime scene so I can't have you stomping around possibly destroying evidence."

Murphy halted, "Got it, Crystal. He pulled out his mini recorder. Please fill me in on what's happening here."

Sheriff King gave him the little information she had, warning him the investigation was just beginning, and the seventeen-year-old may very well have gone off with friends. Murphy gave the sheriff a knowing look, "Sure, Crystal, and I'm the ghost of Christmas past. I think we both know what apparently happened here."

The sheriff wagged her finger at him, "That's right, Murphy. The word is 'apparently' that's all we know for now."

The reporter noticed a couple standing a few yards away, holding each other. He nodded in their direction and asked the sheriff, "Parents?"

"Yes, but I'm sure they don't want to be bothered right now."

Murphy, without a word, walked their way and introduced himself. He got some quotes and then headed back toward the sheriff. "Thanks, Crystal. Good luck. I hope she's just off with friends and nothing bad happened here." Crystal just nodded and walked away, so Murphy headed to his vehicle.

The sheriff instructed the Crows to head home in case there was a ransom demand. A squad car led them to their house, and did a thorough search of the property, along with Addison's parents. They found nothing. The girl's mother made a pot of coffee. Her hands shook slightly as she sipped on the brew, fear gripped every fiber of her body.

Sheriff King called and said they would have squad cars keep an eye out for Addison, and asked her mother to call friends of the queen runner-up to see if they knew anything. She also promised a thorough search the next morning, once the sun lit up the area. The deputy would remain outside their home overnight, and the sheriff would call them with any updates.

Dwayne Murphy sat on his deck, sipping on a Bud Light and running the scenarios through his head. By his count, there were now two drownings and two young women missing from festivals. The only body recovered so far was Cory Rhodes, the young fisherman. *What was going on?* He thought about the possibilities as he swigged more of the beer.

Meanwhile in Kemp, the killer drove into the garage of the Rest In Peace Funeral Home, and placed the now lifeless body of Addison Crow in the cooler. The clear plastic lining from the trunk had some of the young woman's blood on it from when she got rapped in the head with the handgun. The plastic was rolled into a ball and placed inside the crematorium. It would be destroyed as Crow was reduced to ashes.

The killer sat in the dark filled with satisfaction from a flawless mission. While the main target, the rodeo queen had escaped death, grabbing the runner-up was the next best thing, and quite an accomplishment. It was about 10:30. The killer would take a two-hour nap before firing up the crematorium and destroying all the evidence of the now missing teenager.

Seventeen

MURPHY LOOKED AT his watch, it was nearing 11 p.m. He wanted to put out the story on the newspaper's Facebook page and website, but it had to be cleared by the editor who made it plain during several run-ins with the eager reporter, that he was not to be disturbed after 9 p.m. unless World War Three broke out in Athens. Murphy grumbled to himself, "That is no way to run a newspaper. But he needed to keep this job, so he went to bed instead.

Murphy headed to the newspaper early the next morning. It was Sunday, but he had an important story to write. Using quotes from Addison Crow's parents and Sheriff King, Murphy crafted a well written, straightforward account of the situation. The story would be ready for review by editor Huxley first thing Monday morning as they began to plan the Thursday edition of the *Athens Courier*.

After he finished, Murphy headed to Wesley's Marina near Tool, on the west side of Cedar Creek Lake. He went to the covered dock area, and took the canvas cover off his bright white speedboat. It was a Velocity 290, high performance twenty-nine-foot rocket ship. The reporter thought fishing was boring. He loved to rip through the water at seventy to eighty miles an hour, and he owned two water rockets.

His Velocity was about ten years old but looked brand new. It was powered by a 425-horsepower Mercruiser motor. It also had a small cabin with a berth for sleeping. Murphy cranked the starter and the rumble of the engine vibrated through the boat, with the loud roar echoing throughout the covered dock area.

He idled his way past Wesley's Marina in the no wake zone. Once he reached the open water, he shoved the throttle forward and the boat jumped out of the water with a loud roar and a big rooster tail trailing. Murphy was in his special place.

The sun began its journey that would eventually lead it to disappearing in the west. As sunset neared, the lake sky was filled with blue, red and orange colors reflecting off a thin layer of clouds. It was a gorgeous early evening.

A twenty-five-foot pontoon boat chugged along the shoreline, with local wildlife photographer and tour guide George Spade. His passengers on this evening were Autry Tillman III, his wife Grace, and their two children aged ten and twelve. Tillman was the third-generation president of his namesake bank. He was a buttoned-down guy, wearing linen slacks, a crisply ironed golf shirt and a pair of Dude shoes with no socks.

He had no sense of humor, and a pinched face that seemed to add to his boring demeanor. He attempted to cover his early baldness by doing a less than effective combover. His wife was decked out in a white sailing top with horizontal blue stripes, baby blue Capri pants, and jewels dripping from a huge necklace, earrings and matching bracelet. Their children wore name brand, expensive clothing. They were extremely well behaved, quietly sitting on two deck chairs, taking in the sights.

Spade attempted to engage them in some banter to loosen up the group, but it seemed fruitless. The husband and wife, like their children sat together, but hardly said a word. Spade did learn they were considering purchasing a weekend home on Cedar Creek Lake. His wife, asked a few questions, mainly having to do with the crime rate, safety on the lake, and things for the children to do.

Just as Spade turned to head into a wide bay on the south end of the lake, they all noticed something floating in the water. At first, Spade thought someone had tossed, or lost, a large garbage bag. But as they neared the form in the water, all of them let out a collective gasp. It was a dead body.

Grace Tillman let out a yelp and hurried to the back of the pontoon boat, trying to cover the eyes of her children, even as they craned their necks to see the inanimate form in the murky water. As Spade brought the pontoon within a few feet of the body, they couldn't take their eyes off what appeared to be a young woman floating alongside the boat.

If a body is floating in water that is less than seventy degrees (it was sixty-eight degrees on this day in twenty-five feet of water), the tissue turns into a soapy fatty acid known as "grave wax" that halts bacterial growth. The skin, however, will still blister and turn a horrible greenish black color. The woman's eyes were glassy and empty. It was a gruesome sight.

Grace Tillman said, "Mr. Spade, please get us out of here, this is not something my young children should see.

George replied, "I'm sorry, but I must report this to the police, and then remain here until their boat arrives. I believe this is the Olympic swimmer, Melody Highsmith. She was reported missing a few days ago."

Mrs. Tillman harumphed and said, "I suppose you're right, but this has turned into an awful trip." She crossed her arms and sat ramrod straight in her chair. Her husband again admonished the children to avoid looking at the sickening sight.

It took about an hour for the sheriff's boat to arrive. Darkness had settled in. The pontoon boat had a powerful search light trained on the floating body. Using a gaffer hook, a deputy fished the body out of the water. The body was badly decomposed, but it sure appeared to be Miss Highsmith, although the police were puzzled how the body had surfaced over a mile away from where she usually trained.

The sheriff's deputies thanked the tour guide, and slowly turned, motoring toward the boat landing. One of them dialed

Sheriff King's phone and explained the situation away from the ears of those police scanner listeners. King took a deep breath and dialed up Highsmith's mother with the terrible news. She explained the parents needed to meet her at the morgue to make a positive ID on the body. It was a difficult visit for Crystal since she had met Melody on several occasions and was always impressed with her.

Eighteen

THE NEXT MORNING, Sheriff King put out a terse news release, explaining the body of Melody Highsmith had been found. She was apparently a drowning victim. Those who read the news account were surprised that someone with Highsmith's finely honed swimming skills could have lost her life while swimming. They speculated she may have suffered a cramp or something else that caused her to drown apparently during a routine swim she'd made literally hundreds of times.

Murphy read the news release with interest. He'd been awake most of the night with the usual bevy of conspiracy theories churning through his restless mind. This latest drowning fit right in with his theory. It was time to have a talk with *Courier* editor Adler Huxley, even though he knew it was going to be frustrating and difficult.

Murphy knocked on Huxley's door and was waved in. Entering the editor's office was like stepping into a time machine. He worked at a massive rolltop desk that was over a hundred years old. The walls were full of framed front pages of the *Courier* over the decades. It was really true, Huxley had ink running through his veins.

He motioned his star reporter to a battered chair in need of fresh varnish. Huxley looked up, "Very nice work on both of the articles, Murph." Praise was not a word in Huxley's dictionary, so it surprised Murphy a bit. And then he realized, it was because he had written what he felt were boring, "just the facts" stories. Just what Huxley desired from his editorial staff.

Huxley swiveled his chair around to face Murphy, he leaned forward steepling his fingers on the desk, "What's on your mind, Dwayne." Murphy knew he was risking his editor's wrath, but he was determined to plunge into his theory even if he was thrown out of the office.

Murphy took a deep breath and said, "I've been thinking about the four recent deaths around the lake. It averages one drowning per year, and we've just had two in a very short time period." He could see Huxley's eyes narrow, apparently not happy with where this was going.

The editor asked, "And?"

Murphy forged ahead, "In addition two young women have vanished from local festivals. Again, this is a rare occurrence, let alone two of them so close together. I have a theory." And there it was, exactly what the curmudgeonly editor despised from his reporters. Huxley sat back in his chair and crossed his arms.

Murphy noticed the adverse reaction but it was too late to stop now, and he was too stubborn. He leaned in, "Adler, I think we may have a copycat killer on the loose here. The missing women occurred at the same two festivals where that crazy funeral home director, Van Cleave, snatched and killed his first two women." Huxley started to raise his arm in a sign for Murphy to stop, but the brash reporter ignored it and continued. "In addition, we have two people who apparently drowned, and the bodies were found quite far from where they disappeared. That pattern fits the man we dubbed 'The Frogman Of Cedar Creek.' It has to be a copycat because the Frogman was killed by Crystal King. Van Cleave disappeared right after his trial and is assumed to have met with some foul play, although the police never investigated his disappearance. I guess he could be alive and has returned for more revenge."

Huxley had a scowl on his face. "Murphy, it is exactly that wild kind of thinking that almost convinced me not to hire you in the first place. You, unfortunately, have a reputation for these crazy conspiracy theories, with most of them never panning out. As long as I'm in charge of the editorial section of this newspaper, you will report the facts and only the facts with no speculation. Is that understood?" With that Huxley swiveled his chair around and picked up some copy to review, dismissing Murphy, and his theory out of hand.

Murphy was miffed, but realized the meeting was over. He rose without a word and left the office. He was angry but determined to find facts that could support his theory. Murphy was convinced he was onto something important.

While Huxley had shot down Murphy, he had an unexpected ally in the new sheriff. Crystal King was sharp and nothing got past her. She was gazing out of the window in her office, with her mind meshing with Murphy's. She had escaped from Cody Martin and killed him by plunging a SCUBA knife into his neck. Unless he was Lazarus, it could be a copycat drowning two young people in Cedar Creek Lake.

The women vanishing from area festivals was the signature of Thaddeus Van Cleave, the funeral home director from Kemp who was allegedly killing young women to avenge the death of his daughter by a drunk driver returning from the Malakoff Cornbread Festival. Van Cleave had been charged with only three of his murders, but due to shaky evidence, and a hotshot Dallas lawyer, he was acquitted of all charges. The next day he apparently blew town, abandoning the longtime family funeral home and was never seen in the area again. There was no investigation of his disappearance with the popular theory that his business was ruined by the court charges so he just left to start a new life elsewhere.

Crystal heard her name and turned toward her office door to see her assistant standing there. She said, "Sheriff, it's time for your weekly leadership meeting." King nodded, grabbed some paperwork and headed toward the door. She put her ideas on the back-burner as it quickly turned into a busy day.

Nineteen

ROMY MORELAND GREW up as a Navy brat. Her father, Rear Admiral Griffin Moreland's career took the family to eight different naval bases in her first eleven years on earth. Her father named his daughter Romy. Its Latin origin means "dew of the sea."

Her mother was the perfect cliché for a Naval wife. She dutifully followed her husband from base to base, taking care of their home and raising Romy. She was a meek and private person, never bothering to make new friends during their travels.

Poor Romy was quite homely, and following in her mother's footsteps, an introvert. That combination caused her classmates in every town either to shun her completely, as if she didn't exist, or to bully her incessantly. She had very thin, stringy hair, gangly arms and legs, and was a bit pudgy. Her face appeared to be more man than woman, leading people throughout her life to question her sex.

By the time she reached her senior year in high school, Romy Moreland, had grown to nearly six-feet tall. Her manly features had morphed into a chiseled chin as she lost her baby fat. But her hair remained a stringy mess, and an attack of acne created more issues. She remained a resolute loner, no friends, no fun with classmates, but after nearly two decades of this life she had accepted it completely and had no interest in her world changing.

After high school she immediately joined the Navy, making her father proud for the first time ever. Of course, he didn't say that to her. The always stoic rear admiral simply said, "Good choice, Romy. You have a chance to make it a good career." There was no hug, not even a smile. Her mother, on the other hand, was devastated. Romy was the only person she could talk to, and now she'd be moving far away.

Romy and the Navy seemed a good fit. She was used to constant discipline and had no need to make friends. She was trained as a Gunner's Mate, learning to fire all the weapons on the destroyer she was assigned. Turns out, she was very skillful in this position, and also received good reports from her senior officers.

After a year in her position Romy noticed a posting for what was called a high-priority role. The Navy was looking for people to become explosive ordinance disposal technicians. The flyer on the bulletin board promised they'd "work with advanced tools to identify and diffuse explosive threats, above and below the water."

Romy was intrigued by the idea and signed up for the training. To her surprise, for the first time in her life, she was selected to be part of the trainees. Romy sailed through the training, and also became certified in SCUBA diving. Romy, never the athlete, learned she loved diving underwater with an air tank. She was a strong swimmer, and it all came naturally to her.

During the ordnance training, one of the instructors held a class on the Navy's elite underwater team, the Navy SEALs. While SCUBA is an important part of being a SEAL, the name actually stands for the fact they operate in the sea, air and land, wherever their special combat force is needed. One day they could be swimming out of a torpedo tube on a submarine, and the next day they could be dropping out of a helicopter into enemy territory.

There are only about twenty-five hundred Navy SEALs on active duty. Nearly nine out of ten who apply to be a SEAL are washed out. It's about a six-month process to be selected and trained as a Navy SEAL. The training ends with the notorious Hell Week.

It lasts from Sunday evening until Friday morning. It is truly grueling. During Hell Week, students run more than two hundred miles, often with heavy rubber boats held above their heads, swim endless miles and spend hours on physical training while being cold, wet and full of sand. Throughout Hell Week the recruits get a total of about four hours of broken sleep.

Until 2016, women weren't allowed to serve in combat roles, so of course, no woman had ever been a Navy SEAL. Five years later, one woman passed the demanding SEAL training. Romy Moreland was the second woman to earn her place on the SEAL team.

In the course of her training, Romy met a young stud named Cody Martin. He was in his mid-twenties, stood six-feet tall, and was strong as an ox with a rippled body that would make a weight-lifter turn green with envy. He had cold blue eyes that could pene-trate steel, and a tough, no-nonsense demeanor. Like Romy, Martin was a loner who kept to himself. He was relentless in his training and one of the toughest in his platoon.

One morning, the two of them sat on the edge of the Olym-pic-sized swimming pool, catching their breath after swimming nearly two miles. As they sat in silence, staring straight ahead, there was an uncomfortable vibe. Martin, eventually turned toward Romy, stuck out his hand for an awkward handshake and an introduction.

Over the next few weeks, the two became friends. It was a nov-el experience for both of them. There was no thought of romantic involvement on Martin's part. Relationships were prohibited by the commanding officers. In fact, neither of them had ever even kissed another person. Their friendship seemed based on the lyrics of "The Piano Man" by Billy Joel. They were ... *sharing a drink called lone-liness. But it's better than drinking alone.* There was no drinking in-volved but the sentiment fit them snugly.

Through the next two years, they got together for swim ses-sions between assignments. They tried going to lunch once but it was far too awkward, so it never happened again. Yet, there was an unspoken bond—two people who had each other's backs no matter what. They even did several missions together. Romy found it com-forting, and really looked at Cody Martin as the big brother she'd wished for her whole lonely life.

As the weeks went on, Romy's mind began building a fantasy world when it came to Cody Martin. Although their relationship was far from physical, she imagined a place where she and Martin were true lovers. She spent many a night dreaming of places they visited and made love. This was a truly novel experience for Moreland, one that most girls experience in their teens.

She became obsessed with this fantasy world, one, of course, that Cody Martin had no idea existed. He saw Moreland as a friend and a SEAL. Period.

He simply wasn't wired to fall in love or even let anyone get close to him. Moreland was aware of this fault in her imaginary lover, but while she outwardly kept it friendly, inside there was a growing fire of passion for him.

Then one day Martin simply disappeared. His locker was cleaned out in the middle of the night, and he was gone without a word. At first, Romy thought he was on a secret assignment. Later she found out he'd been kicked out of the SEALs for being over-zealous. What exactly that entailed was never mentioned by any-one. Romy, was heartbroken for the first time in her life. Her dream world had been shattered. Moreland went into a deep funk.

She was immersed in a couple of special missions, which kept her occupied for several months and temporarily kept her mind off her loss. When she returned, Romy tried to track down Martin on social media. He, naturally, had no social media footprint. He was too anti-social to get on Facebook or some other app. But when she googled his name, she found an article that felt like a hard punch to her gut.

The *Cedar Creek Gazette* had a long, detailed story about a for-mer Navy SEAL named Cody Martin who'd killed nine people, making it looked like they had drowned. He was eventually a sus-pect, dubbed The Frogman Of Cedar Creek by the media. Then he kidnapped the sheriff's fiancée and held her in an undercover cave. He was killed while swimming out of the cave toward shore after making a deal with police.

Moreland's eyes narrowed with hatred as she read the account of how the fiancée, Crystal Dinsmore, had stabbed Martin in the neck, killing him. Romy's fingers pounded the computer keyboard as she googled Dinsmore, found out she was now the wife of the ex-sheriff, and in fact, had just been elected the first female sheriff in Henderson County. That woman had killed the only person she'd ever felt close to. She became so angry, she began to shake, holding her head in her hands.

Romy Moreland's mind was instantly heading in one direction. She would avenge the death of her only love. She continued her research, getting details on each of the Martin murders. Then she stumbled across information about a funeral home director in Kemp, who was also a serial killer ending the lives of six young women.

She did extensive research into that murder spree and suddenly she had her plan. Her Navy retirement was coming up in five months. Then she'd head to East Texas, create copycat killings in the same places, and with the same methods as her heartthrob Martin, and the funeral home director Van Cleave. The mission was to send chills through people living around Cedar Creek Lake, and eventually to kill Sheriff Crystal King for ending the life of the only person in her life who actually cared about her. Vengeance would be hers. He would be so proud of her.

Twenty

FORTY-THREE-YEAR-OLD Candace Avery was a lifelong resident of the Cedar Creek Lake area. She grew up in Gun Barrel City and graduated from Mabank High School. Candace headed off to Texas Tech for college, majoring in business. After graduation, with some financial assistance from her family, she opened Candace's Candies on Main Street in Gun Barrel City. She had a well-known sweet tooth that drove her to launch her first business.

It was now a local institution, offering a variety of homemade and imported chocolate creations and cakes of all varieties. A few years ago, Candace expanded her inventory to include dozens of products for the home, as well as t-shirts with the Cedar Creek Lake logo. Business was booming.

Every morning at precisely seven o'clock, Candace lowered her bright yellow and orange Perception Kayak into the lake for her daily workout. The twelve-foot kayak had set her back over $1,200 but she believed in the best quality products. Candace lived in a small cabin on a flower-filled property fronting the channel that flowed past Wesley's Marina into the main body of the lake.

Candace Avery was a striking woman. She stood nearly six-feet tall, with a well-toned, slim body and long brown hair that flowed nearly to her waist. Candace had a drawn face, with bright blue eyes, and was always ready with a friendly smile. Many men had asked her out on dates over the years, but she always refused, saying she was just too busy with her thriving business.

Truth be known, Candace had a long relationship with a woman at Texas Tech. In the end, they parted ways and Candace had no interest in any woman or man since. She threw all her energy and emotions into her store, and her daily kayak treks. Her daily jaunts took her around the shoreline on the west end of the lake until she reached the spillway. Then she'd turn around and head back home.

The sun shined brightly as another gorgeous day dawned on Cedar Creek Lake. The cloudless sky was deep blue, and a slight breeze caused the lake water to sparkle like thousands of diamonds. Avery was halfway through her journey, as she used strong strokes to turn around and head back toward home. Candace passed three boats on the way, all apparent fisherman looking for schooling fish at this early hour.

If she'd done more than glanced at those boats, Candace would have noticed a woman with her hair tucked under a blue cap with a Cabela's logo, trolling along the shoreline. She would have seen the cold eyes watching her closely while acting inconspicuously. Romy Moreland was searching for her next drowning victim when she noticed the bright kayak sparkling in the morning sun about a week ago. This was the third time Moreland waited near the spillway to assure the kayaker kept to a regular schedule. Candace Avery had no idea she was going to be drowning target number three for the serial killer.

In Athens, two people were deep in thought on this sunny morning, trying to figure out the truth about the two recent drownings and disappearance of two young women. Sheriff Crystal King pored over the incident reports, trying to glean any clue to help her figure out what happened to the four victims. A few blocks away at the *Athens Courier*, Dwayne Murphy was also researching any information he could find on the four victims.

Murphy was a stubborn, relentless digger and plunged ahead despite the strong rebuke, and warning from his boss at the newspaper. Of course, while the sheriff was looking at the facts through a practiced, open-minded eye, Murphy was searching for the conspiracy theory—something to prove all four victims were connected to some larger plot. So far, he'd come up empty. Murphy was in deep thought, desperately trying to find an angle that would let him sneak a conspiracy article past the editor. So far, he was drawing a blank.

At his ranch outside Mabank, Shane Malaby was checking the local gossip online from the Next Door app on his phone. Once an energetic, boisterous and bully of a boss, Malaby had turned the ranch over to his most trusted field hand after the death of his daughter, and his murder of the man who snuffed out her young, promising life. These days he spent hours rocking on the porch of his massive ranch home, with little ambition. His wife had fallen into the hell of prescription depression drugs. She spent her days wrapped in a colorful horse blanket, sitting in a big leather chair inside the quiet home. The TV blared with a game show, but she pretty much ignored it. Her eyes were glassy and unfocused, her hair uncombed.

Malaby was absorbed in the thread of comments on the local app about the strange disappearance of two young women. One had vanished from the Athens Fiddle Fest, and the other from the Mabank Rodeo. The rancher's eyes narrowed, his forehead furrowed and his hands began to shake a bit as he read about the disappearances. Terrible memories flooded his brain from the time when his most precious daughter had been taken by Van Cleave. Her lifeless body reduced to ashes. Tears trickled down the father's cheeks as he thought of his lovely young daughter.

He knew Van Cleave was not responsible for these latest disappearances, since Malaby had dumped his ashes in the lake. Of course, no one else, not even his troubled wife, knew he had killed the serial killer. Malaby thought of the recent victim's families. He knew what they were experiencing. *How can I help track down their killer?*

72

Twenty-One

AS THE NOON hour approached, Sheriff King walked into McDuff's Restaurant in Seven Points and grabbed a booth in the back. Soon Buddy King joined her with a peck on the cheek, and then former sheriff Billy Richardson slid into the same booth. Crystal smiled, "My two favorite men in the whole world." She'd asked them to join her to talk about the four victims. Crystal was determined to get ahead of this situation.

Within a minute, Melinda Sue strolled over. Today, her ever-changing hair was dyed a fluorescent green. She drawled, "Well, if it ain't the law enforcement brain trust sittin' in my section. This is my lucky day."

Crystal was anxious to get started, "We'll all have the usual, Melinda Sue."

The flamboyant waitress, and chief spy for Dwayne Murphy, was clearly miffed. "Excuse me, Madam Sheriff, for trying to be sociable with y'all!"

Crystal smiled, "I didn't mean to upset you, Melinda Sue, we just have a lot to talk about and not much time to do it. It looks like you're doing well."

Crystal's attempt to appease Melinda Sue was not acknowledged as she said, "I'll get it right out then." She then spun around and headed to the kitchen to place the order. All three of her customers tried to stifle a grin while watching the performance.

The smile quickly vanished from Crystal's flawless face, "I've been thinking about something, and I want your reactions before I do anything." Both Buddy and Billy leaned in a little closer, as Crystal kept her voice low to guard against prying ears. The sheriff said, "We've had two mysterious drownings, and two young women have disappeared. It is all eerily similar to when the three of us were chasing Cody Martin and Van Cleave.

She paused as Melinda Sue brought their drinks. The waitresses' ears were perked up as usual, trying to glean any part of the conversation as she set down the three diet Dr Peppers. Melinda Sue smirked, "Y'all don't need to be quiet on my account. I figure you're talkin' about those four folks who've disappeared?"

Buddy King smiled, "Not at all, Melinda Sue. We're wondering if the Cowboys will finally make it to the Super Bowl this year."

The waitress snorted, as she walked away, "Yeah right." With Melinda Sue safely out of earshot, Sheriff King got to the point of the meeting.

Crystal said, "It seems we were behind the eight ball on both of these incidents from the get go. That's no reflection on either of you and how you handled things, I just wonder if someone with a broader base of experience could help us move forward more quickly."

She had not discussed this with her husband, but Buddy King immediately had an inkling of what Crystal was going to propose. "So, you're thinking about asking for assistance from the Texas Rangers?" Crystal nodded her head in agreement.

The Texas Rangers, a unique, elite state police force has been around for almost two hundred years. Back in the early days they patrolled the Texas frontier, arrested cattle rustlers, and fought in military battles. It was 1823 when Stephen F. Austin decided to augment the Mexican government's militia patrols with a force of ten men paid out of his own pocket. The Texas Rangers was born.

John Caperton wrote, "Each Texas Ranger was armed with a rifle, a pistol and a knife. With a Mexican blanket tied behind his saddle, and a small wallet in which he carried salt, ammunition and tobacco. He was equipped for a month. Unencumbered by baggage, wagons or pack trains the Texas Rangers moved as lightly over the prairie as the Indians." The Texas Legislature approved the first permanent Ranger force in 1874.

One of the most famous Rangers was Captain Frank Hamer. He chased the notorious bank robbers Bonnie and Clyde for 102 days. Hamer and some fellow Rangers finally caught up with the pair in Bienville Parish in Louisiana. They'd hoped to take Bonnie and Clyde alive but when the outlaws reached for their weapons, the Rangers unleashed a volley of fire power that riddled their car and ended the lives of Bonnie and Clyde.

Before that shootout, Bonnie Parker spent the night of April 19, 1932, in a tiny brick jail in Kemp. Townspeople gaped at her through the barred windows. She spit in their faces. The jail, actually called a calaboose, is a free-standing single cell often seen in small towns during that time. The calaboose still stands today near downtown Kemp.

Today there are 234 Texas Rangers. After all these years, only two women serve as captains in the Rangers, Wende Wakeman and Melba Saena. The Texas Rangers is the primary investigative branch of the Texas Department of Public Safety. They mostly conduct criminal and special investigations, along with apprehending felons, stopping major disturbances, and rendering assistance to local law enforcement officials to stop crime and violence.

Billy Richardson said, "I think you may be onto something, Crystal. You have some fine investigators and officers, but the Rangers can send you someone they all can learn from. I like it."

Buddy rubbed his chin stubble, "Yeah, I agree with Billy. Hopefully, these are unconnected victims, but a highly trained set of eyes on what we know so far, couldn't hurt. Do you have someone in mind?"

Crystal said, "I reached out to the commander of the Dallas office. Just a preliminary phone call. I was told they could send us Tolbert Masterson."

Buddy and Billy both perked up.

Billy said, "Wow! 'Night Train' Masterson is a legend in the Rangers. His ancestors, Bat, Ed and James Masterson were all Texas Rangers back in the 1800s."

Buddy asked, "Night Train?"

Billy replied, "He got the nickname some years ago, when he intercepted a shipment of cocaine being sent up from Mexico on an overnight freight train. Busted the entire drug operation single-handedly."

Melinda Sue approached with steaming hot platters, and the three of them quickly went silent. The waitress knew they were discussing something important but was frustrated because she could never get within earshot without being spotted. Crystal said, "Looks great Melinda Sue. Thanks." Melinda Sue, still miffed from her earlier encounter silently left.

Twenty-Two

IN GUN BARREL CITY, Candace Avery brought a strawberry cake from the refrigerator for one of her regular customers. The woman, in her eighties with neatly combed grey hair said, "Oh Candace that looks delicious." She paused, and added, "You know, Candace, I worry about you and your early morning kayak trips with those two recent drownings and now two young women missing from local festivals."

Candace smiled, showing even white teeth, "Oh thanks, Judith, but nobody's going to bother little ol' me and my kayak."

The woman gave her a direct look, "Just the same, Candace. Please be careful." She promised she would, and the woman paid her tab and left. As the door closed, Candace couldn't help but think of the couple who were killed by the Frogman while paddling their kayaks on Cedar Creek Lake. Just then another customer walked in, and Candace gave her a cheery greeting.

Back in Athens, Sheriff King returned to her office, and dialed up the Texas Ranger office in Dallas. She told the commander that the Henderson County Sheriff's Department would be honored to have Tolbert Masterson help with their investigation. She was told that

Masterson would arrive in a few days and help with the investigation as long as needed. Crystal was truly grateful for the expertise heading her way.

⁂

The next morning, early risers were greeted by light showers, a leaden sky, and a bit of a chill for this time of year. Candace Avery gazed at the lake from her front porch. It was wet but the winds were calm. She refused to let a little rain stop her from her morning kayak trip. Candace pulled on a warm sweat suit and dropped her kayak into the water from the dock lift. She settled in and headed for the spillway as the rain continued, bringing a bit of fog with it.

Near the spillway, Romy Moreland, spit into her SCUBA mask to clear the fog, shrugged into her air tank and headed toward the water. She walked through the yard of someone her surveillance had shown was a weekender. The house was vacant this morning, in fact all the houses nearby were devoid of people.

Moreland smiled to herself. The relentless rain drops and cool temperatures generated a thickening fog across Cedar Creek Lake. There wasn't a boat in sight on this dreary morning. The serial killer eased down the bank into the lake. She was about a hundred yards from where Candace Avery's kayak would pass. The plan was to capsize the kayak just as Avery made her turn. It's when she would be most vulnerable.

Moreland treaded water about twenty yards from where she guessed Avery would turn to head back home. The killer was about six feet underwater waiting. Except for the almost imperceptible bubbles, she was completely out of sight.

The rain started falling heavier as big drops pelted Candace Avery. There was no thought of turning back as she used strong strokes to close in on her usual turnaround spot. The fog limited her view to just a few feet. There were no boats in sight anywhere.

As Avery dragged the paddle in the water to begin the turn for home, her kayak suddenly seemed to hit a whale. The watercraft rolled violently to its right dumping Candace in the water. Unfor-

78

tunately, her lifejacket was tucked into the floor of the kayak. Avery was a decent swimmer. She flailed her arms and legs trying to recover from being tossed into the lake. But then, her arms were pinned to her side by someone who was much stronger.

Candace's startled eyes were looking at someone, who appeared to be a woman, wearing SCUBA gear. The woman's eyes pierced into Avery's soul. She'd never seen such a wild look on anyone. The kayaker tried to wrest free, but the woman's grip was like a steel trap. Avery was shocked by how strong her attacker was.

Suddenly, she was dragged underwater, her assailant holding her near the bottom of the lake, as Avery gasped her last breath. Bubbles popped out of her mouth as she attempted to scream. Moreland held the now lifeless body underwater for a good five minutes, and then holding Avery with one arm, and using a strong kick, she took her into about thirty feet of water, a good two hundred yards from shore. She dropped the dead woman to the bottom of the lake and swam toward the kayak.

The serial killer reached the now overturned kayak and flipped upright. Once again using powerful leg kicks, Moreland pushed the kayak in the opposite direction of where she had dropped Avery's body. After swimming a good three hundred yards, she gave the kayak one last push toward the middle of the lake.

Moreland then took one look all around. Satisfied the coast was clear, she dropped about ten feet underwater and swam back to the vacant house where she'd entered the lake. Five minutes later she was gone, and so was Candace Avery.

Three hours later, a regular customer of Candace's Candies knocked on the door of the shop. It was locked up tight, not a soul around, and the lights were off. The "closed" sign was still displayed on the door. She was the first of ten people who phoned the Henderson County Sheriff's Office that day, wondering where Candace Avery could be.

About two o'clock that afternoon a tall, well-tanned, rugged looking man wearing a brown uniform and a cowboy hat knocked on Sheriff King's office door. She rose quickly, and met him halfway into the office, "You must be Tolbert Masterson?"

They shook hands, and Masterson smiled, a bit taken aback by the most beautiful sheriff he'd ever met, "Yes ma'am. That's me." Crystal motioned him to a chair.

Twenty-Three

AS THE TEXAS RANGER settled his six-foot-two frame into the office chair, Crystal gave him the once over. He had the darkest, most piercing eyes she'd ever seen. As he removed his Stetson, she saw that he had neatly trimmed black hair, no facial hair, and had carefully shaved that morning. He had a barrel chest, but not an ounce of fat on his body. His biceps bulged under the shirt, and his hands were huge. His face was rather plain but fit well with his rugged persona. His voice was deep and confident. Crystal was sure he'd make a great partner.

The sheriff said, "I'm so pleased to have you working side by side with us. I've done a little research, and you are a helluva of a peace officer. Congratulations on that cocaine train bust."

Masterson had a crooked smile. "Well, thank you ma'am, but that was a long time ago. Right now, I want to concentrate on your situation."

Crystal smiled. "And I can't tell you how much I appreciate your assistance. Please call me Crystal. How should I address you?"

The Texas Ranger said, "Tolbert is fine, ma'am."

Just then, the dispatcher knocked on Crystal's office door. He seemed to be a bit flustered. Crystal said, "What's going on, Duke?"

The dispatcher said, "I'm not sure there is anything to it, but

I've taken about a dozen calls saying Candace's Candies is locked up with no sign of her anywhere. It's not like her to be closed on a Wednesday."

Masterson's eyebrows went up, while Crystal pondered what she'd just been told. She looked at the Texas Ranger, "Candace Avery is an institution in Gun Barrel City. She's had a popular candy store there for years and years."

Masterson nodded, "She could just be taking a day off, or maybe she didn't feel well today?"

Crystal nodded, "Absolutely, but I think we need to do a welfare check to be certain." She told the dispatcher to send Sergeant Lonny Shields to Avery's house. The dispatcher left, and Crystal and Masterson started digging into the reports on the four victims to bring him up-to-speed with the investigation.

Sergeant Shields pulled into the driveway of Candace Avery's house. He looked in the windows, walked around to the water side and noticed the lift was lowered into the water. The house was locked except for the back door. He called out Avery's name and turned the knob on the back door. Inside the house, the sergeant saw a pot of hot coffee on the counter, as well as her car keys and phone. There was no sign of Candace.

Shields walked onto the dock. He surmised a watercraft was missing. The sergeant hopped back into his car and drove back around to the highway, turning onto a blacktop road that led to Wesley's Marina. He pulled into the marina parking lot and went inside.

The place was nearly empty at this hour in the afternoon. He spotted the owner. Shields said, "Do you know what kind of watercraft Candace Avery has?" He pointed toward the dock across the channel.

The owner replied, "Yeah. She has a fancy yellow and orange kayak. I'm not usually here that early in the morning, but I'm told she paddles to the spillway and back, come rain or shine."

Shields asked, "Did anyone see her heading out this morning?"

The owner shook his head, "Nope our gas pumps don't open until nine o'clock, so there's nobody here that early." The deputy thanked the owner and headed back to his cruiser.

He dialed up Sheriff King's phone, thinking it would be best to keep this information off the police scanners. Crystal answered on the third ring, "What'd you find out, Lonny?"

The sergeant replied, "The back door to the house was unlocked, her purse, phone and car keys were on the counter, her car is parked in the driveway, and her kayak is missing from the dock. I'm told she paddles to the spillway and back religiously every morning."

Crystal said, "It was kinda nasty this morning, rain and fog. Anybody see her paddling out onto the lake?"

Shields replied, "Not that I could find, but Wesley's owner says she never misses a day, no matter how bad the weather."

The sheriff said, "Okay, Lonny. You hang there for a bit. I'll send a boat your way and we can see if there's any sign of her or the kayak on the lake." Masterson and King exchanged worried glances thinking is this another victim. Lonny ordered a sweet tea and sat on the deck at Wesley's Marina waiting for the sheriff's department boat to arrive.

Twenty-Four

IN ATHENS, CRYSTAL took the Texas Ranger to a late lunch. She and Masterson headed to her favorite local restaurant. It was a relatively cool, clear day so they decided to sit outside. They settled into a small wooden table with a colorful red umbrella repelling the relentless Texas sun.

Masterson said, "I read the files you sent and remember those two serial killers from a few years ago. I know those were difficult cases."

Crystal nodded, "Yes. Between the guy the media called The Frogman drowning all those innocent folks, and that crazy funeral home director grabbing young women and cremating their bodies, it was a horrible time for my husband and me, along with our friend Billy Richardson.

The waitress arrived with ice waters and took their orders. Masterson took Crystal's advice and ordered the barbecue sandwich with chips. After their orders were placed, Masterson said, "As I recall you were the one who stabbed that frogman guy to death. That had to be a very scary experience with him."

A distant look came over Crystal's face as her mind returned to those terrible days. She sighed, "Oh yeah. Luckily, I'd just finished self-defense training or I might be dead." Again, her eyes drifted as memories flooded back.

Masterson noticed her discomfort, and smoothly changed the subject, "Now, as I understand it, that funeral home dude... Van Cleave... right? He skated on the murder charges, and then just disappeared?

Crystal was relieved to talk about something else, "Yes. Our case was built on bone fragments remaining in the crematorium, but the jury didn't buy it. It was a real blow. We knew the bastard killed those women, but I guess he came close to the perfect crime."

The waitress arrived with lunch. They each hungrily took a few bites in silence. The Texas Ranger put down his sandwich, wiped the tasty sauce off his mouth, and asked, "Crystal, do you think there's any chance Van Cleave could be back in town, and responsible for those two missing women?"

The sheriff shrugged, "I honestly can't say, Tolbert. I mean the speculation is he skulked off in the middle of the night out of embarrassment and because his business totally stopped after he was charged with murder. But we never launched an investigation. We did look around his property but his personal car was gone, along with his wallet and other valuables. The doors were locked. No sign of forced entry."

Masterson leaned closer, "Well, you should know that before I left Dallas, I had one of our cyber techs track down any sign of Van Cleave and she found nothing. He apparently has no bank accounts, no phone and hasn't renewed his driver's license. He truly seems to have vanished. Do you think someone could have taken the law into their own hands after the not guilty verdict?"

Crystal pondered the question and then said, "I guess that's a possibility, Tolbert. But if that was the case, I think the local gossips would have said something by now. It's hard to keep a secret, especially one as big as that in this small-town environment."

Masterson took another bite, "This is the best barbecue I've had, Crystal, and I've had it all over Texas." He paused, thinking, "Was there anyone involved in the case who could have been angry enough to kill Van Cleave? There is nothing worse to a father than losing a precious daughter, especially if she is your only daughter."

The sheriff instantly had a vision of one furious father before, during and after the trial, "If I had to come up with one person who fits that description it would be Shane Malaby. His daughter was the Mabank Rodeo Queen who disappeared from the rodeo grounds. Malaby is probably one of the most disliked people in these parts. He was a braggadocios bully who thought he was better than anyone else. I always felt bad for his wife. He treated her like a child and was quite an embarrassment."

Tolbert's ears perked up, "And what is Malaby up to these days?"

Crystal sighed, "It's a sad situation. Since the trial Malaby has become a recluse. He just sits in his rocking chair on the porch and seems to stare into space with no interest in the world around him. Everyone was amazed when the control freak put his farm hand in charge of the ranch. His wife unfortunately is in worse shape. I'm told she just sits in a big leather chair in front of their fireplace all day, way over medicated on drugs prescribed by her doctor for depression."

Intrigued, Masterson asked, "Do you think it's possible to pay them a visit? I'm sure he closely followed the trial, maybe he can give us a different perspective on what we're facing now. Hell, maybe he's been trying to track down Van Cleave. He likely has enough money to hire a private eye."

Crystal replied, "It's worth a shot. I'll try to set it up for tomorrow." With that, they both used the rest of their sandwiches to sop up the barbecue sauce.

On the west side of Cedar Creek Lake, Sergeant Shields and another deputy launched the boat and slowly chugged along the shoreline from Candace Avery's house to the spillway. There was no sign of the colorful missing kayak or of Avery herself.

A few miles away, Romy Moreland stopped alongside the road in a small park and pulled a weathered picture out of her purse. It was a shot of Romy and Cody Martin, the man the media called The Frogman. With one foot in her fantasy world, Moreland often talked to the worn picture. As she touched the only love of her life, Romy said, "I'm on the way to avenging your death. But I've just started. I need to pile up some other victims, set the entire lake area on edge, and then snuff out that cute little blond sheriff who thinks she rules the world after ending your life." As she often did, Moreland lovingly kissed the picture, and then put it back in her purse. She continued scouting out the location for the next victim who would vanish from this earth.

The Sheriff Department's boat cruised slowly along the Cedar Creek Lake spillway, the lawmen using binoculars to scan the water and the shoreline in search of Avery and her kayak. The spillway features eight gates that can be opened to lower the lake water level after heavy rainfall in the area. By law, the spillway must start releasing water whenever the lake surpasses 322 feet above sea level. This is to protect the docks and other structures built along the long lake. The released water tumbles into the Trinity River.

Twenty-Five

SHERIFF KING'S PHONE rang. It was the pushy real estate agent, Alice Highsmith. She got right to the point in an angry tone, "Crystal, it's been weeks now. I want to know what you're doing to find out who drowned my daughter? Do you have any leads?"

Crystal, paused before answering, careful not to match the mother's demeanor, "Alice we are tracking down a number of leads, but so far, they have gone nowhere. I'm so sorry."

Highsmith jumped in, "Sorry? I don't want sorry! I want you to find my daughter's killer! Did you know she was supposed to be at the Olympic swimming trials this week?"

Once again in a calm voice Crystal replied, "Again, Alice, I am so sorry this happened to your daughter. But you also need to understand it may not have been foul play. She could have had a cramp or something and drowned. I know she was a great swimmer, but these medical events happen sometimes."

Highsmith snorted, "Give it a rest, Sheriff. That is complete bull!" The phone disconnected. Crystal sat back in her chair. Despite her irate approach, the sheriff felt genuinely sorry for Highsmith's loss, and understood her attitude.

Back at the spillway, the two deputies were also frustrated. Shields suggested, "Let's keep going past the spillway, head south and go around the next couple of points. There was a pretty stiff north wind overnight." The boat continued its slow pace and rounded the first point after the spillway. Shields spotted the kayak in his binoculars, "There it is." He pointed to a dock about thirty yards away. There was an orange and yellow kayak bobbing up and down, caught under the dock.

The deputy sped up the boat and headed to the dock. As they pulled next to the kayak, Sergeant Shields could see it was empty. The paddle was missing, along with Avery. He saw the life jacket stuffed under the seat. The kayak's fiberglass frame was scratched and torn from the constant bobbing under the dock.

Shields hit speed dial on his phone, "Crystal, this is Shields. We found the Avery woman's kayak stuck under a dock in Key Ranch. She is not in it."

The sheriff slammed her fist on her desk, "Dammit. Not another one. Okay, Lonny, stay put. I'm heading your way with forensics. We'll see if we can get any prints or evidence off the kayak. How far are you from Wesley's?"

Shields replied, "Probably a couple miles, Crystal. It certainly does not fit her usual route. Although she could have fallen out of the kayak, and then last night's wind blew it this way until it got stuck under the dock."

Tolbert Masterson strolled back into the sheriff's office, after finding a quiet spot to check in with his wife back in Dallas. All three of his teenagers were doing well. He saw the look on Crystal's face, and asked "Another one?" The sheriff just nodded. They headed out of her office.

Crystal turned on her cruiser's siren and sped down Highway 31 through Malakoff before turning right on Highway 274. She slowed a bit, turned right onto Key Ranch Road and headed to the dock that held the kayak captive. They determined it would be easier to process the kayak if they dragged it onto the shore. Her best forensics officer went to work, looking for anything that would give them a clue what happened to Candace Avery.

At the house next door, Myrtle Johnson sat on her porch and watched the police pull the kayak out of the lake, and carefully dust it for fingerprints. They seemed very intense. Myrtle was a big fan of Dwayne Murphy and was disappointed when the Gun Barrel City newspaper closed and he moved to the *Athens Courier*. She'd met him once, and of course he'd given her one of his new business cards. She dialed the number.

While the other officers pored over the kayak, Crystal walked to the end of the dock, and pointed out the lay of the land for the Texas Ranger. The next unpleasant task was to drag the lake in search of Candace Avery's body. Due to where they found the kayak, the search area was quite large. The sheriff dialed up her rescue team and summoned them to her location, deciding to work backwards from where the kayak was found to the marina. She admonished everyone to keep a tight lid on the situation.

In Athens, Dwayne Murphy answered his phone. He didn't re-member Myrtle Johnson; he gave out business cards like candy on Halloween. But his ears perked up when he heard what she was watching. He thanked her profusely and hurried out the door of the newspaper office.

At that hour in Malakoff, the committee for the annual Cornbread Festival was holding its final planning meeting in the backroom at Bookish, a wonderful not-for-profit bookstore. The popular celebra-tion would be held the next weekend. Everything was in place for a great time.

Thirty miles away, Romy Moreland was also thinking about the festival. She'd opened a thick manila folder with her research of the two serial killers she was imitating. The Malakoff Cornbread Festival was where Van Cleave had tried to grab a third victim, but he failed after some young women noticed his creepy stalking and he fled the area. Moreland was determined to find a victim at the festival this time.

Twenty-Six

A BIGGER CROWD of police officers gathered at the lake house in Key Ranch. Dispatch gave a courtesy call to the homeowners, who were working in Garland, letting them know what was happening. The rescue team launched their boat and began the gruesome job of dragging a heavy hook along the lake bottom hoping to snag Avery's body.

Just then, Dwayne Murphy pulled into the crowded driveway of the home. He got out of his car and started taking pictures before anyone noticed him. Having finished that task, the reporter approached the sheriff. She was less than thrilled to see him. Murphy walked up with his usual crooked smile, "Hey, Sheriff, what's going on here? Another drowning victim?"

Crystal replied, "We're not sure, Murphy. Right now, we just have a kayak that washed up under the dock here. We're trying to locate the owner."

Murphy gave her a look, "You mean the owner who drowned, which is why your rescue team is here?"

Crystal was in no mood to play that game, "Listen, Murphy. I've told you all I know. Now, if you'll kindly get back near your car, I'd appreciate it since this may – and I emphasize may – be a crime scene."

But Murphy's ever-prying eyes noticed a stranger in the crowd of police, "One more question, Crystal. Who's the guy in the Texas Ranger uniform?"

Crystal let out a long sigh, "He's just a friend who happens to be visiting. He's a big fisherman like Billy and Buddy, and they're going out for largemouth bass tonight."

Murphy wasn't buying it, "Or, he could be here to help you solve the mystery of the recent drownings and missing women?"

Crystal turned and walked away, saying over her shoulder, "You're something else, Murphy. You're way off base here. Good-bye."

The reporter watched the sheriff walk over to the Texas Ranger, point at Murphy, and go into a long story. Masterson nodded and turned his back to Murphy. Murphy's brain was churning with ideas for a story about how the Texas Rangers had been called in to help with these mysterious events. Now, he just needed the proof. If he only knew the guy's name, it would be easy to check out, but Crystal was stonewalling him. He glumly sat in the driver's seat of his car, watching the scene in front of him unfold.

The sun was rapidly disappearing as the search came to an end for the day. Murphy had waited in his car the entire time, hoping to get a glimpse of the Texas Ranger's name plate, or to see the body being recovered. Neither happened, and despite all his hours of waiting, Murphy had no idea what the victim's name was. Frustrated, he drove back to Athens. He'd be back in the morning.

Twenty-Seven

AT TEN O'CLOCK the next morning, Sheriff King and the Texas Ranger drove under the large wooden sign that read Malaby Ranch. They parked next to the massive front porch and found Shane Malaby drinking a cup of coffee while sitting in an oversized cedar rocking chair, with the ranch logo on the back. They walked up the steps, and Malaby grunted at them with no effort to get up or make any attempt at offering some hospitality. His dour facial expression never changed.

Crystal attempted to lighten the situation. She smiled at Malaby, shook his hand, thanked him for meeting with them, and introduced Tolbert Masterson. That elicited another grunt from Malaby. Still, making no attempt to get up, he limply took their outstretched hands, and again motioned for them to sit down in matching rockers.

The sheriff was shocked by the transformation from blustery loudmouth to Malaby's zombie-like appearance and disposition. It was as if he had become another person. She said, "Shane, Tolbert and I appreciate your meeting with us. Hope your wife is doing well."

Malaby snorted, "Well? She takes so many pills for depression she can't even tell you what day it is. That damn jury broke her heart and her spirit."

Tolbert said, "I am so sorry for the loss of your daughter, and the obvious pain this has caused your family, sir."

Malaby snorted again, "You don't know squat about what this has done to my family, so don't pretend you do."

Crystal jumped back in, "Shane, we're hoping you might give us a little insight. Two young women have vanished from local festivals, and whoever is responsible is following the same pattern as Van Cleave."

Malaby's facial expression did not change, "So, what the hell do you think I know about that, Sheriff?"

Crystal had a reassuring tone, "We're not sure you do, Shane, but since you followed the case every day in court, we're hoping you might give us your take on these recent events. We all assumed Van Cleave skipped town in embarrassment after his acquittal. There is no trace of him anywhere since then."

Malaby again maintained a poker face, even as his brain warned him to watch what he said. It was Malaby, after all, who had killed Van Cleave the night of his acquittal, cremated his body and dumped the ashes in Cedar Creek Lake, just as the funeral home director had done to his victims. The rancher shook his head, "Sorry, Sheriff, I don't know anything about what happened to that damn killer. I figured he left like a thief in the night. Did you check the funeral home?"

Crystal shook her head. "Not yet, Shane, but that's a good idea. As far as I know it's been vacant since Van Cleave disappeared. I think it went into foreclosure and someone bought it, but it hasn't been open for business as far as I know."

Malaby shrugged, appearing totally disinterested. He said, "Got me, Sheriff. I just sit here thinking about the most wonderful daughter a father ever had, and how that som'bitch killed her and got away with it." He crossed his arms defiantly over his chest.

Masterson gave it a shot. "So, Mr. Malaby have you ever tried to track down Van Cleave? I understand your pain and anger, so it would be a natural thing to do."

Malaby smelled a trap and shrugged. "Nope. He's gone. My

daughter's gone. That's the end of it. Now, I've got to go and check on my wife. Goodbye." With that he pushed himself out of the rocking chair and ambled into the house without so much as a glance back at the lawman. The door slammed and he was gone.

Masterson rose from his chair, "Well, that didn't go anywhere. I can't really get a read on Malaby, but something tells me he knows more than he's telling us."

Crystal replied, "I don't know, Tolbert. But I do like his idea about looking into who bought the old funeral home. It might give us a lead." They got into Crystal's police cruiser and drove back to Athens.

While the meeting with Malaby was going on, the Henderson County Sheriff's Department Rescue Team was back on the west side of Cedar Creek Lake, dragging that steel hook along the shoreline, searching for the body of Candace Avery. So far, they'd no luck finding the missing woman.

Twenty-Eight

ON THE EAST SIDE of the lake, Romy Moreland zoomed down Highway 198 on her way to scope out the sight of this weekend's Malakoff Cornbread Festival. Suddenly, a police cruiser was visible in her rearview mirror, blue lights flashing and siren wailing. A startled Moreland had a brief moment of panic, and then pulled over to the side of the highway, trying to keep her fears under control. *Did someone see my vehicle at one of the crime scenes? Are the cops onto me?* She reached under the front seat and felt the reassuring handle of a .357 magnum.

Moreland watched in her side mirror as a Texas State Patrol officer exited his police cruiser, carefully put on his Resistol hat with the custom color called Textan, and walk toward her car with his right hand on the gun in his holster. She'd already taken out her driver's license and insurance. She hit the power switch, lowering the driver's side window. Her body was poised to grab the gun under the seat in one swift move.

The officer stopped at her side door, tipped his hat, and asked in a slow Texas drawl, "Driver's license and insurance, please ma'am." He was polite but all business.

Moreland tried the innocent approach, trying to ferret out why she was pulled over by the state trooper. "Hello, Officer," she said in a sweet, non-threatening voice. "What seems to be the problem?"

The trooper didn't answer her question, saying instead, "Please stay in your car, ma'am. I'll be right back." She watched him climb back into his cruiser and type something into his computer. He kept one wary eye on her. His face was serious. His demeanor spooked the serial killer. Despite her extensive SEAL training, she was finding it difficult to control her breathing. Her mind was racing overtime, *Have they caught me already? Do I need to shoot this trooper? What is my next move?* To make the situation worse, cars continued to drive by, making it impossible to shoot him without a witness.

After what seemed like hours, but in truth was about two minutes, the trooper exited the car, and with his right hand still resting on his service revolver, walked back toward her car. Instinctively, Moreland leaned forward a little, and put her hand on the pistol under her seat.

The trooper, still looking serious, said through the window, "Miss Moreland, your driver's license says you live in South Carolina. Have you been in these parts for a while, or just passing through?"

The killer replied, "Just visiting, Officer. I haven't been in Texas before. It sure is pretty country." She smiled at him.

The trooper said, "Well, Miss Moreland, we have speed limits in Texas for your safety and that of other drivers on the road. I clocked you going eighty in a zone with a speed limit of fifty-five. That means I can arrest you and you could face felony charges for reckless driving."

Moreland was shocked. Was her quest to gain vengeance for the love of her life going to end because she had a lead foot? Moreland, stammered, "I'm so sorry, Officer. I had no idea I was going that fast. I just can't believe it." The truth was, she was relieved it was only speeding ticket instead of being hauled in for murder.

The state trooper ignored her plea, "And this road has many dangerous curves. It's a miracle you didn't get killed or kill somebody else."

Moreland seriously nodded, "Yes sir. I understand."

After a pause of about twenty seconds, that seemed like an eon, the trooper handed her a piece of paper as he said, "Since you're not from here, you may have not been paying attention to the speed limit, so I'm going to give you a break. I've knocked the speed down to eighteen miles an hour over the limit. That means you won't be arrested. You'll still need to pay a $309 fine."

The killer let out a sigh of relief. "Thanks, Officer. I understand your concerns, and I really appreciate your help. I promise I'll keep my speed right at the posted limits in the future."

He handed her the ticket, tipped his hat and said, "Good day, ma'am. Please slow down while you are in our fine state." He turned on his heel and walked back to his cruiser.

Moreland's breathing returned to normal as she shifted her car into gear, and carefully pulled back onto the highway. She set the cruise control at fifty-four miles an hour. The police cruiser pulled out behind her and followed at a discreet distance all the way into Malakoff. The serial killer was angry with herself. Her goal was to be inconspicuous, but now they had her name on file as being in the area. She slammed her fist on the dashboard. *Why was I so stupid?*

Back in Athens, Dwayne Murphy sent a text to Henderson County Sheriff's Sergeant Lonny Shields.

Can I buy you lunch? Need to talk.

A minute later came the reply.

OK. McDuff's at 1?

Murphy smiled as he replied. His cousin Caitlin had done a great job in cementing the longtime deputy as a source before she'd headed to Milwaukee.

Twenty-Nine

MORELAND DROVE INTO the historic downtown area of Malakoff. The town of just over two thousand souls had the usual array of gas stations, barbecue joints, quaint stores, and one McDonald's restaurant. Malakoff was founded in 1854 and was a hub of coal mining in the 1920s.

The Malakoff Cornbread Festival started nearly thirty years ago. The main event is the battle to come up with the best cornbread concoction. There are also the usual festival activities including food trucks, axe throwing, a corn hole tournament, corn eating contest, a dunking booth, and a car show. Many poor dogs are also subjected to a wide range of crazy costumes and, of course, there is live music.

Moreland parked her car in front of the Bookish Book Store. Her eye caught a sign that said they offered a variety of coffee and other drinks. She entered the store and was greeted by the smiling face of the owner, "Welcome. Can I help you with anything?"

The killer smiled at the vivacious blond, "Yes. I'd like one of your lattes, please."

Moreland walked around the bookstore, acting interested in various novels.

The owner brought her the steaming coffee drink, "I'm Jen. What's your name?" Moreland took the coffee, "I'm Sally."

Jen asked, "Are you new in town? Haven't seen you around here before?"

The killer nodded. "Yeah. Just passing through on my way to Kansas. Thought this was an interesting town, and your coffee sign got my attention."

Jen replied, "You should stick around a few days. Our annual Cornbread Festival is this weekend. It's a great time."

"Sounds great but I've got to keep driving." Tired of the conversation, the killer paid for the coffee, and walked back outside and down the street, acting like an interested tourist. She wanted to memorize all the roads and buildings, so she could grab a young woman undetected by security cameras or anyone else.

At precisely one o'clock, Lonny Shields ambled into McDuff's, tipped his hat to the owner, Shelly, and found Dwayne Murphy sitting at a table in the back of the dining room. The deputy wanted to have a late lunch, so the restaurant was nearly empty. He looked around. There was only one couple in the dining room, and they were deep in conversation. Mission accomplished.

Murphy rose to shake Shields' hand. The men sat down, and Lucinda Sue hurried over to take their orders. After she left, Shields leaned in toward the reporter, asking, "What's up, Murphy?"

Dwayne replied, "First off, thanks for meeting with me, Lonny. I need some confidential information."

The deputy smirked, "That's a shocker!" They both chuckled.

Murphy said, "I was over in Key Ranch this morning."

Shields jumped in, "Yeah, they're dragging for a missing kayaker. Her name is Candace Avery."

Murphy jotted down the name, and other information that his secret source gave him.

Of course, Shields admonished the reporter, "You didn't get any of this from me, Murphy."

The reporter stopped scribbling. "That goes without saying, Lonny. I would never burn a source, especially one as valuable as you."

They ate for a few minutes in silence. Murphy set down what was left of his juicy cheeseburger and asked, "So who is that Texas Ranger I saw with the sheriff this morning? And why is he in town?"

Shields, set down his fork and wiped his mouth, "Name's Tolbert Masterson. King called him to get a fresh set of eyes on these recent drownings and missing women. He's got quite the bloodline. He's a long-lost cousin to Bat Masterson."

Murphy was impressed, "Wow. That's a story in itself. So, what's the 4-1-1 on these victims, Lonny? It almost seems like The Frogman and that crazed funeral home owner are back in town?"

Shields nodded, "Yup. Except Martin is dead, and Van Cleave has apparently vanished from the face of the earth."

Murphy took a sip of sweet tea and glanced around the now empty dining room. "Lonny, I know people get upset about my conspiracy theories, but we now apparently have three drownings in a short time, which is unusual, and two young women missing from festivals. On top of that, I checked, and the two women disappeared from the same two festivals that started Van Cleave's spree."

Shields nodded in agreement. "I've looked into that, too, Dwayne. My question is—is this a copycat killer of both Martin and Van Cleave? And, if that pattern holds, he will try to abduct a young woman at the Malakoff Cornbread Festival this week."

Murphy was getting excited. "Did you run that past Sheriff King?"

Shields snorted, "I'm trying to keep a low profile. I already lost to her in the election, and I only have five months until I can retire with a full pension. I'm staying away from this one as much as possible."

Thirty

AFTER THE SHERIFF and Texas Ranger left his ranch, Shane Malaby's brain kicked into gear. After losing his daughter, and getting revenge by killing Van Cleave, the formerly energetic rancher had been wasting away each day rocking back and forth on his porch. But the information about two missing young women seemed to shake Malaby out of his malaise.

He'd already disposed of one serial killer when law enforcement and the court system failed to act, maybe he could help catch the person responsible for these two disappearances. The police were trying to find Van Cleave, but Malaby knew his ashes were resting on the bottom of Cedar Creek Lake, never to be found. *While they chase a ghost,* Malaby thought, *I can find the person who took those two young women before he grabs anyone else.*

For the first time in months, Malaby sprang out of the rocking chair, and strolled into his house with purpose. He'd find that bastard himself. He had nothing but time and a strong will.

While the police, the newspaper reporter, and the angry father all obsessed over the mysterious deaths, and who may be responsible, the subject of all this angst sat in the small den of the lake home she'd rented in Point La Vista, a community of about five hundred homes, thirteen miles south of Gun Barrel City. It is located on over one mile of shoreline, on the southeast end of the lake. The development has a pool, a pavilion, tennis courts, and a boat ramp for residents.

It is also an out of the way spot tucked in a rather secluded area, with little traffic, and most importantly to Moreland, few prying eyes. Her neighbors, she'd discovered were all weekenders, giving her privacy for most of the week. She could come and go without anyone noticing.

On this day, the serial killer was googling everything she could find about the weekend's Malakoff Cornbread Festival. Her reconnaissance of Malakoff showed it was going to be an arduous process to grab a young woman from the festival. First off, the festival occurred during the day. Secondly, the location was wide open. How could she grab someone without being noticed? She was becoming discouraged, but still determined to complete the task where Van Cleave had failed. She took another sip of her energy drink, and kept searching, hoping an idea would appear.

In Eustace, Chloe Campbell was busy decorating a colorful array of cupcakes. As she expertly applied the frosting, Chloe dreamed of a big weekend selling her wares at the Malakoff Cornbread Festival. The baker was average height and weight with large almond eyes, and a bright smile that matched her sparkling blond locks. She had a beautiful face which always attracted plenty of guys when she visited area drinking establishments.

But Chloe always turned them down. She was true to the guy she had dated since high school. He was serving a hitch in the Navy, stationed in Guam. They planned on getting married when he finished his service. At that time, they'd both be twenty-seven. Chloe already had the wedding planned out. It was going to be outside on her grandfather's ranch under the moonlight with longhorn cattle grazing in the background.

She'd started Chloe's Cupcakes a year ago, and she was struggling. Everyone agreed her cupcakes were delicious, but there was a lot of competition all over the lake area. Most of her sales were either online or at various festivals and events. She needed a big day at the festival to afford more ingredients. With a long sigh, Chloe continued to add colorful red, white and blue swirls to her cupcakes. Unfortunately, on the day of the festival her mother had a mild heart attack. Missing the festival may have saved her life.

That afternoon, Sheriff King phoned a friend of hers at one of the local title companies, "Hey, Sue. Hope you're doing well. I'm wondering if you can help me with something?"

A friendly, warm voice responded, "Of course, Crystal. Whatcha need?" King explained that she was wondering if anyone bought the old Rest In Peace Funeral Home in Kemp. As Sue's fingers flew across her computer keyboard, she asked, "Why do you care about the rundown place, Crystal?"

The sheriff knew that Sue was quite the gossiper and talked to a lot of people every day. She replied, "Oh, just checking. We never have heard anything from the owner since he left town, so I'm wondering if he sold the place."

Sue snorted, "Yeah, after killing those helpless young women, and then having that jury let him skate."

King sighed, "Unfortunately that was the case, Sue."

Sue was silent for a moment as she read from her computer. Then she said, "Well, Crystal, it looks like it was purchased by a shell corporation about a year ago. It was in foreclosure for failure to pay back taxes, so they bought it from the county. Whoever bought it paid the back taxes and basically was handed the property."

Crystal was puzzled, "What's the name of the shell company, and why would someone go through all that to buy a building in such disrepair?"

Sue explained, "A shell corporation has no active business interests or significant assets. They're not always illegal, but they are used to disguise business ownership from law enforcement and the public. The way this one was done they did not want anyone to know the name of the true owner or owners."

Crystal asked, "And the name of the shell corporation?"

Sue said, "It's Vindicta Ventures. Unfortunately, there is no business address, no list of officers. It is well disguised, Crystal."

The sheriff thanked Sue and hung up the phone. She stared out the window of her office, deep in thought. Just then Tolbert Masterson walked in.

He noticed the faraway look on Crystal's pretty face, "Hey, Sheriff, you look like somebody just kicked your dog. What's up?"

Crystal explained about the shell corporation. "Why would somebody go through all that bother, buy the place, and then leave it just rot away?"

Masterson was also a bit confused. "I've dealt with lots of shell corporations, usually drug dealers, or arms suppliers, but this is a strange one."

In fact, Romy Moreland, during her research on Van Cleave noticed a small blurb that said the old funeral home was up for auction because of unpaid back taxes. A woman she'd met during her time in the Navy was an expert on the dark web and started a business creating untraceable shell corporations for clients with deep pockets. She gave Moreland a sweet deal on her fee, one Naval servicewoman to another, and walked her step by step through the process of buying the property, while at the same time hiding her identity from preying eyes.

Masterson looked at Crystal and said, "What makes this shell corporation so unusual is that someone bought the business, and then apparently did nothing with it. Have you been out that way recently?"

The sheriff shook her head. "No. Had no reason to even think about the place until now."

"Well, just because the funeral home isn't open for business doesn't mean someone is using it as a base for an illegal operation or is even living there." They agreed to drive to Kemp in the morning.

Thirty-One

IN ATHENS, DWAYNE Murphy was researching Masterson. He was definitely a heavy hitter in the Dallas office of the Texas Rangers. He had an amazing pedigree being related to Bat Masterson, and two more Masterson Rangers. Having him in town was a big tip-off to the newspaper reporter that this case was being given urgency and priority. *But what is the case? So far, two people have drowned with really no signs of foul play, and two young women have vanished from festivals.*

It was the latter situation that caused bells to go off in Murphy's conspiratorial brain. *Those two victims vanished from the same two festivals in the same order as Van Cleave's victims. Has that demented funeral home director come back to cause more havoc and pain. If so, where has he been in recent years? What would be his motive this time?* So many questions, but no answers to this point. Murphy gathered up his notes and headed to the editor's office.

He found Adler Huxley poring over copy. His infamous red pencil poised to roughly scratch out any words he deemed unnecessary. Murphy knocked on the door. Huxley, without lifting his eyes from the pages in front of him, motioned him to a chair in front of the editor's huge desk. He continued reading for several minutes. In his short time at the Athens newspaper, Murphy had learned not to interrupt the grumpy editor.

Finally, Huxley laid down the copy and peered at Murphy with eyes half hidden by the bushiest eyebrows the reporter had ever seen. Huxley tilted his head toward Murphy, his movement silently asking, "What do you want?"

Murphy said, "I've just learned a Texas Ranger has been called in to help the Henderson County Sheriff's Office with these recent deaths." He paused, as Huxley sat forward a bit, taking more interest in what his reporter had to say.

That's when Murphy added exciting information that he felt would really grab Huxley's attention, "And is name is Tolbert Masterson, as in a relative of Bat Masterson. His nickname is "Night Train" for single-handedly taking down a big drug dealer who was using freight trains overnight to transport his product." Murphy smugly sat back in his chair, arms crossed, waiting for the praise he expected from his editor.

Huxley said nothing. He crossed his arms across his chest and sat back in his chair. He cleared his throat, "As far as I know, Murphy, no police official has said anything about these so-called victims being met with foul play."

Murphy was clearly angry and frustrated. He quickly said in a loud voice, "What do you want from me? Just having a famous Texas Ranger here is a helluva a story. And what if there is a copycat killer on the loose here?" Murphy stood up, pacing the room as he spit out those words.

Huxley pointed at the chair, "Sit down, Dwayne. I told you when I hired you that I would not allow you to publish your crazy conspiracy theories without solid proof. So far, you don't have anything even resembling that. Secondly, I do like the idea of profiling the famous Texas Ranger and if you do, you may be able to glean more information about these four people. So, calm down, set up an interview with Masterson, and continue to dig into your other ideas. But we will not publish anything on that until I have solid proof. Got it?"

Murphy calmed down a bit. At least he'd get a solid story with the famous Tolbert Masterson, and maybe he could trick him into saying something that would lead him to proof of his other theories. He said, "Okay, boss. Got it." He rose from the chair, turned on his heel, and without so much as a look back, or a goodbye, he quickly walked out of the editor's office. Huxley returned to his editing.

It was a rare day indeed when Crystal King's thoughts aligned with Dwayne Murphy's, but today her mind was walking down the same path as the pushy reporter. *Was there a copycat killer?* She wasn't sure about the two drownings which seemed to be totally disconnected with no signs of foul play, but the two young women vanishing from festivals, and in the same order as the women who disappeared during Van Cleave's spree, gave her pause.

She'd never said anything to her husband, Buddy, who was sheriff during the Frogman murders, or to their great friend Buddy Richardson, sheriff during Van Cleave's mayhem, but she felt they both denied any connection too long, allowing the murderous sprees to rage on. Maybe it was her woman's intuition, but in her heart of hearts Crystal couldn't help but think there was a murderer, or two, on the prowl around Cedar Creek Lake.

Thirty-Two

IN TOOL, DESTINY Jackson, had her smoker fired up as she prepared to make her famous brisket sandwiches for the Malakoff Cornbread Festival. The twenty-two-year-old had the figure of a beauty contestant. Her mocha-brown face had the sharp features of a model, and her eyes, a penetrating jade-green that mesmerized every man in the room. She checked the smoker temperature and brushed her dad's special rub on the thick slabs of pork and beef. They'd be ready in ten or twelve hours.

Destiny was a bit nervous, although she sold a lot of brisket at her little cement block store every day, the festival was her first big event since taking over Booker's Barbecue. She'd been helping her father at the store since high school, but when Booker Jackson suddenly died of a heart attack at age fifty-nine, she was left in charge of keeping his dream alive. Her mother had died of cancer when Destiny was a teenager.

Booker's restaurant and catering had been in business for nearly twenty years and was extremely popular with people making the drive from Dallas and all-over East Texas to buy her dad's barbecue magic. Destiny wanted to expand the business and believed selling her brisket at the big Malakoff Cornbread Festival would help gain that goal. She'd paid her vendor fee a bit late, and Destiny was not pleased with her location at the festival, which was at the very end of the rows of sellers. People have to walk past many food vendors to reach her.

Destiny also had no idea the serial killer had picked her location as the most vulnerable at the festival. As she studied a map of vendors, Moreland circled Booker's spot. It was at the end of everything, and it was a bit darker there than elsewhere in Malakoff. It was her prime target.

Dwayne Murphy decided an in-person visit might be the best way to snag an interview with the famous Texas Ranger, so he drove over to the sheriff's office. The dispatcher on duty, one of his best sources, greeted him warmly and enthusiastically shook the reporter's hand. Murphy asked to see the sheriff. The dispatcher called her office. He hung up and motioned Murphy toward the office.

As Murphy walked into King's office, he was pleasantly surprised to see a stranger sitting in a chair at the side table. He walked right up to him, hand extended, "I assume you are Tolbert Masterson?" The Texas Ranger rose from the chair and shook his hand. He said nothing, as he glanced at Crystal.

The sheriff smiled and introduced the reporter. "Tolbert, this is the number one pest in this part of the country. Name is Dwayne Murphy and he's a reporter for the *Athens Courier.* Dwayne this is indeed Tolbert Masterson. What can I do for you and your conspiratorial brain today?"

Murphy looked hurt and said, "Now, Sheriff, we don't want to give this distinguished guest the wrong impression of me." He turned to Masterson, "Actually, sir, I am the senior reporter at the newspaper, and up until a few months owned my own newspaper in Gun Barrel City."

Masterson again said nothing, just nodded. Murphy, undaunted, plunged ahead, "I'm actually here to see if I might secure an interview with you, sir. I've read about your exploits, and I'm sure my readers would love to learn more about you in a Sunday profile."

Masterson sat stone-faced. He looked toward the sheriff. King said, "As you can see Murphy, Mr. Masterson really isn't interested in talking to you."

Now Murphy was miffed at the cold reception, "Well, Sheriff, maybe you can tell me what this famous Texas Ranger is doing in our little town?"

Crystal shook her shiny blond locks. "Afraid there's nothing to it, Murphy. He's just visiting a few days. It's part of a new Texas Ranger outreach program for county sheriff departments."

Murphy snorted and then said sarcastically, "Right, Crystal. I'm sure it has nothing to do with the four recent murders." He defiantly crossed his arms and thrust out his chin.

King said in a quiet, even tone, "What murders, Murphy? We've had two recent drownings with no sign of foul play, and two young women who have disappeared. We haven't found any bodies?"

Again, Murphy snorted, "Yup, just like when the Frogman was drowning all those poor people, and Van Cleave was kidnapping and killing woman, and law enforcement kept saying 'There's nothing to see here.'"

Murphy was on a roll now, "Here's what I think, Sheriff. There is a copycat killer or killers mimicking the Frogman and Van Cleave. At this point I don't know who or why, but I do know the two missing women were taken at the Fiddle Fest and Rodeo, just like the first two women Van Cleave murdered. But I guess you already know that, and like me, at this point you have no idea who is behind this." He gave her a smug look.

The expressions on the faces of King and Masterson did not change during the reporter's rant. Crystal finally said, "That's exactly what I'm talking about, Murphy. You are obsessed by conspiracy theories. Facts be damned." Murphy started to respond, but Sheriff King held up her hand, "Stop, Murphy. You've taken enough of our time. As of right now, Mr. Masterson is not interested in doing an interview. Now, if you'll leave, we have work to do." She shooed him out the door, much like a gnat that had been bothering her.

The next morning, King and Masterson drove to the former

funeral home in Kemp. The place was a mess. Weeds, standing two feet tall encircled the property. The paint was peeling off the wooden sign that read "Rest In Peace Funeral Home." One of the boards had fallen down and was hanging on by one nail. There was no sign of activity and it didn't seem like there had been for a long time.

The sheriff and Texas Ranger walked around the building that contained the house and attached crematorium. The doors were locked. The windows were dusty and dirty. The paint on the building was peeling just like the sign. King said, "It sure doesn't look like anyone's been here in years, Tolbert."

The Ranger nodded, "It sure doesn't, Crystal. Why would somebody buy this place, and go through the hassle of creating a shell corporation and then just let it rot away?"

The unsuspecting pair had no idea that they were being watched at that very moment. There was a thick wooded area next to the funeral home property. There, carefully hidden in thick brush, Romy Moreland peered through her binoculars. Her SEAL training had drummed into her to always be a step ahead of the enemy. That's why she'd decided to stake out the funeral home for a few days before removing the ashes from victim number two.

The sheriff and lawman spent about fifteen minutes walking all around the property, checking for broken windows, and open doors. It was locked up tight. It sure seemed to be just an abandoned building left to rot away. The serial killer took it all in. She smiled to herself, it appeared they found nothing, and would most likely cross the place off their checklist. That would give her the freedom she needed to cremate other victims, and to store their ashes until she had a chance to put them in the lake so they disappeared forever.

King and Masterson climbed back in her police cruiser and headed off. Moreland, aware of the old trick of doubling back once someone felt safe, stayed hidden for two more hours. Satisfied they were indeed gone, the serial killer walked around the back of the house, unlocked the door, and went inside. The air conditioning kicked on and cool air flowed from the vents in the ceiling as she took a blue urn off a shelf. It contained the ashes of Addison Crow.

The shell corporation had prepaid the electricity and water for a year. Moreland was happy the A/C hadn't come on during the sheriff's visit. It helped with the illusion that the place was abandoned. Moreland put the urn in the trunk of her car, locked the door and left.

The serial killer had no idea another set of eyes was secretly watching her property. Shane Malaby had staked out the funeral home for three days, hiding in a clump of trees, sitting in a lawn chair with a pair of binoculars. He was so dedicated to keeping watch, that he fell asleep in the chair at night.

Malaby watched the sheriff and Ranger check out the funeral home, and then was surprised to see a woman emerging from a different hiding spot on the other side of the property. Once the law left, the woman went around the back of the property, unlocked the door and went inside. Several minutes later, Malaby watched the garage door open. She drove away.

The Mabank rancher waited a few minutes, in case she came back for some reason, then gathered up his chair and binoculars and hiked a half mile through the woods where his truck was parked. *Who was that woman? What connection did she have to Van Cleave? Was she the one who grabbed the two young women?* He had many questions, but no answers as he headed home for lunch. One thing was certain – he had found a potential suspect while the police were still trying to trackdown Van Cleave. Malaby knew they'd never find him or his ashes resting somewhere in Cedar Creek Lake.

Meanwhile, Moreland drove to a storage compound in Payne Springs and hooked up her boat and trailer. The killer launched her boat and headed toward the south end of the lake with the urn containing Addison Crow's ashes. She checked in all directions. Not another boater in sight. The boat chugged along at two miles an hour as she poured the ashes into the murky water and watched them disappear.

Thirty-Three

IN ATHENS, ADDISON Crow's parents decided it was time to pay a visit to the sheriff. They'd heard nothing about the disappearance of their daughter from the Mabank Rodeo. It was time for some answers. They walked to the dispatch desk and asked to see Sheriff King.

The dispatcher said, "I'm sorry she's in a meeting right now. Can I tell her who you folks are and the purpose of your visit?"

Crow's father was a bit indignant, "We're the parents of Addison Crow. She's been missing for weeks and we need to get some answers about your investigation." He glared at the dispatcher but his eyes betrayed him as a father fearful about what happened to his daughter. The dispatcher called the sheriff.

After hearing who was in the lobby, King said, "Okay. Send them back here. I'll talk to them."

The sheriff met Crow's parents at the door to her office and motioned them to take a chair at her side table. King began, "First off, please accept my concern about your daughter. I know how difficult this must be for both of you."

The father abruptly interrupted her, "No. I don't think you do, Sheriff. As I recall you have no children, so there is no way you can possibly have any idea how difficult this is."

King softly replied, "No. You're right. I don't know how terrible this is as a parent, but as the chief law enforcement officer of Henderson County, it is my job to keep everyone safe. So, this is personal to me as well."

Crow's mother, who had seemed timid, suddenly said loudly, "I voted for you because you promised to keep our children from harm. So, where is my daughter?" She began to sob loudly, as her husband rubbed her back and gave the sheriff a nasty glance.

Sheriff King said, "We've been monitoring her banking activity, and so far, her bank accounts have not been touched and her phone was found that night at the rodeo grounds. I know this is a difficult question, but could she have met someone, or run off with a boyfriend?"

Crow's voice grew louder this time, "Hell no! She's not that kind of young lady. She's a straight-A student for God's sake. She volunteers in nursing homes. She is a fantastic person."

The sheriff replied, "That's what our research shows as well, sir, but I hope you understand I had to ask that question. It does happen frequently, even with girls a lot like your daughter."

Crow said in a low voice, obviously fighting back tears, "That is not Addison Crow!" He turned away, attempting to hide his emotions.

After the disgruntled couple left, Sheriff King sat at her desk staring straight ahead, deep in thought. This was the part of her job she knew she'd dread, but in many ways, it was much worse.

She was shaken out of her malaise when Ranger Masterson walked into her office. "You look like you'd rather be somewhere else today."

King nodded, "Just met with the parents of Addison Crow. It tears me up."

Masterson slowly nodded. "I know just what you mean, Crystal. It's the worst part of this job." With a wry smile, he rubbed his hands together. "So, let's catch this bastard!"

The tricky part of catching a clever serial killer is anticipating their next move. Crystal said, "If he is a copycat killer, it means he'll try to strike at the Malakoff Cornbread Festival this weekend. So far, he's followed Van Cleave's path. First the Fiddle Fest, then the Rodeo. So, using that logic the Cornbread Festival should be next."

Masterson agreed, "Sounds right. What do you think, flood the place with undercover officers?"

Sheriff King nodded, "I think that's our play. Van Cleave was stalking women at the festival, but he was spotted acting strange by the women he was following and left empty-handed. The problem is he grabbed a woman at a bar in Caney City and killed her. So, it would make sense that the copycat would try to complete the task where Van Cleave failed."

It was the day before the Malakoff Cornbread Festival, and Destiny Jackson was preparing her special brisket as well as beans and cole slaw for what she hoped would be a big day of sales. As she wiped a sweat bead from her forehead, Jackson had no idea the copycat killer was lurking.

Dwayne Murphy was once again in the editor's office, pleading to be allowed to do a story about Tolbert Masterson, despite the fact the Texas Ranger would not do an interview. He had widened the scope from a simple profile, to a larger story explaining the famous lawman was in town to help with four unsolved murders. Newspaper editor Adler Huxley was unmoved. He was definitely old school. He wanted just the facts, never speculation. The compromise was that Murphy would cover the Cornbread Festival so he'd be there if anything did happen. If it was a peaceful celebration, Murphy would write a straightforward report on fun at the festival.

At her bungalow, Romy Moreland once again studied a map for vendors at the Cornbread Festival. This would be a daring and tricky mission. Snatching someone in broad daylight was dangerous. The good news is darkness would be settling in as the festival ended, and the vendors started to pack up. She circled the last booth in a long row of vendors. It would be her best chance with the aid of a little darkness, and no streetlight at the end of vendor's row.

Her target would be the owner of Booker's Barbecue. At the last second, Moreland decided paying a visit to the restaurant might give her some good information, and she could see what the owner looked like. She hopped in her car and headed toward Tool.

In Athens, Sheriff King called a meeting of her entire staff. She asked for volunteers to go undercover at the Cornbread Festival. Fifteen deputies and office staff raised their hands. King thanked them, told them to put in for overtime, and laid out her plans. The undercover police would be on the lookout for anyone acting suspicious. King admitted they had no idea what the possible copycat killer or serial killer looked like, so she told them just be aware of all activity at the festival.

Thirty-Four

SATURDAY STARTED WITH a beautiful sunrise as low-lying clouds filtered the light into bright red and orange fingers reaching across the sky. Vendors were busy setting up their canopies and putting out their wares for sale. Destiny Jackson arrived early and was ready to go an hour before the festival opened. She'd paid extra for electricity to keep her brisket warm and delicious. Nearby vendors walked over telling her how wonderful the aroma was coming from her table. Destiny smiled. *This is going to be a great day,* she thought. She had no idea someone else had a dire ending planned for her day.

The undercover police assembled three blocks away from the festival grounds, received their orders, and fanned out to blend in with the gathering crowd. Sheriff King and Texas Ranger Masterson would work together. All communication would be by phone. King didn't want to risk having the suspect listen in on a police scanner.

Romy Moreland, drove into Malakoff, and pulled into the Mc-Donald's a block off the downtown area. She wanted to spend time checking everything out, since she'd never been to a festival here before. She motored to the drive-thru, ordered a cup of black coffee, and pulled into a space at the edge of the parking lot facing the busy area of Malakoff.

119

✾

The weather was spectacular and that brought a big crowd to the festival. Families with kids in tow, couples, and groups of young women walked the grounds, buying the homemade goods, and noshing on a variety of foods and desserts. Destiny was ecstatic, she'd had a long line at her food stand all day. These proceeds would really help her keep the restaurant going.

The undercover deputies had been watching everyone all day. So far, it had been peaceful with not one suspicious person lurking around. Sheriff King was both relieved, and unhappy. Relieved that apparently everyone was safe, but unhappy that a suspect didn't reveal themselves. She said to Masterson, "Well we're in the final hour and we've got nothing. I just spent a lot of tax dollars for nothing."

Masterson replied, "It was worth a shot, Crystal. These guys are always difficult to catch. They need to make a mistake."

Crystal's mind drifted back to the serial killer the media had dubbed The Frogman Of Cedar Creek. They were nowhere in finding a suspect when he made a mistake, breaking the neck of a fisherman. That's when they had concrete proof the drownings were not accidental.

✾

Moreland had kept a low profile all day. She'd blended in with the crowd, and even bought a small handmade set of earrings so she'd have a bag to carry around like many of the revelers. She'd walked past Destiny's food stand several times, joining a crowd of shoppers. Destiny had no idea that a woman who meant to end her life was just a few feet away as she made still another brisket sandwich.

As the sun disappeared from a sky that had suddenly become filled with dark clouds, the festival came to an end and the crowd headed quickly to their cars, hoping to avoid what looked like a rainstorm headed their way. Sheriff King did a group call to all of her undercover operatives, "Okay, folks. Let's call it a day. Thanks for your assistance." She was sullen as she said to Masterson, "Thanks for your help, Tolbert."

Masterson replied, "I know you're extremely disappointed, Crystal, but it was worth a shot." With a wave he headed for his car. Crystal headed out as well.

Big rain drops began to fall, and the sky grew dark. Destiny rushed to pack her truck before the storm got worse. Moreland couldn't believe her good fortune. It was suddenly as dark as night and there was no one standing around in the area. The only people were other vendors scrambling to pack up. All concentrated on the task at hand, paying no attention to other folks around them.

Destiny had just finished stowing her food warmer in the truck. She was on the side away from the other vendors. Suddenly, someone was behind her. Startled, she spun around to see a woman holding a gun. The stranger roughly grabbed her arm. Destiny was surprised how strong the woman was. Moreland said in a low, menacing voice, "You scream...I'll shoot you dead. You struggle...I'll shoot you. Got it?" She emphasized the point by squeezing Destiny's arm even harder.

Destiny half-whispered, not wanting to upset this crazed person, "If you want my money, go ahead and take it. Just don't hurt me. I promise I won't go to the police, and I will not remember what you look like."

Moreland cackled, "I don't want your damn money. I want you." With that, she shoved the gun hard into Destiny's ribs, causing her to yelp in pain. "Now we walk like two friends to my car. If you try anything I will kill you!" Once again, she jammed the pistol harder into Destiny's rib cage.

Moreland took a quick look around as the wind picked up, and the rain pelted down harder and harder. Anyone nearby was focused on one thing—packing up and escaping the stinging rain drops. Not one person was looking their way. Moreland said, "Okay. Time to move. Don't try anything." She grabbed the arm tighter guiding Destiny toward her car which was parked on a side street a block away.

They reached her car. Using her key fob Moreland popped the trunk, and roughly pulled Destiny toward it. Destiny's mind was racing. Should she try to escape? Will this crazy woman really shoot her? Would anyone hear her scream and get to her in time? Just then a loud thunderclap crashed nearby. Destiny jumped, it seemed to be so close. Moreland jammed the syringe with the combination of morphine and embalming fluid into her arm. Destiny started to fall toward the ground. Moreland grabbed her, stuffed her now lifeless body in the trunk and slammed it shut.

The rain was now falling so hard the serial killer could barely see three feet in front of her. She put the car in gear, and carefully headed out of town. This was no time to get into an accident and have police check her trunk. Moreland took the route around the west side of the lake and headed to Kemp. Destiny's truck was left behind with the rear door open, and bags of buns still sitting on the table getting soaked by the storm. No one paid any heed as they drove away with the rain pouring down.

The serial killer drove about ten miles an hour under the speed limit with the rain continuing to pelt down in huge drops. A bit of fog had also rolled in. Visibility was near zero. Moreland loved every minute of it. She finally reached the rundown funeral home and pulled into the garage. Since no one would be out in this weather, Moreland decided to immediately fire up the crematorium and reduce Destiny Jackson to ashes.

The serial killer was unaware that the rain had also given her another bonus. Shane Malaby, who had once again staked out the funeral home, was forced to race to his truck as the storm rolled in. He decided to call it a day as the rain poured down. Malaby left his post less than fifteen minutes before Moreland returned.

Thirty-Five

ONCE THE THUNDERSTORM moved off toward Louisiana, the broken clouds that remained created a beautiful multi-colored canvas as the sun set in the west. It had turned into a calm, cool evening. Crystal King headed out on the patio of their lake home, and using a large towel wiped the water off the deck chairs and table. Buddy placed thick T-bone steaks on the grill, along with corn on the cob still in their silky cocoon.

Tolbert Masterson settled into one of the deck chairs and sipped on his cold beer, "Buddy, this has turned into a beautiful evening."

Buddy wiped the hands on his chef's apron, "Yeah, it's always great when we get a storm that leaves behind cool air that smells so fresh." The King's had invited Masterson over for some great food, and hopefully a conversation that might get them on track to find the missing victims.

After a quick prayer, the three of them hungrily dug into the steaks and corn. The good food created a few moments of silence as they enjoyed the night and the meal. Crystal recapped what had occurred so far. One man and two women had apparently drowned in Cedar Creek Lake. The young man was fishing on his personal watercraft, the second victim was a strong, experienced, Olympic-level swimmer, and the third a well-known kayaker. All three victims had never met each other, didn't have any of the same friends, and had no known enemies."

Buddy spoke first, "I'm really concerned these apparent accidental drownings weren't accidental at all. They remind me so clearly of our experience with that serial killer Navy SEAL. If there is a person doing this, they are extremely strong, and well-trained at avoiding detection. All three victims had to be watched before they disappeared in the lake because each of them had a pretty rigid schedule of when they were in or on the water."

Masterson agreed, "I've read all I could find on that Naval serial killer, and it sure appears the same pattern could be true here."

Crystal joined the conversation, "And speaking of patterns, the two women who vanished from the area festivals also are in sync with the killing spree by Van Cleave, the old funeral home director. His first victim was at the Athens Fiddle Fest, and his second was taken at the Mabank Rodeo. That's exactly what is happening again." She let out a long, deep sigh. These deaths were really weighing on the first-time sheriff.

Buddy said, "Well, we know the guy they called the Frogman, Cody Martin, is dead. Crystal saw to that. But is it possible Van Cleave is back in town? He sure left in a hurry and hasn't been seen since the day he was acquitted."

Crystal said, "We've checked every avenue possible to find out where Van Cleave is. But he has no credit cards, didn't renew his driver's license, there are no bank accounts and he has no social media footprint."

Masterson recounted, "There was a guy named Edmund Kemper who killed his grandparents in California when he was fifteen. He was sent to a psychiatric hospital, but when he turned twenty-one, he convinced the doctors he was rehabilitated. After his release, he ended up killing eight more people, targeting young female hitchhikers. They were gruesome murders. He would take the corpses home, decapitate and dismember them. After he killed his mother, he finally turned himself in to California police and is in prison serving eight consecutive life sentences. I bring it up because he stopped killing for six years then started up again when he was released. There is a possibility, Van Cleave is back seeking more revenge on young women?"

Crystal shuddered at the thought, "That is one of the possibilities we can't ignore for sure. My question is, how do we get these investigations on track. We're stymied right now. I need to make some progress on getting answers for our department and the public, not to mention the parents of these victims."

Buddy turned to Tolbert, "Crystal is in a tough spot. Newly elected and now faced with the possibility there is another serial killer on the loose. She needs to show some action."

The Texas Ranger stroked his chin, deep in thought. Then he said, "Crystal, I'm as lost as you on this one. The only suggestion I have is to go back and try to follow the evidence, or in this case find some evidence. We should revisit the autopsies on the two drowning victims whose bodies have been recovered, as well as re-interview everyone connected in any way to the two missing women."

Crystal liked the plan, at least it would create some possible new information on the victims, as well as maybe develop a lead or two. She felt better, took a sip of wine and relaxed for the first time in weeks. Then her phone rang.

It was the dispatcher, "Good evening, Sheriff. Sorry to bother you, but we apparently have a vendor missing from the Malakoff Cornbread Festival. After the storm, a Malakoff deputy was cruising through the festival area and saw one of the vendors had left a table still set up, and there was a truck parked nearby with the passenger door left open. Of course, the inside is soaked now after the heavy rain." Crystal felt her world falling away. Not another one. They'd staked out the festival with no sign of anything troubling.

Her dinner companions closely watched her reaction to the call. She got up from her chair, and said, "We need to head to Malakoff looks like we may have another victim missing from a local festival!" As Crystal headed inside to grab her gun, Buddy and Tolbert quickly cleared the plates from dinner, and carried them into the house. By that time, Crystal was halfway out of the front door. They grabbed their guns and hurried after her.

They piled into her cruiser and with siren blaring and lights flashing, sped toward Malakoff. At that same time, Dwayne Murphy received a text.

There's another one. Malakoff.

Without hesitation, the reporter hustled out of his house, and headed for the crime scene as well.

As she entered Malakoff, Crystal could see the flashing blue lights a few blocks away at the site of the festival. She shook hands with the Malakoff patrolman who had happened on the crime scene and introduced her two companions. The patrolman said, "I was drivin' through the area and happened across this." He pointed at the vendor booth, "As you can see it looks like the vendor was packing up, and my guess is, she was interrupted by someone. The truck door was left open."

The *she* reference caught Crystal's immediate attention. The patrolman responded, "Yeah, I checked with the organizers and according to the vendor map this spot was rented to Destiny Jackson from Booker's Barbecue."

Crystal just shook her head, "Her father, Booker, was an expert brisket smoker. Ran a restaurant and catering service in Tool. He died recently, and his daughter Destiny took over. She is a beautiful young lady with real smarts."

Masterson asked, "Young lady?"

Crystal sadly nodded, "Yes sir. Early twenties just like the two others. Let's get a BOLO out right now with her description. Maybe someone saw something this time." The sheriff glanced down the street, "Oh, hell no! How'd Murphy already find out about this? I swear if I find who is feeding him information, I'll fire the SOB on the spot."

The reporter ambled toward them, snapping pictures of the scene. The sheriff said, "Murphy, what the hell are you doing here?"

Murphy smiled, "Just covering the story of now a third missing person, Sheriff."

King said, "And what gives you the idea that's what happened here?"

This time Murphy gave her a snarky smile, "Come on, Crystal. I've been around long enough to recognize a crime scene when I see one."

The sheriff took a step toward him, her fists clenched, "And who the hell told you this was a crime scene?"

Buddy King could see his wife was about to blow a fuse, so he quietly stepped between her and Murphy, "Sheriff, why don't we check out the truck." As he gently guided her away from the reporter. He was truly concerned she was about to punch him. Crystal glanced back at Murphy, "You don't come any closer, Murphy. I don't want you traipsing through my potential evidence."

Murphy, ever the protagonist, replied, "So, I can quote you as saying you now have a third missing young woman, Sheriff?"

She wrested her arm from her husband and took a step toward Murphy. Once again Buddy calmed her down. The crime scene unit showed up. Despite meticulous work, they found no fingerprints or any other clues that might lead them to Destiny, or her abductor. Murphy kept his distance, took more pictures, and didn't say a word, feeling he'd antagonized the sheriff enough for one night.

Thirty-Six

THE NEXT MORNING, Bernice Ashe finished sweeping the sidewalk at her lake house in Key Ranch and walked toward the dock. The eighty-three-year-old still had the slim figure she'd had in high school, but her knee replacement slowed her down a bit as she shuffled toward the water. She had platinum hair, cut short, but always neatly combed.

Mrs. Ashe walked onto the dock and started brushing off the deposits from the ducks who enjoyed sunning themselves on her pier. As she swept near the empty boat cradle—she'd sold the boat after her husband passed away from cancer—Bernice was startled to see what looked like a ball of hair in the shallow, dark green water.

Taking her glasses from her pocket, she put them on for a closer look. She was aghast when she nudged the hair with her broom, and a decomposing body rolled over exposing itself in the water. She dropped the broom, hurried into the house as quickly as her repaired knee would allow, and called 9-1-1 to report the body resting under her dock.

Sheriff King was having a cup of coffee at home before heading to the office. It had been a long night, and she slept in a bit. But it was time to get to work. That's when her phone rang, "Crystal, this is Bennie. We just received a call from a citizen. It looks like the body of Candace Avery has finally surfaced under her dock."

King slammed down her coffee cup, spilling some of it on her marble countertop, "I'm on the way. Text me the address. And I want no radio traffic on this one. The dispatcher replied, "That's why I called you directly, Sheriff."

On the way to Key Ranch, King phoned Masterson, giving him the address and asking him to meet her there. She said, "We found her kayak a week ago, so I've been expecting this but on top of the disappearance of Destiny Jackson this is more bad news. That makes three drowning victims, and three women who have vanished. This has to stop. We've got to catch this guy or guys before they take another life."

At that same time, Romy Moreland was cruising the lake, heading for the south end to dump the ashes of Destiny Jackson. As she passed Key Ranch, the police activity caught her attention. Moreland turned the boat toward the shoreline, slowed to trolling speed, and put a pole with a silver slab in the water as if she was just another fisherman.

She had to be careful to keep her identity hidden. Moreland pulled her blue cap with the Cabela's logo on the front tightly on her head, partially hiding her face, which was also covered by deep blue colored sunglasses. She watched as the police pulled something out of the water. It looked like a person. Moreland surmised that it had to be Candace Avery. After another quick glance, she reeled in the lure, stowed the pole and headed for the north end of the lake.

Once there, the serial killer slowed to trolling speed once again and cast the pole with the devil diver and silver spoon out the back of the boat. She took her time to carefully take a 360 degree look around. She saw another boat approaching. The driver veered left away from her, giving her the courtesy of not creating a wake while she was trolling. Without a glance back, the fisherman piloted his bass boat farther south on the lake.

Once alone, Moreland unwrapped the urn from the towel, opened the cover and slowly poured the ashes into the lake. She was in twenty feet of water. The last remains of Destiny Jackson quickly fluttered out of sight. Moreland put the boat in gear and sped back to the boat launch. She smiled to herself, another perfect crime.

Predictably, Dwayne Murphy was sitting across from his editor, once again making a plea to tie the three missing women, and two drowning victims to a serial killer. Once again, his frustration was bubbling over because of the cautious attitude of his old-fashioned boss. He was pacing the room, "I tell you, Adler, there is a big story here. This guy has followed the exact pattern of Van Cleave with now three missing women. And then you have drowning victims, two bodies found so far and one still missing. There has to be a copycat killer or two."

Just then Huxley's phone rang. He answered, glanced at Murphy, and then thanked the caller. "That was a police source of mine. They just found the third drowning victim, Candace Avery, under a dock in Key Ranch."

Murphy sat down. "So that's six victims, Adler. We've got to do a big spread. These aren't six random incidents and having that Texas Ranger in town just adds to the fact that something big is going on. Let's get on the record ahead of everyone else."

Huxley rocked in his old wooden desk chair, arms folded across his chest, face deep in thought. He finally said the words that Murphy had been craving, "Alright. You write the story but I want the sheriff on the record as well. And probe into this Texas Ranger too. I want to do it right though. That means a minimum of speculation. No conspiracy theories. Just the facts as we know them today. You can add the history of the other two serial killers, but at this point you will not refer to a copycat killer until we get more facts. I will get the final say on the article and its contents. Got it?"

Murphy was already halfway out the door, "Got it, boss. I assume we're talking a spread in the Sunday edition?"

Huxley nodded, then added, "And put a small blurb on our website and Facebook page about the body of Candace Avery being found."

Murphy immediately put a call into Sheriff King. She, against her better judgement, agreed to sit down with Murphy at one o'clock. She didn't relish battling with the reporter's theories, but she had to admit his instincts were amazingly on target most of the time. Maybe he'd jar something in her brain to get the investigation on track.

Masterson walked into her office just as her phone rang. He flopped into a chair and waited. It was the Henderson County Coroner. She put the phone on speaker, "Go ahead, Doc. I've got Texas Ranger Tolbert Masterson with me as well.

The coroner, as usual, was all business, "I've completed the autopsy of Candace Avery. Her lungs were filled with water. She definitely drowned."

Sheriff King asked, "Can you tell if someone held her under water to cause her drowning death?"

After a short pause while she re-read her notes, the coroner replied, "No ma'am. There were no ligature marks, no bruises. Nothing to indicate this was anything but a tragic drowning."

Masterson jumped in, "She's the third drowning victim in recent weeks. So, I understand, you are saying none of them had any indications of a struggle before they died?"

The doctor tersely replied, "That's what I'm saying. You'll have my full report on your desk, Sheriff by COB today." She hung up.

King and Masterson sat in silence for a few moments. Their frustration was palpable. The Texas Ranger broke the silence. "Anything turn up as your troops reviewed the evidence, and re-questioned anyone who might know something?"

King vigorously shook her head from side to side. "Not a damn thing. It's like this guy is a ghost."

Masterson steepled his fingers in front of him, "Well, it might be wise to eliminate any Navy SEALs who live around here. Maybe we can put the potential copycat theory to rest?"

Again, King shook her blond locks "Impossible. Buddy tried to get that information when he was sheriff during the Frogman's killing spree, apparently their names and whereabouts are a deep dark secret."

Masterson looked surprised, King continued, "He finally got a congressman to give him some names. But it was a bust. The Frogman's name wasn't on the list."

Masterson grunted, "Another dead end I guess." They returned to their own thoughts, as silence filled the office.

Thirty-Seven

ROMY MORELAND SAT along the shore of Cedar Creek Lake's Tom Finley Park. It's a pretty little area next to the bridge, on the left side of the road as you travel from Gun Barrel City to Seven Points. There are two boat launches, a treed picnic area, covered pavilion, and an inviting swimming spot. Moreland sat under the shade of a tall live oak and fondly held the well-worn picture of her and Cody.

As she often did, she talked to the picture as if Martin was sitting next to her, "Hello the best thing that ever happened to me. I miss you so much, but I want you to know I'm tired of offing other folks. It's time to move on to the main event. I can sense fear in the locals, but I want that damn sheriff. The one who took your life. She must pay for taking away the only person who ever cared about me."

Over the years, Moreland's recollection of her time with Cody Martin had taken on a life of its own. Her brain imagined that they spent every possible moment together while they served in the SEALs, and that it was a romantic relationship. The truth was Cody Martin had eaten a few meals in the mess hall with her, but that was it. They had attended a movie on the base together. Moreland re-imagined that as a wonderful evening of holding hands and snuggling. Truth of the matter was that Martin brought her a bag of free popcorn and sat with her during the movie. He looked at her as a fellow SEAL. Nothing more. In her mind, he loved her, and would be the first one in her lonely life to care about her, and make sure she was safe.

She gently smiled at the badly worn snapshot of them together, "I'm going to plan the final mission. I will kill that woman! I'm going to build an IED and put it under her police cruiser. She'll turn the key and boom! Goodbye killer!"

During her days as a Navy SEAL, she spent twenty-four weeks learning basic underwater demolition, the basics of parachute jumping and many other grueling skills followed by tests and finally the infamous "Hell Week" when the SEALs hopefuls go without sleep while performing many exhausting tasks. Moreland really proved skillful during the demolition phase of the Land Warfare training segment that last nine weeks. She was known for building the deadliest IEDs (Improvised Explosive Devices) in her class. She brought those skills to bear during her various missions after graduation.

About thirty yards away, Rhonda Melrose and her two small children were enjoying a picnic in the park on an idyllic day. As they munched on peanut butter sandwiches, Melrose noticed a woman sitting alone under a tree, rocking back and forth and talking to herself as she apparently looked at a small snapshot. The young mother became concerned about the strange woman who was wearing a brown t-shirt and cutoff jean shorts, along with a grey baseball cap. There were no logos on either the shirt or the ball cap. Melrose worried that the person was mentally ill based on the way she was acting.

Her kids clamored for more Kool-Aid. When she finished filling their glasses and looked up, the woman was gone. Melrose couldn't get the woman's odd behavior out of her mind. Unfortunately, she never did a get a good look at her face, which was in the shade, and partially covered by the cap. The kids started acting up, and the strange woman was quickly forgotten.

Promptly at one o'clock, Dwayne Murphy sauntered into Sheriff King's office without knocking, like he owned the place. Sheriff King and Masterson were deep in a discussion. King was irked by his rude entrance, "Nice to see you, Murphy, but next time check in at the front desk instead of just strolling into my office. Got it?"

Murphy nodded. This was no time to put her in a bad mood, he wanted to ask some pointed questions. Besides, he was stunned by an unexpected bonus. The Ranger was also apparently going to talk to him.

He stood in front her desk. "Yes ma'am. I apologize. May I sit down?"

His hint of sarcasm was not lost on anyone as King motioned him to a chair, "So what's on your mind today, Murphy?"

He scooted to the end of his chair, leaning toward the sheriff, "Well, ma'am, I've been assigned to write a front-page story about the recent spate of drownings and disappearances around these parts."

King let out a long sigh, "That's what I figured. So, is this going to be one of your speculative articles that needlessly scares the locals?"

Murphy, doing his best to look like a choir boy replied, "No ma'am. We at the *Athens Courier* have some concerns and questions and so do the citizens of Henderson County."

King smiled. She had been through these dances with the mettlesome reporter before. "That's a good speech, Murphy. But let's get down to business. I actually think you may be able to get the word out so people can be on the lookout for the person or persons who might be involved in the disappearance of the three young women. The coroner assures me all three drowning victims died of natural causes. They all had lungs filled with lake water."

Murphy loudly scoffed at her, "C'mon, Crystal. We've known each other for a long time. We were both involved in the Frogman drownings. Y'all didn't suspect anyone then until he carelessly broke that fisherman's neck! You must have had concerns. We don't usually have more than two or three drownings in a year, and there have now been three in just a few weeks. One of the three was a world class swimmer. There's no way someone with her skill level would drown on her own."

Masterson jumped in, "We haven't been formally introduced. I'm Texas Ranger Tolbert Masterson, and I have over thirty years of chasing murderers and other bandits." He glanced at the sheriff, "If I may, Crystal?" She nodded in the affirmative. Tolbert continued as Murphy quietly turned on his tape recorder, "When the county coroner does an autopsy and finds no evidence of foul play, no bruises, no scratches, nothing under the victim's fingernails, and their lungs are filled with water, I believe her when she says they drowned."

Murphy changed the subject, "I'm honored to meet you sir. May I ask what has brought a famous Texas Ranger to our little spot on the map if foul play is not suspected? Masterson replied, "I'm assisting the sheriff in locating the three women who have vanished. We go all over the state, as you know, assisting law enforcement when possible. Nothing more, nothing less."

The reporter turned to the sheriff, "So, Crystal, is this your attempt to get ahead of this serial killer?"

The question, as he anticipated had the desired effect, Crystal glared at him, her voice rising, "There you go, Murphy. Nobody said anything about a serial killer."

Murphy plunged on, trying to get the sheriff worked up so she might say something she wanted to keep secret, "So how do you explain the fact three women have disappeared from local festivals in the exact same order as they did when Van Cleave was on his murder binge?"

The sheriff rose from her chair. For a moment, Murphy thought she might smack him. Instead, she sat on the front of her desk, a menacing couple feet away from Murphy, wagging her finger in his startled face, "That's the kind of speculative reporting I'm talking about. Stick to the facts instead of trying to create news and scare the hell out of our citizens!"

Murphy recoiled a bit and said, "I want the facts, for instance, what has your investigation turned up concerning the fact (he stressed the word) three women have vanished from the same festivals, in order, as they did with Van Cleave?" He felt some courage returning, as he defiantly crossed his arms across his chest and jutted his chin toward her.

The sheriff calmed down a bit, "First of all, Murphy. Two women were taken from the same festivals as Van Cleave, in the same order. But the Malakoff Cornbread Festival doesn't fit the pattern because he failed to grab anybody there during his rampage."

Murphy gave her a shrug and a crooked grin, "So, this guy succeeded where Van Cleave failed. It's still in the same exact order. He is definitely a copycat killer!"

Masterson didn't like the direction of the conversation, so he jumped back in. "Murphy, you obviously don't know the difference between a fact and speculation. The fact is three women have disappeared. The speculation you offer is there is some sort of copycat killer on the loose. That, son, is a long leap from what we know so far. I've dealt with reporters like you before, more bent on making a name for themselves than writing a true, factual story." Murphy opened his mouth to respond to the Ranger's rebuke, but Sheriff King held up her hand, signaling him to stop talking.

"We're out of time here, Murphy. Here is my message to the public. We are currently looking for their assistance in finding three young women who have gone missing after attending a number of area festivals. So far, we have no proof of foul play. We're asking anyone with information to please call the Henderson County Sheriff's Department." With that she walked to the door, and motioned Murphy to leave. None of the three said another word as he exited the sheriff's office.

The sheriff dialed up longtime *Athens Courier* editor, Adler Huxley. She'd known him well for years. When Huxley answered, Crystal said, "How are you Adler? Haven't seen you in a while."

Huxley chuckled, "Just trying to keep my head in the foxhole, Crystal. What's going on?" King recounted their conversation with Murphy, "Adler, I have not, and will not ever ask you to not report a story, but I'm afraid your boy Murphy is knee-deep in another of his conspiracy theories. It is dangerous for him to throw around the word copycat killer with no evidence, and even worse if garbage like that is printed in your newspaper."

Huxley, ever the diplomat, assured Sheriff King he would have the final edit responsibility for the article. "I'm well aware of Murphy's proclivity for sensationalism and I will not allow it as long as I hold the editing pencil at this newspaper, and I warned him about that."

King felt better, "Thanks, Adler. I've always known you to be classy and straightforward, and I'm sure you will be with this story. I feel better just talking to you. It was hell when Murphy owned his own newspaper and had no one like you to keep him in line."

There was a chuckle on the other end of the phone, "I understand, Crystal. When I hired him, I warned him that we only deal in facts here. Now, having said that, is there anything you can tell me about these unexplained disappearance and drownings?"

The sheriff replied, "Like I told Murphy, the coroner says all three drowning victims had water in their lungs with no signs of foul play. Young women disappear all the time, and that's the focus of our investigation right now. We need to find them. If you could ask the public to give us any information they have on any or all of the three, it would be very helpful." The editor assured her it would be included prominently in the article.

Thirty-Eight

WHILE CONVERSATIONS continued in the sheriff's office, the serial killer drove to the old funeral home in Kemp. She wanted to do a reconnaissance mission to see if the police were staking out the place. Moreland had installed a few wireless game cameras and hung them from some trees around the property. She'd paid cash for internet service using the name of her shell corporation. The cameras alerted her phone if anyone came onto the property, sending her a video clip as well.

The cameras had warned her when the sheriff and Texas Ranger walked around the property. She was glad they didn't enter the building, and especially the crematorium which would still give off the odor of hot ashes, even a couple days after she had cremated one of her victims. Moreland parked her car about a quarter mile from the funeral home, and worked her way through the adjoining wooded area, staying out of sight while surveying the scene.

Even though she was heavily trained in ground combat, Moreland failed to see a man with powerful binoculars watching her from a great distance. Malaby had built tree forts from the time he was just a little boy. Using those skills, he'd constructed a small wooden platform about a half mile from the funeral home. It was impossible to see through the trees unless you were standing right under it.

The angry father purchased GSCI Long-Range Tactical Thermal binoculars. They were crazy expensive costing over $10,000. But they had a range listed at one-and-one-half miles. With his location, just a half mile from the funeral home, Malaby had a great view of the property. The binoculars also had the capability to snap pictures. He was determined to get a clear shot of this woman's face. Hoping to have one of his police friends run it through facial recognition on the sly.

Romy Moreland took a walk through a portion of the woods until she came to the rear of the crematorium. Satisfied no police were watching her, she unlocked the door and walked inside. The super-hot crematory had cooled down after reducing the flesh and blood of Destiny Jackson into a five-pound pile of gray ashes. She sniffed the air. There was no sign of the crematorium actually being used. Moreland exited the rear door, locked it, and walked back through the woods, taking one last look around the property, searching for any signs of police surveillance.

Her path took her within a couple hundred feet of Malaby's perch, but her head was down looking for any footprints or cigarette butts on the ground. The serial killer passed by Malaby without so much as a glance his way. He finally took a breath after not daring to make any movements or sounds while the killer was walking nearby. Moreland reached her car, climbed aboard and drove away.

Shane Malaby waited a full hour in the tree, just in case the woman doubled back. He was excited after capturing a clear shot of her face. He was convinced that she had to be copying Van Cleave, grabbing women at festivals, probably using the same lethal combo of embalming fluid and morphine that he'd used. Like Murphy, he too noticed that the women were vanishing from the festivals in the same order as when the funeral home director was on his mission of death.

Darkness was settling into East Texas when the rancher finally climbed down from the tree, carefully cradling his expensive binoculars, and their precious picture. Malaby looked at the picture dozens of times as he sat in the tree waiting for the cover of night.

He did not recognize the woman. He was convinced that he'd never seen her around town before. But who was she? He had to know. Malaby had already decided that since the police seemed to be nowhere, he'd once again have to end this killing spree on his own, just as he had with Van Cleave.

Earlier that afternoon, Dwayne Murphy and Adler Huxley had their worst disagreement since he was hired on at the newspaper. Murphy was furious that Huxley talked to the sheriff after his visit, and basically caved on the story. The careful editor had already rejected three versions of the article for the Sunday paper. Murphy felt hog-tied on his own story, and he let Huxley know of his displeasure. Huxley was not swayed. Late that day he agreed to hold off on more discussion about the article until the next morning. In the meantime, Huxley "invited" Murphy to do a more tamed down re-write. Murphy stomped out of the office.

In her tiny, rented cabin, Romy Moreland chugged down a Monster Energy Drink, and went to work crafting a powerful IED to place under Sheriff King's police cruiser. There are a number of components that come together to create an effective IED. First, you need an initiator, a switch, the main charge, a power source and a container to hold everything together. An IED is usually also packed with what are called "enhancements" such as shards of glass, nails or metal fragments. Moreland had become an expert at building these devices thanks to the Navy SEALs. She had some of the components but would have to track down the parts she was missing.

Shane Malaby returned to his ranch and using his computer made prints of the mystery woman. He had a smug smile on his face, sure that he had located the person grabbing young women at the festivals, while the police seemed unable to locate her. He called the mobile phone of one of the Mabank police detectives who had moonlighted at his ranch, providing security when Malaby would throw big parties or host fundraisers.

She answered on the second ring. Malaby made small talk for a few minutes before asking her for a huge favor. "I have a picture of a woman who has been kind of snooping around the ranch. I'm not sure what she's up to, but I'd like to find out who she is and what she does."

The police officer asked, "What do you want me to do, Shane? Do you want me to find some men who can keep an eye on your ranch for you in case she comes back?"

Malaby replied, "What I'd really like is for you to try to find out who she is, using the picture I took and facial recognition software."

There was a long pause before the detective answered, "I'm not sure that's possible, Shane. Our computer system is undergoing an update, and none of us has access to the equipment right now."

Malaby was not happy. "How long is that supposed to take?"

The officer responded, "Everything is supposed to be up and running in a week. If you want to send me a copy of the picture I could sneak in and do it then."

Patience was not in Malaby's vocabulary. "Naw, that's alright. I'll figure out something." He hung up before she could respond. But he really had no other choice so he shipped the pictures to her anyway.

Thirty-Nine

EVEN THOUGH HE had slowed down a lot since the murder of his daughter, and killing Van Cleave, Malaby was not one to just wait around until something happened. He grabbed a dark jacket, and a stocking cap along with the keys to his truck. Without saying goodbye to his wife, he jumped into his truck and headed to the funeral home. It was time to take a look around inside.

Malaby drove onto the property, killing his headlights as he neared the funeral home. He parked off to the side of the property, grabbed a powerful flashlight from his toolbox in the truck, and set off toward the crematorium. He stopped halfway and spent a few minutes looking in every direction for any sign of anyone else. Satisfied he was alone; Malaby approached the back door of the crematorium and picked the lock. It was a skill he'd learned from his father years ago.

As the rancher concentrated on getting the door unlocked, he failed to notice a red light blinking on a nearby tree. He'd triggered one of the game cameras. He opened the door and headed inside.

At that moment, Romy Moreland was in her shed, digging through an old can filled with nails of every size, gathering ammunition for her IED. She went back to her workbench in the garage. Her attention was immediately drawn to her phone. There was an alert from one of her game cameras. Someone was snooping around the funeral home property.

She unlocked her phone, and tapped on the game camera app. There was a saved video of some guy wearing dark clothes and a dark stocking cap, breaking into the crematorium. She couldn't make out who it might be. *Was it the police? Some thief looking for whatever they could steal and sell from the abandoned property?* Moreland grabbed the pistol from the work bench, ran to her car, and sped toward the funeral home.

Shane Malaby left the lights off, using a powerful military-grade flashlight for illumination he worked his way through the funeral home, the house and the crematorium looking for evidence to connect the mystery woman with the disappearance of the three victims. Outside, there was only a sliver of a moon that occasionally poked through the thick cloud cover. The weatherman had predicted heavy rain sometime after midnight.

Moreland parked her car a quarter mile down the road from the funeral home property, and silently and stealthily worked her way to the back door of the house. She peered inside a window and could see the beam of a strong flashlight as someone poked around in the dark. The serial killer opened the door, being careful not to make any noise. She entered a few feet into the darkness, stopped, pinned herself as flat as possible against a wall, and listened.

Malaby, unaware he was no longer alone, continued to poke around. He checked the urns lined up on a shelf in the backroom of the funeral home. They were all empty. He worked his way into the crematorium and shined the flashlight beam on the latch of the cremator door. He could smell the faint odor of Destiney Jackson's cooling ashes before being pulverized into a pile of fine dust.

Malaby was startled, as he closed the cremator door when the lights suddenly turned darkness into a bright fluorescent glow. He spun around to find the barrel of a gun pointing at his head. The woman holding the pistol was the same one he'd snapped pictures of. In a gruff voice she said, "Put your hands on top of your head and don't move or I will shoot you dead where you stand."

The rancher quickly complied as he asked, "Who are you? Why are you holding that gun at my head?"

The woman's eyes were like ice, "The real question is who the hell are you and what are you doing in my house?"

Malaby was surprised, "Your house? I thought this property was abandoned."

She waved the gun at him, motioning for him to sit down in a nearby chair, as she simply said, "Sit!"

Malaby's eyes and brain were processing the situation. He had no doubt this strange, rather unpleasant looking woman, was going to kill him. He decided to try to get her talking, "I'm curious. Why did you buy this place and then just let it continue to rot? You're not interested in the funeral home business?"

Those icy eyes never seemed to blink as she snorted, "My business is none of your damn business."

She set the gun down on a nearby counter, almost daring him to go for it. Malaby didn't move, still planning what his next move would be. The woman gave him a disdainful look, "I'll ask you for the last time. What is your name and what are you doing snooping round here in the middle of the night?"

Malaby thought about what to say next. He decided one of them was not going to leave alive, so why not tell her the story of Van Cleave. Taking that approach would buy him more time, and maybe she'd tell him why she was apparently copying Van Cleave, grabbing and killing young women.

Malaby took a deep breath and said, "My name is Shane Malaby. My daughter was killed by Van Cleave but the dumb asses on the jury let him skate. So, I took justice into my own hands, killed him, cremated him and dumped his ashes in Cedar Creek Lake. The cops think he just left town. I was the only one who knew that I killed him, and now you know, too. Now, who are you?"

The woman picked up the pistol, and snorted, "Why do you want to know that? Do you really think you're leaving here alive?" She made that statement without showing any emotion at all, sending a chill down Malaby's spine. Then the woman looked at him with some new respect, "So, you killed the funeral home director? When was that?"

Malaby was carefully measuring the distance between the two of them. She was not very tall, but he could see that she was quite muscular and obviously strong. He replied, "I was waiting for him the night the jury let him go. I injected him with the same embalming fluid and morphine he'd used to kill my wonderful daughter and the other young women. There was no way I could let him go free. He was a deranged serial killer and I had to take care of it myself. I've never told anyone about it until now, not even my wife who has been on too much medication since my daughter's death."

The steely-eyed woman was curious, "How did you know how to work the crematorium?"

Malaby replied, "Probably the same way you did. I know you killed those three missing women and I'm sure dumped their ashes in the lake."

The mysterious woman again showed no emotion, "You think so, huh? Why the hell are you here tonight?" She pointed the pistol at him. "I've studied that killing spree, and I recognize your name. So, I ask you again. Why are you snooping on me. You don't have a dog in this fight?"

Malaby silently weighed his response, "I guess I'm smarter than the cops. When those women started to go missing from exactly the same festivals and in the same order as Van Cleave's murders, I figured someone was using this place to dispose of the bodies. I was curious, especially when everyone but me thought Van Cleave had just blown town right after the not guilty verdict."

Moreland nodded her head. "So once a vigilante always a vigilante huh? What was your plan? Were you going to kill me like you did Van Cleave?"

Malaby measured his words carefully, "No. I was just curious if

146

someone was using this place to dispose of evidence again, and then I saw you here a few days ago."

The former Navy SEAL was shocked, and angry at herself for not spotting this obviously untrained rancher. She had to ask, "Where were you that I couldn't see you checking me out?" Malaby honestly answered, "I used very expensive, very powerful binoculars hiding in a tree, quite aways from the house. I was hoping to snap a few pictures and see if a buddy policewoman of mine could run it through their facial recognition software. I wanted to know who the hell you are?"

She waved the gun at his head once again. "And where is your vehicle right now?"

Malaby hesitated. He figured not answering that question could either buy him some more time or result in a bullet in his brain. He said, "It's about a half mile from here."

Moreland was growing weary of this game. She took a step forward and cocked the hammer on the pistol. "You have one more chance to tell me exactly where that vehicle is parked, right now!"

The serial killer was now less than three feet from Malaby, far too close based on her SEAL training but she had to find out where the vehicle was parked. She had to find it and get rid of it once she ended Malaby's life. Suddenly Malaby, who towered over her and was quite strong himself, lunged at her, knocking the pistol out of her hand with a quick slap to her wrist. It clattered to the floor.

He was surprised at her quick reaction time, as she sent a kick from her right foot into his knee with a crunching sound. The pain shot through Malaby as he bull-rushed her, wrestling her to the ground, and sprawling on top of her. But Moreland was lightning quick. In a split second she'd escaped from him, jumped to her feet and delivered a powerful kick to his throat. He was left gasping for air on the floor.

She jumped toward the counter, sweeping the gun into her hand as she did a spin kick that shattered Malaby's nose. Blood was oozing everywhere. He was staggering, obviously feeling tremendous pain. Moreland pointed the gun at him, "You move, Malaby, and I'll put a bullet through your brain." But the rancher knew she was going to kill him one way or the other, so he tried one last lunge at her. Moreland pulled the trigger, shooting him dead center in his heart. Malaby fell in a heap to the floor.

Moreland took one look at the lifeless eyes of Malaby and knew he was dead. She quickly grabbed a towel and stuck it into the hole in his chest, trying to keep blood from flowing onto the nearby rug. She pressed the towel hard into the wound, and the blood stopped. Moreland moved to the crematorium and fired it up.

Within an hour, Shane Malaby had transformed from a strapping wealthy rancher, into a pile of ashes weighing about five pounds. She poured the ashes into a black urn she'd grabbed off the shelf. Malaby, it seemed, was going to keep his secret, his murder of Van Cleave, with him to his watery grave in Cedar Creek Lake.

Forty

AT THEIR RANCH outside Mabank, Malaby's wife woke up from another three-hour nap, caused by her long list of medications. She glanced at the clock above the fireplace in the great room of their sprawling home. It was almost 2 a.m. She got up from the recliner where she spent nearly every hour of her day and ambled into the bedroom. She was surprised to find it empty. Where was Shane at this late hour?

He'd been acting strange again lately, coming and going at all hours of the day and night. She knew he was working on something, but he refused to tell her what it was. She turned off the lamp on the bedside table and was asleep in moments as the pills she took put her in a stupor.

As Moreland waited for the crematorium to cool down, she scrubbed Malaby's blood off the hardwood floor. Satisfied there was no evidence of the murder, Moreland sunk into the over-stuffed chair in the office and pulled out the tattered picture of Cody Martin. As she did most nights, the troubled former Navy SEAL talked to the visage of the love of her life for the next hour.

Besides meticulously cleaning up the crime scene, Moreland

had found Malaby's truck keys in his pocket, and removed them before cremation. She walked around the property for thirty minutes looking for his truck, using the key fob and listening for the horn to beep. Once she found it, Moreland jumped in the truck, and drove it to the nearest public boat ramp. She drove into the middle of the boat launch driveway, and parked the truck, blocking anyone else from putting their boat into the lake. Then she hiked the three miles back to the funeral home. Her watch read 3:25 a.m. when she locked the crematorium door and headed home for some rest.

✿

Three hours later, Max Bellecourt, drove into the boat ramp towing his battered aluminum fishing boat. He was surprised to see a pickup truck parked smack dab in the middle of the boat ramp, blocking access to the lake. Bellecourt, best described as a crusty old dude with a scraggily beard, flecked with white among the black hairs. He was tall and thin, with a face that could tell a hundred stories of drinkin' and womanizing. These days, nearing his eightieth year on the planet, he did nothing but fish every morning. Of course, he had a battered silver flask in the boat full of his favorite single malt scotch.

Bellecourt got out of his truck, used his well-worn baseball cap to swat away a wasp, and ambled toward the truck with a slight limp due to a bar fight and a baseball bat a decade ago. He pulled out a pack of unfiltered Camel cigarettes, placed one between his lips using his nicotine-stained, bony fingers, and lit it. The old fisherman took a big drag on the cigarette, as he pondered what to do next. It was the first of two packs that would burn up today.

✿

At the ranch outside Mabank, Amanda Malaby woke up from a deep sleep and rolled to her right to see the bedside clock. The glowing numbers said it was 7:04. She got out of bed, pulled on a bathrobe and walked into the great room. There was no sign of her husband. She walked through the entire home. He wasn't there. She

150

went into the kitchen. The coffee pot sat untouched in a corner of the counter. That was strange, her husband was an early riser, starting every morning by brewing a strong pot of coffee. In all their years together, she could not remember a day when he didn't make coffee first thing.

Her brain was still foggy from all her medications, but Amanda Malaby was lucid enough to be concerned. Shane had been acting a bit stranger than usual lately, coming and going at all hours of the day and night, without any explanation. At first, she was worried that he might be having an affair, but there was never anything that pointed her in that direction, so she erased the thought from her mind.

Amanda was at a loss. What should she do next? Unfortunately, her husband was probably one of the last holdouts in America who did not have an iPhone or some other device. He always said he believed in face-to-face discussions and didn't want to haul one of those phones around with him. That made it impossible to try to call him or locate him using one of the apps available these days. Amanda desperately needed coffee, so she brewed a pot, sat down at the kitchen table and pondered what to do next.

As the clock neared 8 a.m., Dwayne Murphy walked into Adler Huxley's office, ready for the second round of their battle over the cover article Murphy was writing for Sunday's newspaper. Huxley sat passively at his desk, his fingers interlaced in front of him, waiting for his overzealous reporter. He motioned Murphy to a chair. Neither combatant wished the other a good morning. This was war.

Murphy handed his latest re-write to the *Athens Courier* editor and sat back in his chair with his hands behind his head. Waiting. The reporter watched closely as Huxley, red pencil poised in his right hand, carefully read the article. Neither spoke for ten minutes.

Huxley was quite impressed, Murphy had toned down much of his more sensational prose, although it was still more inflammatory than he wanted. Huxley was well aware how important a friendly, safe place to cool off from the city heat was necessary to the economy of the Cedar Creek Lake area. Years ago, he had vowed never to damage the local merchants through a reckless newspaper article.

Back at the boat ramp, three other fishermen had driven in and were confronted by the same problem of Malaby's truck blocking them access to the lake. They decided the best action was to phone the sheriff and have the truck towed away. A few minutes later, a Henderson County Sheriff's cruiser parked near the ramp. Sergeant Amelia Sampson pulled on her hat and exited the vehicle.

She quickly assessed the situation and then asked, "Any you guys know whose truck this might be?" All four men shook their heads from side to side.

Bellecourt said, "No idea, but it's damn sure keeping me from catching some crappie this morning."

Sampson nodded then proceeded with her duty. "Unfortunately, we don't know if this truck was stolen, or where the driver is so this might be a crime scene. I'm sorry, fellas, but I can't move that truck until we get a detective out here. You're going to have to find a different boat launch this morning." Grumbling, the men got into their vehicles and headed out.

Sergeant Sampson walked to the back of the truck, and radioed the dispatcher, "I need you to check on the owner of a pickup truck with Texas license plate XJC-67K."

In a few seconds the radio crackled as the dispatcher replied, "Amelia, that license plate comes back to a Shane Malaby from Mabank."

The sergeant said, "I think that's the guy who owns that big ranch just outside Mabank."

The dispatcher replied, "That's the one. His daughter was one of the victims of that Van Cleave nutcase back when she was Mabank Rodeo Queen."

Unknown to the two sheriff's deputies, Chester Roman was listening in on his police scanner. He immediately hit speed dial on his phone for Dwayne Murphy. Roman, who had a myriad of ailments, was Murphy's ears around the lake. He had difficulty sleeping, so he spent countless hours every day and night listening to his police scanners. Murphy would slip him a crisp hundred-dollar bill at times for his tips.

Forty-One

MURPHY WAS DEEP in discussion with his editor as they continued to argue over various points of his article when his phone rang. He glanced at the caller ID, "Gotta take this call, boss. It's one of my most valuable informants." Huxley motioned him to go ahead, as he got out of his chair and headed for another cup of coffee.

Murphy answered the phone, "Hey, Chester, how ya doin', buddy?"

Chester replied, "Just listened to an interesting exchange on the Henderson County Sheriff's Office radio." He filled Murphy in on what he'd heard, as the reporter scribbled notes. He thanked Roman profusely, and hung up, just as Huxley re-entered the office with a big, steaming cup of black coffee.

Huxley noticed the puzzled look on the reporter's face, "What was that all about?"

Murphy scratched his chin stubble, "They just found Shane Malaby's truck abandoned at the boat ramp near Kemp. It's on the edge of the water, blocking any boats from using the ramp. There was no sign of Malaby."

Huxley tilted his head in thought, "That's seems odd. He was the guy whose daughter was the Mabank Rodeo Queen when she vanished never to be seen again, right?"

Murphy nodded, "That's him. He was always a fast-moving, mean son of a gun until he lost his daughter. He was at the trial every day and has pretty well disappeared himself since Van Cleave was acquitted. Why would his truck be at the boat ramp?"

Huxley replied, "Well, it could have been stolen and then abandoned there."

Murphy, always taking the big leap said, "Or he could have finally reached the end of his rope, parked the truck at the ramp and committed suicide by jumping into the water?"

Huxley put up his hands in disgust, "Murphy, that is the kind of thinking that will eventually get you fired from this newspaper. That is a crazy idea and it damn well better not get printed in my paper."

In the sheriff's office, King and Masterson were having a conversation about the next festival where someone was taken by Van Cleave. King said, "That would be the annual Aley Picnic. It's a big deal, a week from Friday that raises money to keep the historic cemetery going. He actually snatched a friend of mine from there, Tina Williams. She used to work at Wesley's Marina back when I was there helping out part-time during busy weekends."

The dispatcher knocked on the door jamb of the office, "Sheriff, you probably want to be aware of something." The dispatcher filled the two of them in on Malaby's truck being found at the boat ramp. I've got a detective headed that way."

Sheriff King said, "Has anyone thought about calling the ranch to see if he's there? She'd worked with Malaby when she and Buddy were building the private eye business, and she was aware that he never carried a mobile phone.

With that, King picked up her phone, found the Malaby Ranch in her contacts, and dialed the number. It took a long time until someone finally answered. A meek, slurred voice came through the phone, "Malaby residence."

King said, "Hi, Amanda, this is Crystal King. I'm wondering if Shane is home?"

"No he is not, Crystal. He didn't come home last night, and I haven't seen him this morning. I have no idea what he's doing."

The sheriff noticed the fear in her voice, "Amanda, what do you mean you have no idea what's he doing?" Amanda explained how he'd been gone for hours and hours the past couple weeks, both day and night. Crystal asked, "Do you know what he's been up to?"

Amanda, with a bit of a sob in her voice replied, "I don't know anything, Crystal. We really don't talk anymore since we lost our daughter. Shane just comes and goes with no explanation. But I suspect he was working on something, but what that is I have no clue."

The sheriff said, "Okay, Amanda. I'm going to look into this situation. Once I know something I'll give you a call, and if you hear from Shane, or if he comes home, please let me know right away." Amanda promised she would. The line disconnected as King stared into space, deep in thought.

As the two women were talking, Romy Moreland was in her boat heading to the dam on the south end of Cedar Creek Lake. She was pretty sure it would be a quiet place this time of the morning. After a twenty-five-minute trip, she'd reached the dam, and had tied on to the platform that drew water out of the lake for the East Cedar Creek Freshwater Supply District.

There wasn't a boat in sight as Moreland took the cover off the black urn and dumped the ashes under the structure. She watched as the last remains of Shane Malaby headed for the bottom of the lake. After a few minutes, satisfied that all the ashes had disappeared, Moreland put the boat in gear and headed home. The man who had killed the serial killer Van Cleave, went to his watery grave with only he and Moreland knowing what really had happened to the funeral home director.

Sheriff King and Dwayne Murphy arrived at the boat ramp at the same time. Crystal pounded her steering wheel in frustration. How does Murphy always know what's happening at the same time as she does. They parked side by side. King said, "Murphy, can't I go anywhere without you snooping around?

The reporter took that as a compliment, "Thanks, Sheriff. That's my job." She just shook her head. Nothing bothers this guy.

She ordered Murphy to wait in his car, "I'll talk to you in a few moments, but I can't have you traipsing around a potential crime scene."

Of course, Murphy immediately jumped on that comment. "So, you do suspect foul play then!"

King again shook her head from side to side in frustration, "No! I'm not saying that at all. Quit making up your own facts. Right now, I'm not sure why that truck is parked here." She looked at Murphy and continued sarcastically, "That's why we call it an investigation." She stressed the last word.

The sheriff walked to the truck. The detective was dusting for fingerprints. King asked, "Anything so far."

The detective replied, "Afraid not sheriff. I grabbed a set of Malaby's fingerprints from when he applied for a concealed carry permit. They're all over the truck, but I haven't found anyone else's prints. I do have a slight suspicion the truck was wiped clean, because some of Malaby's prints are wiped off."

Sheriff King walked over to Sergeant Sampson, "Once they're done checking out the truck, have it towed back to the impound garage so this ramp can be open again."

Sampson replied, "Yes ma'am. Will do."

King asked, "Find anything in the truck that might lead us to why it's parked here or where Malaby might be?"

Sampson replied, "Nope. Nothing so far."

The sheriff called Masterson on her mobile phone and filled him in on what was happening. Then she said, "I'll head back to the office to pick you up, and let's take a drive out to the Malaby ranch. Maybe we can figure this out by talking to his wife and snooping around the place a bit. She thinks her husband might have been working on some secret project."

As she started up her police car, Murphy was at her side window. She rolled it down, "What?"

Murphy was indignant, "What? You promised to talk to me."

King replied, "That truck belongs to Shane Malaby. We are going to talk to him and ask him why it's parked there. That's it." She rolled up the window as Murphy loudly protested. The police cruiser drove away letting Murphy standing there with his hands on his hips, still calling her name.

Forty-Two

THEY FOUND AMANDA rocking back in forth in one of the huge hand-carved wooden chairs on the porch. She gave them a weak wave as they got closer.

Masterson said, "What about the wife? How has she been since their tragedy?"

King shrugged, "She always was a meek housewife who was controlled by her husband. Unfortunately, she has been heavily medicated since her daughter's death as she deals with it in her own way."

The three of them sat on the porch for a while as Sheriff King gently asked her a series of questions about her missing husband. Amanda Malaby seemed to drift in and out as they talked. King thought to herself, looks like she took even more pills today since she can't find her husband.

After ten minutes of small talk, Masterson asked, "Mrs. Malaby, would you give us permission to search the house to see if there any clues to her husband's absence?" She nodded, and they walked in the house. Malaby remained in the chair, gently rocking back and forth.

The Texas Ranger let out a low whistle as they walked through the front door with its beveled glass windows, and into the massive great room. Masterson said, "Well this sure qualifies as a great room. This place is huge and worth a ton of money, I'm sure."

King smiled for the first time all morning, "Yeah. It's quite impressive."

They took a slow walk through the seven thousand square foot house with its five bedrooms, six baths, private movie theater and a full gourmet kitchen. Nothing jumped out at them. Eventually they came to Shane Malaby's incredible private office. It had to be almost a thousand square feet. One wall was lined with five television monitors. The desk and chair were massive. The desk was hand-carved out of a brightly polished chunk of oak. The chair was deep blue leather with the Malaby Ranch logo on it. There were the usual perfunctory pictures with local and national politicians.

Masterson found the desk to be unlocked. He opened each drawer, sifting through a lot of paperwork. King was working her way through Malaby's computer. She came across a file that read "In Case Of My Death." King called Masterson over to the computer, as she opened the file.

It began with Shane Malaby sitting at his office desk, looking into the computer's camera. He began, "If you're seeing this, then I must be dead. I want to confess to the murder of Thaddeus Van Cleave. When that gutless jury acquitted that murderer, I had to take care of it myself. I surprised him the night he was set free, used the same combination of morphine and embalming fluid and then cremated the SOB! His ashes are somewhere in Cedar Creek Lake."

Amanda put her hand to her mouth as she watched the confession. She was trembling and big tears welled up in her eyes. King was shocked, and Masterson was surprised. King said, "Holy crap! I had no idea he could do something like that. I mean he was always a bully but murder. I'd never suspected that."

Amanda, sobbing said, "That's not my Shane. He was really devastated when our daughter died but to do something like that. I just…" Her voice trailed off without completing the sentence.

After a brief pause, Malaby reappeared on the computer screen. It was obviously a different day. He looked at the camera and said, "After those recent disappearances of young women I started staking out the old funeral home. I really believe they are being done by a copycat killer. I spent hours watching the place from a half mile away with powerful binoculars. On several occasions I saw a woman on the property. I snapped some pictures of her. Tonight, I'm going inside to investigate." The tape ended.

The room was filled with silence.

Amanda screamed, "Oh no! Do you think that woman killed him and drove his truck to the boat ramp?"

King and Masterson stared at each other. *A woman?* They replayed the recording, listening carefully to every word. King said, "Yup. He says there's a woman. What the hell?"

Masterson looked at her, "And he mentions that he took pictures of her. Where are the pictures?"

Sheriff King and Masterson spent the next half hour carefully going through everything in the large office, looking for a flash drive that contained pictures. Crystal used all her best computer skills but could not find a file with pictures of a woman. King called headquarters and requested three detectives to help them search. After three hours, they came up empty. They had no clue that the uber-expensive binoculars that Malaby used in his surveillance of Moreland contained pictures of her. Unfortunately, Moreland had grabbed the binoculars from Malaby's truck and hid them in the crematorium.

After Murphy was stonewalled at the boat ramp, he headed back to the newspaper office and started making phone calls to his sources in the police departments in the Cedar Creek Lake area. To his chagrin, none of his contacts knew anything, other than the obvious, the rancher was missing and his locked truck was parked at the boat ramp. It was time to talk with his editor.

He knocked on Huxley's door and was motioned inside. Turns out Huxley had been working his sources too, and they knew nothing more than Murphy's spies. After another hour meticulously going through Murphy's Sunday article, Huxley finally laid down his despised red pencil, satisfied they'd created an excellent article that pretty much stuck to the facts. Murphy, wanted to fight some more over

161

pieces of the story, but Huxley held up his hand, "Enough Murph. This one is put to bed."

Then they turned their full attention to the missing rancher. It was decided that the story of Shane Malaby would be a separate piece on page one. Huxley admonished Murphy, "Remember, stick to the facts, including the fact that his daughter had been taken and killed by someone. You can't put the finger on Thaddeus Van Cleave because the jury found him innocent." Murphy started to protest but Huxley waved him away, "Show me the copy when its finished." He started rifling through some other papers piled high on his desk ignoring the reporter.

A few blocks away, Sheriff King and Ranger Masterson were kicking around ideas about the disappearance of Malaby. Crystal said, "I always knew that Malaby was a bully, but until I saw that recording, I would never suspect him of killing Van Cleave."

Masterson nodded, "He was obviously driven to the brink by the death of his precious daughter, and then when Van Cleave was acquitted, he snapped." They were both lost in thought for a few minutes.

Finally, Masterson said, "And what about his claim that he has pictures of a woman he suspects of kidnapping three young women, just like Van Cleave, and then using the crematorium to dispose of the evidence?"

The sheriff shook her head, "It is certainly plausible. If we can find those pictures, we can use facial rec to determine her name. Until then, I guess we can start watching the funeral home day and night to see if she returns."

Masterson looked at the sheriff. "And we also have to consider the possibility that this mystery woman killed Malaby and used the cremator to dispose of his body. Then she drove his truck to the boat ramp so it looked like he may have committed suicide."

King let out a long sigh, "I hate to admit it, but Murphy's theory of their being a copycat killer on the loose might just be on target. We've got three apparent drownings, just like the Frogman murders, and there are now three women and one well-known man missing. Those disappearances mimic Van Cleave, right down to the same festivals in order. Is it possible someone, maybe this woman, is creating all this havoc?"

In Mabank, the police detective that Malaby had spoken with about identifying pictures of the mystery woman, saw the information come over their computer system. The sheriff had sent a BOLO to all area law enforcement asking them to be on the lookout for a missing rancher named Shane Malaby. The detective was surprised to see that Malaby had vanished. She checked with the dispatcher, "Has anyone delivered a package for me?"

The dispatcher dug through some papers, checked all around his built-in desk, and then shook his head, "No ma'am."

The detective walked back to her cluttered desk and searched it thoroughly in case someone had thrown a package on it while she was out. Nothing. She slumped into her chair, pondering the next move. The sheriff could certainly use the information about the pictures, but what Malaby had asked her to do was technically illegal. She decided to see what the rest of the day had to offer before exposing herself. Maybe Malaby would show up. She picked a folder and started working her way through a cold case.

Forty-Three

ROMY MORELAND WAS itching to return to the funeral home for a thorough inspection of the murder scene. She replayed the cleanup in her mind, picturing her every move. She determined it would be too dangerous to head there now. She was unaware of the Malaby recording but felt sure the police might check out the abandoned funeral home because of the death of Malaby's daughter. Moreland decided to head to lunch at McDuff's instead. If there was any gossip going around on the disappearance of Malaby, they'd be talking about it there.

Moreland walked into McDuff's and looked for a table. She noticed a Henderson County Sheriff's Deputy sitting alone in the small backroom that held a few booths. She sat two booths away from the policeman. Lucinda Sue was there in a flash offering her a menu and asking for her drink order. She ordered a Dr Pepper on ice and pretended to pore over the plastic menu.

A couple of minutes later, Melinda Sue headed to the deputy's table with a platter of fried catfish, green beans and grits. She set down the food, and then slid into the booth across from the cop. Her hair was a bright pink today. She leaned toward the deputy and said in a quiet voice, "Lonny, what the hell is this about the disappearance of Shane Malaby?"

Lonny, was a bit startled that she already had heard about the episode, "Who told you that Melinda Sue?"

She scoffed at him, "Ya know I hear stuff all the time in this joint. So is it true? Come on dish me some dirt here."

Sergeant Shields gave her a troubled look, "C'mon, Melinda Sue, you know I can't say anything about this."

She smiled, "Well, I know I ain't as purty as that Caitlan reporter, but you know you can trust me."

Shields chortled, "Yeah, I can trust you to call Murphy two seconds after I say something."

Moreland's food had arrived, and she tried to listen inconspicuously while she munched on a tasty cheeseburger.

After several more minutes of cajoling by the sassy waitress, Shields took a deep breath, leaned in closer and in barely a whisper said, "Yeah, Malaby is missing but that's not even the big news!"

Melinda Sue was all ears, ignoring the cook calling her name with an order. Shields looked around, "I haven't seen it but apparently there's a videotape from Malaby where he confesses killing Van Cleave." Melinda Sue gasped. Shields continued, "But there's more,. He has pictures of some mysterious woman who is using the old abandoned funeral home."

Two booths away, Moreland nearly choked on a crispy french fry. A chill ran down her spine, as she digested that bit of information. She had forgotten the rancher had taken pictures of her at the funeral home. *Who had them?* Her mission quickly changed to one where she finds the pictures and makes sure whoever has them doesn't live to talk about them. She pushed her half-eaten cheeseburger away and motioned Lucinda Sue to bring the check. Then she hastily left the restaurant. Melinda Sue and Shields were quietly talking and never noticed her the entire time she sat so near to them.

True to form, Melinda Sue was on the phone to Dwayne Murphy a few minutes later. She filled him in on the murder confession and the pictures of a mystery woman. Murphy was quiet for moment, then thanked her profusely for her information. "There'll be a hundred-dollar bill for you on this one Melinda Sue. Keep your ear to the ground. See if you can find out anything else." The phone went dead.

Murphy was in a quandary. Should he immediately tell Huxley or would it be more prudent to wait until he confirmed everything and had the facts the editor keeps talking about. He decided to keep silent and work his sources. His plan was to dig up all the facts, craft a story, and present it to Huxley as a finished product.

Romy Moreland sat in the restaurant parking lot, sifting through the clutter on the floorboard of the front and rear seats. She really kept a messy car. She climbed into the back seat and dug under a few shirts and other clothes. That's where she found the special binoculars she had taken from Malaby's truck before abandoning it on the boat launch ramp.

She hadn't really examined the binoculars until now. She turned them on and noticed a recording button for both video and still pictures. After fiddling with the complicated state-of-the-art binoculars, she found the saved photos. Moreland was astonished to see about a dozen pictures of her taken while she was entering and exiting the funeral home. She was angry at herself. Her SEAL training taught her to always be aware of her surroundings and whether she was being watched, but she obviously missed the fact Malaby was keeping an eye on her.

The serial killer pushed some more buttons on the device and figured out how to delete her pictures. She felt better, but the cautious voice in her head warned her that Malaby had sent a copy of the pictures to the Mabank police officer. Her main mission now was to find the cop, make sure they had the pictures, and then snuff out their life leaving no witnesses behind. All she knew at this point that it was a policewoman in Mabank. She was surprised to see some pictures of a woman in a police uniform along with the pictures Malaby had taken of her

In Athens, Murphy was hammering away at the keys on his computer as he worked on his exclusive story. The reporter had started his career punishing the keys on an old Selectric typewriter and had never learned to gently push the computer keys. After he finished the first draft, and put himself in his editor's shoes and realized he needed the sheriff to give him a quote or two for the stunning article. He called her number.

Moreland returned home and went on the Mabank Police Department website. It was a small department, with only a couple of female officers. One of the women had just joined the force a few weeks ago. The other was a lieutenant, Brenda Wright. She'd been on the Mabank police department for ten years and had previously served in the Army for a dozen years. Moreland was convinced that was who Malaby sent the pictures to.

Wright sat at her desk as the day wound down, still trying to decide on her next step. That's when UPS delivered a package from Shane Malaby. Wright took the package into an empty interrogation room so prying eyes would not see what was in the brown manila mailer. She ripped open the package and found a half dozen pictures of a woman she'd never seen before. She studied the photos, still torn on whether to phone the sheriff.

Forty-Four

SHERIFF KING ANSWERED her office phone on the fourth ring. Her face quickly turned dark as she heard, "Hi ya, Crystal," and recognized the irritating voice of Dwayne Murphy. In an impatient, clipped tone, she said, "Whatcha need, Murphy. I'm a little busy." Murphy quickly explained he knew about the video tape confession and the existence of the photos of a suspect.

Crystal muttered under her breath, then said, "Don't know what you're talking about, Murphy."

There was a pause as Murphy decided on his next move, "Look, Crystal, I have a strong source on my information. I'm just giving you the courtesy of a call for a quote or two. The disappearance of a wealthy, well-known rancher, whose daughter also disappeared and was apparently murdered is a huge story."

Crystal had played this game before. She said, "Murphy, we both know that Huxley won't let you run a speculative story."

Murphy quickly replied, "C'mon, Sheriff. I was at the boat ramp. I know Malaby is missing. Those are facts."

The sheriff quickly retorted, "And that's the only story, Murphy. His truck was found abandoned at the boat ramp. Hell, it could have been stolen. That's why we investigate these things to find out what exactly happened."

Murphy was undaunted, "Okay. Let me ask you this. Have you heard from Malaby? Have you found him or is he missing?"

King replied, "Murphy, let me say this slower so your feeble mind can follow what I'm saying, and this is an official quote. The Sheriff's Department found Malaby's truck abandoned on the boat ramp. We're investigating. Period." The phone line went dead.

Mabank detective Brenda Wright stuffed the pictures back in the envelope. She'd decided to pay the sheriff a visit with the photos. She told the dispatcher she had a meeting and would be back in tomorrow. As the detective walked into the bright late afternoon sunlight, she had no idea an evil set of eyes followed her to her unmarked police cruiser. She climbed in, shut the door and put on her seatbelt as she started the cruiser. She turned left out of the parking lot and drove toward Highway 175 to head to Athens.

Moreland took a back route to the highway, putting her a couple miles down the road ahead of the detective. She had to be sure the detective would not reach the sheriff with the photos.

Moreland parked her car on the side of the road just before the detective would arrive on the outskirts of Eustace. She turned on her hazard lights and pulled to the shoulder of the highway. There were just a few cars on the road at this time of day.

Detective Wright saw the car ahead with the hazard lights flashing, and a woman sitting on the highway beside the driver's door. She turned on her lights and drove to a stop just behind the car. The woman appeared to be unconscious.

Wright hurried over to the woman, bent down, and asked, "Are you alright, ma'am?" Moreland continued to play possum, as she noticed a semi heading their way down Highway 175. The driver sped by with nary a look at the cars on the side of the road. There were no other vehicles in sight in either direction.

Detective Wright reached down to feel the woman's pulse as she said, "Ma'am. Are you okay?" Suddenly the woman on the ground pulled a pistol, held it on the detective and said, "I'm fine. Don't move or I will kill you!" The detective backed away a few feet as Moreland said, "That's far enough. Get in my car now. And hand over your gun."

Wright hesitated, "Can't do that. What do you want?"

Moreland pointed the gun at the policewoman, "Do it now or I'll put a hole in your head." For the first time, Wright looked closely at the woman's face. It was the same woman from the pictures Malaby had sent to her. Moreland noticed the flicker of recognition on the woman's face. This convinced her that Wright had the photos.

She moved the pistol closer to the officer, wary of the fact she was trained to disarm a suspect, "I'm going to give you two seconds to do what I say. We are going to get up, we are going to grab the photos you have, and we're leaving in my car."

Wright was defiant, "And where do you think we're going?"

A deadly look swept over Moreland's face, "Get the damn pictures!"

In Athens, Murphy finished the first draft of the article, printed out two copies, and headed to his editor's office. He anticipated having to make some edits. Murphy had tried hard to walk right up to the speculation line without crossing over it. His hopes of having a discussion were quickly dashed.

Huxley grabbed the copies as he said, "I'm in the middle of some reports I need to finish today. I'll read this tonight, and we'll discuss tomorrow." He turned back to his reports. Murphy was angry and deflated as he left the office.

Along Highway 175, Wright opened the cruiser door and took the manila envelope from the passenger seat, with Moreland now sticking the gun roughly into her back. The killer had been lucky so far, as no cars had passed by, but she knew that traffic would be coming along any minute. Wright reluctantly got into Moreland's car, running potential scenarios through her mind of possible ways to turn the tables on this mystery woman.

Holding the gun on Wright, Moreland made a U-turn and headed back toward Gun Barrel City. A mile down the road she took a quick right turn onto a farm-to-market road that had nothing but fields on both sides. There was not a house or another car in sight. Back on the highway two cars passed the empty cruiser with the blues lights still flashing. They called the Sheriff's Office to report the strange scene. The dispatcher sent an officer to quickly investigate.

A couple miles away, Moreland turned off the bumpy, pothole-filled road, and onto a dirt driveway. Her car was hidden from view by the tall crops growing in the field. She stopped the car still holding the gun menacingly at the deputy. Wright measured the distance it would take to lunge at the gunman while grabbing her pistol at the same time. She needed the element of surprise, so she tried to engage in conversation.

Wright said in a quiet, calm voice, "Let's talk about this. Just let me go. I'll give you the envelope with the photos and you can be on your way."

Moreland let out a harsh laugh, "Yeah. Right. And you'll just forget we met and the fact you know what I look like. Nice try." In a gruff voice she waved the gun at her, "Get out of the car right now." Wright knew once this happened her life would end quickly. She was convinced this mystery woman was serious and capable of anything.

Moreland grew increasingly agitated and impatient, "Get the hell out of the car. NOW!" Wright opened the passenger door, still mulling a number of escape scenarios. Unfortunately, her life was about to end.

Forty-Five

IN ATHENS, SHERIFF King and Masterson were kicking around ideas about Malaby. Three women had disappeared, and one of the possible outcomes is they had been taken to the abandoned funeral home and cremated just as Van Cleave had done to his victims. Malaby admitted on the video that he had killed Van Cleave. Now, he apparently had taken the law into his own hands, staking out the funeral home. That had allowed him to take photos of a strange woman. Was she the one responsible for the three women who vanished?

Sheriff King said, "We have to find those photos."

Masterson replied, "Yes. That's the potential lead we need to solve this case. But if Malaby did indeed have the photos, then where are they. Who did he send them to?"

As the sheriff left the room to check in with her staff. Masterson took the opportunity to phone the Mabank Police Dispatcher, "Can you tell me if you received a package today, and who it was sent to?"

In the hidden field, Moreland ordered Wright to lay flat on the ground on her stomach, with her fingers laced behind her head. The detective was desperately trying to stop what she feared was coming next. But it was too late. Moreland, took Wright's weapon out of

172

her belt, held it just inches from the back of her head and pulled the trigger. The detective lay motionless with a large pool of blood surrounding her head and soaking into the dirt of the field.

In Mabank, the dispatcher told the ranger that an envelope had arrived from UPS addressed to detective Wright. Masterson, felt a sense of relief, "May I speak with Officer Wright, please?"

The dispatcher said, "Sorry, sir, but she left with the envelope an hour ago and said she'd be back in the morning."

Masterson was deflated. "Did she say where she was going?" The dispatcher said she had not.

As Masterson hung up the phone, the intercom immediately buzzed. It was the department dispatcher passing on information about an abandoned Mabank Police car parked on the side of the road just outside Eustace. There was no sign of the officer. They alerted the Mabank Police Department. The car was driven by Brenda Wright.

Moreland dragged the dead deputy's body farther into the tall grass of the field, concealing it as much as possible. She'd determined that it would be too risky to bring the body to the crematorium, since it was most likely under police surveillance after Malaby's disappearance and confession. She put her car in gear, and continued down the dirt road until she came to a crossroad, where she turned left staying out of sight, and getting farther away from the abandoned police cruiser.

Sheriff King and Masterson jumped into her squad car, and with siren wailing and lights flashing, sped down Highway 175 toward the abandoned police car. When King arrived, there were two other police cruisers already on the scene. One was the sheriff's officer who had been sent to investigate, the other belonged to the Mabank Police Chief who had been alerted to the situation.

They examined the cruiser, searched the ground around the car, as well as the interior of the vehicle. There was no sign of a brown manila envelope or Brenda Wright. Since there appeared to be no clues about what happened, a Mabank deputy, who had ridden along with the chief, drove Wright's car back to the police station for further inspection and dusting for fingerprints.

King filled in the police chief about Malaby's on-camera confession, and his claim he had photos of a strange woman. The Mabank chief said, "Well, it would make sense that he'd contact Brenda if he wanted to keep this on the downlow. Malaby had hired her many times to provide security for parties at his ranch."

King nodded, "Especially if he was on a vendetta to find the person responsible for the three recent disappearances. He probably wanted her to run facial recognition without alerting any law enforcement."

Masterson spoke up, "But none of that explains what happened here. Unless the mystery woman found out Wright had the photos of her and stopped her right here."

King nodded, "That's a plausible scenario. But where is Brenda? Was she kidnapped by the killer?" None of them had a clue.

※

After wending her way down a number of dirt roads, Moreland found herself back on Highway 175. She'd actually emerged near where she had grabbed the detective. But now the police cruiser was gone, and there was no one on the scene. She drove past in the opposite lane and headed to her rental property.

The first thing she did after arriving was take a hammer and smash the high-caliber binoculars into little pieces. She went out to the burn pit in her backyard and lit the printed photos. They quickly curled up, turned black and became unrecognizable ashes. Moreland knew killing the deputy was going to raise the heat. She hoped coyotes destroyed the carcass before anyone stumbled across it.

Moreland unscrewed the cap on a cold bottle of water and sat on the deck of her home. It was time to change her plans. She determined it had become too dangerous to grab more young women and use the crematorium. It was time to find another drowning victim to keep the police busy with still another crime scene. She grabbed the mobile phone she had taken off of Wright and once again using the hammer smashed it into tiny pieces. She'd turned off the phone as they left Wright's cruiser behind. It would show that was her last location. Indeed, the police had already tracked her phone, and discovered its last location was the side of the road.

Forty-Six

THE NEXT MORNING, the lake area was abuzz with rumors of the missing rancher and policewoman from Mabank. Sheriff King had called a news conference and walked into the room packed with local newspaper reporters, one from the *Dallas Morning News,* and a myriad of area television reporters from Dallas and Tyler. King scanned the room and asked them to all be seated.

King began, "I know there's a lot of talk around town about missing rancher Shane Malaby and Mabank Police Lieutenant Brenda Wright. I want to inform everyone that we are investigating both disappearances and could use the public's help." Pictures of Malaby and Wright appeared on the big screen TV behind the sheriff. She referenced the photos, "If anyone has seen either of these people, please call the Henderson County Sheriff's Office."

A picture of Malaby's truck popped on the screen, as the sheriff continued, "This is Shane Malaby's truck. We found it parked on the boat ramp near Caney City. If anyone has seen this truck, please contact us." A picture of Wright's police cruiser appeared as King said, "This is the Mabank Police cruiser that Lieutenant Wright was driving. It was found abandoned on the shoulder of Highway 175 just outside Eustace. A lot of cars use the highway, so someone must have seen something. If you have, call us right now."

As she paused, Dwayne Murphy shouted, "What about the three missing young women? Do you have any information on them? Are all of these disappearances connected?" Murphy crossed his arms and waited for a reply. He was miffed the sheriff had hijacked his exclusive story before it could be published.

King shot him a displeased look, "So far, we have no evidence that any of the disappearances are connected, Murphy." She decided to dress him down in front of his peers, "And one of your ridiculous conspiracy theories certainly isn't needed as we all work to find these folks."

She recognized another local reporter who asked, "We're hearing from quite a few people that Shane Malaby had made a videotape confessing to the murder of Thaddeus Van Cleave. Can you confirm that?"

Sheriff King paused, then decided since the information was spreading, she might as well address it. She said, "I can confirm that we found a videotaped message on Mr. Malaby's computer where he did confess to killing Mr. Van Cleave. As you know, Malaby's daughter was one of the alleged victims of Van Cleave. At this point, we are looking for any specific evidence that proves he did indeed kill him."

Murphy jumped to his feet, "And what about Malaby saying on the same videotape that he had pictures of a woman going in and out of Van Cleave's funeral home? Is she a suspect?"

King was getting irritated, "Yes, that is true. So far, we have not located any photos either at Mr. Malaby's home or on his computer. So, we are working to verify his story. Thank you all very much." With reporters shouting at her back, King strolled out of the room in silence without so much as a glance at anyone.

Romy Moreland watched the sheriff's news conference that was carried live by one of the local TV stations. She smiled. So far, it seems, the police are mostly in the dark about the eight people she'd killed. She was happy to see her killing spree had achieved its purpose of getting the local townspeople talking, worrying and wondering who might be next. Moreland was assembling the pieces of an IED as she pondered her next move.

The IED would be used to blow up King's police cruiser as she entered it in front of the sheriff's office. It would take careful planning to attach the device while the car was parked at King's home, and then set it off remotely as she turned the ignition key. In the meantime, Moreland wanted to kill another victim by drowning them in the lake. She wanted to make a splash with a high-profile person whose death would keep the buzz going strong.

An hour after the news conference, Sheriff King called an all-hands-on-deck meeting, even bringing in members of the department who had the day off. She had to come up with a concrete plan to move these investigations forward. King began the meeting with an impassioned speech about how critical it was to make progress on various fronts in their investigation. She said, "We simply have to find the Mabank policewoman and Malaby. Once we do that, we have to start crafting a list of potential suspects. I'm cancelling all days off and vacations for the next two weeks so y'all can help us make progress." There was a low murmur of grumbling in the room. King ignored it.

She'd built a small PowerPoint presentation for the troops. The pictures of the missing three young women appeared on the TV monitor. King said, "Luna Ortiz disappeared while helping on her father's food truck at the Athens Fiddle Fest. Addison Crow was a queen candidate who vanished from the Mabank Rodeo. Destiny Jackson was a well-known local business owner who disappeared at the Malakoff Cornbread Festival. It should be noted that this pattern of young women vanishing from local festivals follows the exact order as that of Van Cleave when he was grabbing and killing young women.

Three different pictures popped up, as King said, "We also have three drowning victims. Cory Rhodes, drowned while fishing from a personal watercraft on Cedar Creek Lake. Melody Highsmith, a world-class swimmer and Olympic hopeful, drowned apparently while in the midst of her morning swim practice on the lake. And, Candace Avery, an avid kayaker drowned after apparently falling out of the watercraft, which was later found under a dock in Key Ranch."

She faced the room, "And then we have Brenda Wright and Shane Malaby. The first question we need to answer is this – do we have a copycat killer on our hands mimicking the killing sprees of the dude they called The Frogman, Cody Martin, and Van Cleave." She pointed a finger at the staff for emphasis, "And if I hear or read that I said we might have a copycat killer running around the lake I will immediately fire whoever told a reporter or anyone else." She put her hands on her hips, "Understood." There were nods around the room and a smattering of "Yes ma'am" could be heard. King continued, "That pain in the ass Murphy has already floated that theory past me so if any of you are his source, you damn well better keep this information to yourself."

This coming Friday was the annual Aley Picnic, a well-attended annual fundraiser for the cemetery. If the copycat killer followed Van Cleave's pattern they would strike at the picnic. King asked for volunteers to form an undercover squad to police the Picnic and keep everyone safe. Then she handed out sheets of paper with a list of assignments for every single member of the sheriff's department. King ended by saying, "Let's catch this SOB right now!" The meeting broke up.

While that meeting was in progress, the copycat killer sat in a booth off to the side at McDuff's Restaurant eating a grilled chicken salad for lunch. She kept her head buried in her phone as conversations buzzed all around her during the lunch rush. That snotty waitress, Lucinda Sue bounded over, took her order, and disappeared into the kitchen. A few minutes later, as Moreland finished her salad, she heard Lucinda Sue talking to a cute young guy two booths away.

Moreland's ears perked up when she heard Lucinda Sue say, "Yeah. I love to go for a late-night swim right before I go to bed. It's refreshing and I sleep really well." The guy asked her what time she went swimming, and asked with a smile on his face if she went skinny-dipping. Lucinda Sue waved away his comment, "Oh, Lord, no. I'm too shy for that. I usually jump in for about ten minutes right after the local news, about 10:30. I always watch to check the weather forecast."

The guy said, "Does your cousin Melinda Sue join you?"

Again, Lucinda Sue waved away the question, "Heavens no. First off, she's afraid there might be a snake swimming around, and she's always in bed by ten o'clock sharp. Says she needs her beauty sleep."

Moreland paid her tab and left McDuff's. She was elated. She now had the perfect high-profile victim, and it looked like an easy kill. She'd scout out Lucinda Sue for a couple nights to verify her late-night swims, and then strike.

Forty-Seven

FRIDAY WAS A picture-perfect day on the lake, a front moved through in the morning, holding down temperatures with a cool breeze from the north. The clouds had cleared by late afternoon. It was great weather for the annual Aley Picnic. The Picnic was a fundraiser for the ancient Aley Cemetery. There's live music, and what are touted as the "best hamburgers" on the lake. It always draws a big crowd.

As night fell, the country music cranked up, and the crowd had a great time. Most had no idea that ten Henderson County Sheriff's deputies were melding into the crowd, keeping an eye out for the copycat killer. Meanwhile, the person they were searching for was home watching an old John Wayne movie on her iPad, waiting to head out on her scouting mission.

Moreland had decided there would be no more vanishing women. It was simply too risky with police trying to get information on the mystery woman Malaby had seen on the funeral home property. If she could no longer cremate them, it meant she had to risk someone finding their bodies. Moreland was not willing to take that chance. She was not going to veer from her mission of killing that King woman.

Sheriff King had phoned Shane Malaby's widow with the unfortunate news that she had nothing to report on her missing husband. She did ask if they could search his office one more time. King explained they wanted to pore through everything one more time to see if they could find the photos of the mystery woman, or a thumb drive containing the photos that may be stashed away somewhere. The visit was set for 10 a.m. Saturday morning.

At ten o'clock Friday night, Melinda Sue gave her cousin a hug and headed to bed for her beauty sleep. Lucinda Sue watched the late news and found out it was going to be sunny and hot for the entire weekend. She smiled, since that meant the morning breakfast rush at McDuff's would be busy on both weekend days. She shut off the television, grabbed a towel and headed out the door toward the lake. She had on a blue swimming suit just purchased at Beall's in Gun Barrel City.

As the young waitress backed down the dock ladder and slipped into the dark water, she had no clue a pair of eyes were on her, watching every move. Lucinda Sue swirled around in the water and held on to the ladder. The water was about eight-feet deep right off the dock. Two houses away, Moreland took in the scene and smiled. This was going to be easy.

She continued to watch as Lucinda Sue climbed back up the ladder after about ten minutes in the water, grabbed her towel and stood on the dock in the moonlight, wiping down her arms and legs. Then she turned and headed into the house. Five minutes later the lights snapped off. Moreland checked her surroundings one last time and walked over to her car. She drove home.

About twelve hours later, Sheriff King and Ranger Masterson were in her police cruiser heading to the Malaby Ranch. Masterson asked, "Anything happen at the Picnic last night?"

King shook her flowing blond locks. "Nope. As far as we know everyone had a good time, and everyone made it home safely."

"Well, I guess that's good news but it doesn't help us find this killer."

King agreed, "That's true but at least no one was taken. My guys worked the scene hard, while also staying inconspicuous, but saw nothing and no one acting strange. Just the usual folks who might have had a little too much beer."

Amanda Malaby greeted them at the door, asked if they'd like some coffee, and led them back to her husband's office. King and Masterson spent the next two hours carefully and meticulously sifting through every paper, every book and every drawer and shelf in the office. Their hearts raced a bit when Masterson found a thumb drive taped under the desk. They quickly popped it in the computer. The screen was filled with numbers. Masterson examined it closely, "Well, it looks like Mr. Malaby was keeping two sets of books. One for himself and one for the IRS."

King smiled, "That doesn't surprise me. He always seemed to live on the edge when it came to this ranch."

Mrs. Malaby appeared at the door, "Did you find anything?"

King didn't have the heart to tell her that Shane was basically cooking the books. Instead, she replied, "I'm afraid not. But thanks for letting us take another look." Amanda looked like she had slept little over the past few days, her hair was tangled and scraggly, she was not wearing makeup and her face seemed to have deeper lines than a month ago. They thanked her and left.

Forty-Eight

AFTER THREE NIGHTS of surveillance, Moreland was ready to carry out her mission of drowning Lucinda Sue. Her pattern was well established. She always headed to the water promptly at 10:30, spent ten minutes splashing around and cooling off, and then headed to bed. It was the perfect night for the mission. The moon was only a sliver, and clouds obscured the usual blanket of stars that filled the Texas sky.

Moreland, wearing a black wet suit, and using SCUBA gear, watched from two docks away. Her mask barely broke the waterline. Lucinda Sue walked onto the dock and down the ladder into the dark water. The wind was out of the south at ten to fifteen miles an hour, making the water a little choppy. That provided extra cover for Moreland as she silently and stealthily neared the waitress.

As Lucinda Sue enjoyed her last night of splashing in Cedar Creek Lake, Moreland swam into deeper water and came around to the dock facing open water. Lucinda Sue was holding onto the ladder on the other side of the dock. Moreland dove down and was suddenly right next to her victim.

This startled Lucinda Sue who began to thrash in the water as she desperately tried to scramble up the ladder. But the former Navy SEAL was far stronger than the waitress. She grabbed both arms and quickly took her underwater before she could let out a scream. But Lucinda Sue proved to be a real fighter, as she tried to bite Moreland on the arm. But the thick wet suit made the bite ineffective. Lucinda Sue fought her way back to the surface by kicking Moreland in the head. They both created quite a stir as the water splashed loudly into the quiet of the night.

Finally, Moreland was able to tightly wrap her arms and legs around Lucinda Sue and drag her down to the bottom of the lake. Fighting for air, Lucinda Sue tried mightily to get free, but Moreland was far too strong and soon her body went limp. Moreland caught her breath after the big wrestling match and decided to drag the body underwater far from the dock. Using powerful leg kicks, Moreland carried the dead weight past four docks before swimming into deeper water. The glow of her gauge showed she was in twenty-four feet of water. That's when she brought Lucinda Sue to the bottom of the lake and headed home.

The incessant buzzing of her alarm clock finally penetrated the ear plugs Melinda Sue wore each night to get her maximum beauty sleep. She pulled off her fur-lined sleeping mask, blinked her eyes a couple time and brought the clock on her nightstand into focus. It was 7 a.m. Time to rise and shine to have a little breakfast and get ready for her shift at McDuff's. She slipped out of bed, shrugged into her fluffy blue terrycloth bathrobe and headed downstairs. Along the way, she tapped on Lucinda Sue's closed bedroom door, "Good morning, sunshine. Time to rise and greet the day." She continued on her way, as Lucinda Sue was a notorious slow riser.

In the kitchen Melinda Sue was greeted by the wonderful aroma of freshly perked coffee. As usual, the timer had started the coffeemaker right before Melinda got out of bed. She sat at a small table in her breakfast nook as the streaming sunshine sent a warm glow through the room. Melinda Sue sipped the delicious blend and munched on a day-old doughnut. She glanced at the wall clock. It was now 7:17.

Melinda Sue walked to the bottom of the stairs and loud-ly called Lucinda's name. No answer. Just then her eye caught a glimpse of a large beach towel neatly folded on the dock. That's odd, she thought, why would Lucinda Sue leave the towel on the dock, apparently unused, after her usual evening plunge into the lake. She called her name a bit louder this time. Still no answer.

Melinda Sue walked back upstairs, stopping at Lucinda's door. She hesitated. They'd promised to respect each other's privacy. What if her cousin had a man in her bed this morning? She removed her hand from the doorknob and instead knocked on the door. This time knocking louder and more urgently. She was greeted by dead silence.

Melinda Sue stood still for another minute, and then made up her mind. She twisted the doorknob and opened the door. She was surprised to find not only no sign of Lucinda Sue, but that her bed had not been slept in. *Where was she? And why was the apparently un-used towel sitting on the dock?* She noticed her cousin's purse and cell phone sitting on a table in the empty bedroom.

Melinda Sue hurried outside and strolled quickly onto her dock. She grabbed the towel and sniffed it. It smelled fresh and definitely unused. The waitress started to breathe harder as an icy fear invaded her thoughts. *Had Lucinda Sue drowned? Had she been attacked by the serial killer? Where was she?*

At the same time, Sheriff King and Ranger Masterson slid into a booth at McDuff's for an early breakfast chat. They were surprised that neither Melinda Sue or Lucinda Sue hadn't already sauntered to their table. Instead of the two sassy waitresses, restaurant owner Shelly appeared, "Good morning, y'all. How are you doing today?"

King said, "We feel honored to have the boss taking care of us, Shelly." They placed their orders for veggie omelets, hash browns and a hot, fresh biscuit with gravy.

After Shelly left to turn in their order, Sheriff King turned her attention to Masterson, "Do you really think a woman is our killer, Tolbert? Do you think they'd have the strength to snatch people from festivals, and to hold people underwater without any bruise marks?"

Masterson drank some of his coffee, "I believe so, especially if our killer was or is in the military. If that's the case we're probably dealing with an exceptionally strong woman, highly trained and skilled in hand-to-hand combat, similar to a Navy SEAL like Cody Martin."

King nodded, as Masterson continued, "There was a criminologist named Eric Hickey who really researched this, and he found that just over eleven percent of serial killers are women. None of them really seemed to gain the notoriety of male serial killers like the Boston Strangler or Dahmer. But in fact, the first female serial killer actually dates back to the turn of the sixteenth century. A Hungarian Countess named Elizabeth Bathory who supposedly tortured and killed hundreds of young girls. Now, Hickey disputed the fact she killed that many women, but he did find out that women seem to follow a more subtle modus operandi than men."

King said, "We had a pretty notorious serial killer around these parts named Betty Beets. Supposedly killed a number of her husbands. She was executed in 1985."

Shelly arrived with two steaming platters that smelled wonderful. She said, "I remember Beets caused quite a stir around here."

King nodded, then asked, "Speaking of causing a stir, where are your twin sassy waitresses this morning?"

Shelly shrugged, "Don't know. Neither of them showed up and we've been so busy I haven't had a minute to give them a call. But it is unusual for them to miss a shift especially without letting me know."

Just then Sheriff King's phone rang. All eyes shifted to her as Crystal said, "Hello, Melinda Sue. Please calm down and slow down. What happened?" King grew very serious as Melinda Sue explained the situation. She motioned to Shelly and Tolbert to hold on a second, as Melinda Sue breathlessly continued to talk. Finally, King said, "Okay, Melinda Sue. Just hang tight. We'll be there in a couple of minutes.

The sheriff motioned for Shelly to slide into the booth next to her, as every pair of eyes and ears in the restaurant seemed to be paying attention to the phone call. In a low voice, Sheriff King explained the situation to Shelly and Tolbert. They wolfed down breakfast, while Shelly told a few of her staff that she was leaving for a few minutes. The three of them hurried outside and got into King's cruiser. Shelly gave them directions to Melinda Sue's lake house.

They found Melinda Sue sitting on her front porch anxiously waiting and nervously puffing on a cigarette. As they walked toward her, Melinda Sue got up, crushed the cigarette onto the sidewalk with her foot, and hurried to meet them. She led them onto the dock, pointed out the unused towel and explained how Lucinda Sue always jumped into the lake at 10:30 to cool off before heading to bed. Melinda Sue explained how she always turned in right before ten to get her needed hours of beauty sleep, and that she shut out the world with a mask and ear plugs. So, she didn't hear anything all night.

Shelly held Melinda Sue in her arms and tried to console her as she sobbed loudly, saying through her wails, "I promised I'd watch over her and now she could be dead!" Shelly tried to reassure her that Lucinda Sue could be any number of places, but Melinda Sue heard none of that. She knew Lucinda Sue was dead and it was her fault. She sobbed even louder, her body shaking.

King and Masterson stood off to the side, quietly talking. The sheriff said, "I hate to say it but this looks like another mysterious drowning. If that's the case the town will be buzzing and the fear level will rise. McDuff's is a very popular restaurant, and the two Sue's were really well known."

Masterson nodded, "And I'm afraid that's exactly what we're dealing with, Crystal. With the disappearance of Malaby, and now Lucinda Sue it seems the killer has decided to murder well-known people. That means no one is safe." King nodded grimly.

Forty-Nine

THE SHERIFF HAD no idea how on target Masterson's comment was. At that moment, Romy Moreland finished wiring the IED she planned to use to blow up the sheriff's police cruiser. Her plan was to attach it to the car, which her surveillance showed was parked in the King's driveway every night. Once King drove the car to work, she would arm the IED and the next time King started the police cruiser, the sheriff would be blown to smithereens.

The serial killer set the IED down on the bench, satisfied with her powerful device. She took out the wrinkled picture of Cody Martin and as she did so often, talked to it as if he was alive and sitting in the room with her. She softly promised him that soon the woman who had killed the love of her life would be dead.

Sheriff King called the office to order a crime scene investigator, but she already knew they'd find no proof. She also asked the rescue boat to drag the lake around Melinda Sue's dock, admonishing the dispatcher to explain the importance keeping a low profile with no sirens.

King and Masterson searched Lucinda Sue's bedroom, found her purse and cell phone undisturbed but nothing that might give them a clue what happened to the popular waitress.

That evening, Crystal invited Masterson to a cookout that included her husband, Buddy. It was a gorgeous night. Across the lake, the sun was slowly sinking out of sight radiating fingers of orange, blue and yellow light into the night sky. The three of them sat on the deck enjoying a cold beer as the brisket finished cooking on the smoker. The conversation turned to female serial killers.

Masterson had done a great deal of research on female serial killers and he was spinning the tales. "Aileen Wuornos was in her thirties in 1989 and 1990 when she killed seven men in Florida. Shot them at point-blank range."

Buddy took a swig of beer, "What was her motive?"

Masterson continued, "She claimed it was self-defense because they raped her while she was working as a prostitute. They captured her after she had a minor traffic accident driving one of her victim's cars. They made a movie about her called Monster. It starred Charlize Theron and had great reviews. Wuornos was sentenced to death and died by lethal injection in 2002."

Buddy added his contribution, "I read an article recently about a woman they called 'Jolly Jane.' She was a nurse who killed dozens of patients using different combinations of medicine and chemicals. Her name was Jane Toppan, and she was a nut case. At times she crawled into bed with her victims after delivering the lethal dose. She eventually confessed to thirty-one murders, was found not guilty by reason of insanity and went to a loony bin for the rest of her life. She died there in 1938 at age eighty-four."

The former sheriff got up to check on the brisket. It was ready. Soon the trio was enjoying a great barbecue meal of brisket, cole slaw and grilled corn on the cob. As they munched, talked and laughed and told more stories, they had no idea a woman dressed in all black was in their driveway attaching the IED to the county squad car. She finished her mission, undetected, and walked the three blocks back to her car before disappearing into the night.

Word circulated around Cedar Creek Lake about the disappearance of Lucinda Sue and her possible drowning. At McDuff's, loyal customers arrived with flowers and soon a shrine was set up inside the restaurant with a picture of the missing waitress and many heartfelt signs. As they dined, customers throughout the restaurant swapped tales about the waitress and her cousin Melinda Sue. One of the longtime waitresses phoned Dwayne Murphy and alerted him to the memorial and the missing Lucinda Sue. He had no idea about the situation since his best spy, Melinda Sue was home too grief-stricken to return to work.

Sheriff King put her empty coffee cup in the sink, kissed Buddy goodbye and hopped into the Henderson County cruiser. She had no idea there was a device blinking under her car with enough C4 and nails to blow up the car and kill her in seconds. The sheriff drove to work and parked the car in her reserved space right in front of the Sheriff's Office.

It was eight o'clock when King walked into her office. Tolbert Masterson was already sitting at her small conference table enjoying a cup of coffee. Crystal's husband Buddy was working on a big investigation of his own, but he'd agreed to stop by at 8:30 for a meeting. The topic on the table was the possibility of the copycat killer being a current or former Navy SEAL. And most importantly, how they could get names of area SEALs when the information was highly secret.

Melinda Sue sat on the deck of her lake house, sipping herbal tea, and watching the Sheriff's Department boat dragging Cedar Creek Lake looking for her missing cousin. Tears rolled down her cheeks. She could not shake the terrible sadness that enveloped every fiber in her body. It was the second day of dragging the lake bottom with no sign of Lucinda Sue.

Her doorbell rang. Melinda Sue dragged herself out of the deck chair and walked to the front door. She saw Dwayne Murphy standing on her porch, and let him in. Murphy gave her a sympathetic hug, and explained he'd have been over sooner but had no idea that Lucinda Sue was missing until an hour ago. Melinda Sue seemed to melt into his arms. She was shaking all over, "Oh, Dwayne it is just so terrible. Do you really think this serial killer drowned her like the others?" She continued sobbing and felt like she was going to collapse onto the floor. Dwayne guided her to a nearby chair.

In Athens, Buddy joined the sheriff and Texas Ranger at the table in Crystal's office. While they'd kicked around ideas the night before, all three became convinced that the copycat killer had to be a Navy SEAL. It was also apparently a woman based on the information on the videotape from Shane Malaby. They continued to search everywhere possible but could not turn up the photos the dead rancher claimed to have.

Buddy said, "During the search for Cody Martin, we really found out just how secretive the Navy is when it comes to former SEALs. They sent his checks to a P.O. Box in Tool, so we staked that out but we had no idea what his name might be. I finally went to one of our East Texas Congressmen Pete Dicus and after quite a bit of convincing he found a friend in the Senate who was a former Navy SEAL and managed to get us the names of former SEALs who live around here. But it was a difficult path to get those names for sure."

Masterson said, "Well, since you have such a good relationship with him maybe he'll help us get the current names. I'm sure your original list is a bit outdated by now."

Buddy King shook his head from side to side. "I'd like to give it a shot, but right now we don't have any solid evidence that it's a woman. I believe he'd tell me to get more before he goes to the Senator for help. I tell ya, they guard that information like the gold in Fort Knox."

Sheriff King looked at her watch, "Sorry, gentlemen, but I have to run. I've got to attend a meeting of the county commissioners." She had no idea the copycat killer had now activated the lethal IED under her car and when she turned the ignition key, she would be dead. King grabbed her car keys, purse and a briefcase, kissed buddy on the cheek and said, "I'll be back in an hour or so."

Meanwhile Dwayne Murphy was jotting down notes as he sat on the deck of Melinda Sue's lake house. He was planning a big story on the popular waitress who had made so many friends and loyal customers in a short time. Out on the lake, the sheriff's boat had been joined by boats from fire departments in Gun Barrel City and Seven Points as they dragged the lake in a synchronized grid search.

Fifty

SHERIFF KING WAS a few feet from the police cruiser and about to unlock the doors with her wireless key fob. Suddenly there was a shout behind her. It was Hollis Duncan, the sheriff's department chief mechanic. King stopped in her tracks and looked his way, "Hollis, I'm about to run late to a meeting with the county commissioners. What's the matter."

Duncan, a stickler for following mechanical guidelines said, "Sheriff, my records show your police vehicle is almost two thousand miles overdue for a scheduled oil change. If we don't follow the recommendations, you could harm the engine, and cost the taxpayers a great deal of money."

King was a strong believer in following the rules, but she had grown weary of Duncan's fastidiousness interrupting her busy days. She turned to him, "Hollis, I'm only going a few miles. I'll be back in less than two hours and then you can do whatever you need to do." She slid into the driver's seat of her cruiser and put the key in the ignition.

But Duncan was stubborn. He walked right up to her and handed her a set of keys, "Sheriff, these are for that vehicle right over there. Please take that one, and I'll have your oil changed, and all the fluids topped off when you return from the meeting."

Crystal started to turn the ignition key. But Duncan persisted, "Please, Sheriff, I don't want you to have any engine issues." Again, she grasped the key to start the vehicle, but then she decided to appease her top mechanic.

Reluctantly the sheriff gave him the keys and headed for the other vehicle. As she opened the door and slid behind the wheel, she waved at Duncan who waved back and mouthed 'thank you' to her. The mechanic jumped in, and turned the ignition key. Suddenly, the sheriff's cruiser was blown several feet into the air as the powerful IED denotated. A ball of fire engulfed the car. Duncan was killed instantly.

The blast was so strong it blew all the windows out of the vehicle the sheriff was in, and the concussion momentarily knocked her unconscious. The blast shook the sheriff's building, and suddenly deputies streamed out of the front door. Buddy also emerged, and when he saw the now blackened and burning sheriff's cruiser thought Crystal was inside. He sprinted to the car but was repelled by the intense heat of the flames.

Several deputies dragged him back from the inferno as he screamed Crystal's name. As the deputies kept a firm grip on him, holding him back, Crystal woke up just as a deputy reached her. He shouted, "Hey, the sheriff is over here in this vehicle. I think she's okay." The scene was chaotic, with thick black smoke billowing into the sky, and the sound of fire department vehicles piercing the air.

The deputies let go of Buddy, and he ran over to Crystal. She had a few cuts on her face, and her hair was full of shards of glass, but she was alive. Buddy reached in and held her tight. Soon paramedics joined them and tended to Crystal. As they treated the cuts on her face, and her right arm, they gently pulled the glass pieces out of her hair. They reassured Buddy that she was fine, but because of the concussion from the blast they were going to take her to the hospital to get checked out.

Crystal looked at Buddy, "Hollis is in the car. He wouldn't let me leave without an oil change and it saved my life. But it cost him his life." She shuddered. The firemen had doused the flames and fi-

195

nally reached Duncan. It was a terrible scene. The fire had consumed his body. He looked like a marshmallow that had caught on fire and melted into an ashy black mess.

Crystal turned away, just as Tolbert Masterson walked up next to her, "Are you alright, Sheriff?"

Crystal nodded, "I guess you're a bit of a prophet when you said that no one was safe from this lunatic."

Masterson replied, "I've already talked to my boss and asked for some reinforcements. We can't have anyone in Texas trying to blow up an elected official." With that, the paramedic led Crystal to the ambulance, and Buddy hopped in to accompany her to the hospital. Masterson took over the crime scene.

Soon the area around the Henderson County Sheriff's Department was flooded with nosy townies, police, and the media. It was a mob scene. Nothing like this—blowing up a sheriff's police cruiser—had ever happened around here. Uniformed police set up yellow crime scene tape around the perimeter of the explosion. The squad car was nothing but a shell of black metal. Pieces were blown over a hundred yards away. The poor mechanic never knew what hit him.

With the media clamoring for a statement, Ranger Masterson promised a news conference in an hour. He wanted to give the Dallas and Tyler television stations time to reach the scene so he wouldn't have to do it twice. Meanwhile, Dwayne Murphy was buzzing around the crime scene like a bee in search of nectar, trying to get information from his police sources. But with the boss being checked out at the hospital, and the Texas Rangers now in charge, none of them wanted to even be seen with the aggressive reporter.

As detectives continued to scour the area for pieces of shrapnel, metal and other fragments, a bomb squad team moved in to assure there were no more bombs, but also to locate the device used to set off the explosion. The Sheriff's Department had been evacuated until bomb sniffing dogs could search every floor. They came up empty, and people were allowed back into the building. A number of Athens Police patrolman went to the nearby courthouse. A thorough search there also found no more bombs.

Sheriff King, with Buddy holding her hand all the way, arrived at the Athens Hospital. Crystal refused a gurney, and instead agreed to enter in a wheelchair. Photographers were waiting at the hospital, and she didn't want to have her picture taken lying down on a gurney. As the sheriff was wheeled into the hospital by Buddy, reporters shouted questions. "Crystal, who did this?" "Sheriff, who would want to kill you with a bomb?" "Sheriff, how do you feel?" She answered no questions, instead with a big smile she gave them a thumbs up, knowing it would be the picture they used.

Once in the emergency room, Crystal changed into a hospital gown and was given a thorough examination. Even though she'd been almost twenty yards from the blast, broken glass and shrapnel were tangled in her hair. One piece of glass pierced her right bicep and that wound required stitches. The doctor also wanted to do x-rays just to be sure. Crystal started to protest, but Buddy gave her that look, and she reluctantly gave in.

When they had a moment alone, Buddy gave her a strong hug, and asked, "You sure you're okay, honey. That was one hell of a blast."

Crystal nodded, "I just feel so bad for Hollis and his family. He was just doing his job and now he's dead."

Buddy took her hand, and looked into her eyes, "Honey, I'm sorry about Duncan, too. But that could have been you."

Crystal shuddered recalling the blast, with her mind processing what would have happened if she was in the driver's seat. She turned back to Buddy, "The most important question is who the hell wanted to blow me up?"

Buddy thought for a minute, then said. "Well, with the same pattern as The Frogman, I'm more and more convinced it could be a Navy SEAL just like Cody Martin. And they're so damn secretive, it's going to be really difficult to get information on who it may be."

Crystal nodded, "I believe you may be right. Is this some sort of revenge thing? I mean, I'm the one who killed Martin. Now one of his buddies is coming after me?"

Buddy agreed, "That's where I'm heading, honey. I don't understand the copycat killings that mimic Van Cleave, but more and more this seems like this person is trying to embarrass you with unsolved cases, some high profile like Malaby and Lucinda Sue, and then planning on killing you. That car bomb was no accident."

Crystal frowned, "What has me a bit confused is Malaby's statement that it is a woman. I thought all Navy SEALs were men. And we still haven't located Brenda Wright. If Malaby sent her the pictures of the suspicious woman, she's probably already dead if the killer found out she had them. This is one helluva mess."

Buddy replied, "From my research on Cody Martin, not all Navy SEALs are men any longer. There are a few women who passed their extremely inhuman 'Hell Week' training and made it as SEALs. But that list has to be very short. If we can get solid proof that it is a woman, I can take the information to Congressman Dicus and once again ask him for help. I mean she could have been Martin's girlfriend. One thing is certain, if it is a woman, she is extremely strong, well trained in killing skills, and apparently knows how to construct a powerful IED."

The doctor came into the room, and informed Crystal it was time for x-rays. She reluctantly got into a wheelchair and was taken down the hall. Buddy took a seat next to the emergency room bed, and called his pal, and former sheriff, Billy Richardson, thinking maybe he had some ideas to share on this situation.

Back at the explosion scene, the crowd continued to grow. It was time for the news conference. Tolbert Masterson stepped to an outdoor podium filled with microphones and wires snaking everywhere. The Texas Ranger introduced himself and began. "We are in full investigation mode regarding this car bomb. Unfortunately, it has claimed the life of Hollis Duncan. Sheriff King, who was supposed to be in the cruiser is being checked out at the hospital, but it appears any injuries to her are minor. Mr. Duncan was about to take the sheriff's cruiser into the shop for an oil change. The sheriff was about twenty yards away when Mr. Duncan turned the key in the ignition and the IED exploded." He paused for a moment, and the air was filled with shouted questions.

Romy Moreland sat in her rental house, watching the news conference live on a Dallas TV station. She was angry at her bad luck. If that damn mechanic hadn't intervened, she would have accomplished her mission of killing Crystal King. In her hand she held the battered picture of Cody Martin. She told the picture what happened, and then pledged that the sheriff would soon be dead. She would gain vengeance for King murdering the only one she ever loved. A tear rolled down her troubled cheek.

Fifty-One

At the news conference, Ranger Masterson agreed to answer a few questions. Murphy shouted the quickest, "What about the missing Mabank Police Detective, Brenda Wright?"

Masterson replied, "At this time the lieutenant remains missing. We're searching everywhere for her. As you know her cruiser was recovered along Highway 175, but there has been no sign of her." He pointed toward a well-known Tyler TV reporter who asked about the drowning deaths, and the four people who have disappeared including Shane Malaby who admitted on videotape that he killed Van Cleave to avenge his daughter's murder. Masterson, who was skilled at holding these sessions with reporters replied, "It is all part of our investigation. I've also asked for a contingent of Texas Rangers to join us in solving these cases."

That brought a crescendo of more shouted questions. Masterson held up his hand, "We hope to have more information to share with you in a few hours. That's all for now." The reporters continued shouting questions at his back as Masterson walked away from the microphone. The Ranger never looked back or acknowledged any of them.

Sheriff King and Buddy arrived back at police headquarters. She'd been checked out, received a few stitches and was released from the hospital. They quickly huddled with Masterson in the conference room. Four more Texas Rangers had already arrived, so Masterson introduced them to the Kings. The lead bomb squad sergeant joined them. They asked him for an update. The bomb expert said, "It was definitely an improvised explosive device. It was held under the car by a powerful magnet and once activated from a mobile phone, exploded when the ignition key was engaged. It was filled with nails which acted as powerful shrapnel. We believe the death of Mr. Duncan was instantaneous." Crystal's body shook at the thought it could have been, should have been, her.

Masterson asked, "I don't figure you found any evidence that would point us to the perpetrator?"

The bomb squad expert shook his head, "I'm afraid not. All that was left were tiny pieces. Of course, we did not find any fingerprints. However, from my time with the bomb squad in the Navy, I firmly believe this had all the traits of a Navy SEAL IED. They have certain little signatures like how the IED is constructed." Buddy looked at Crystal. It appeared their speculation was on target.

While this discussion occurred at police headquarters, about fifteen miles away a local farmer climbed aboard his tractor to cut hay. He made three passes through the field with the heavy steel blades cutting the Bermuda grass meadow. Suddenly, the farmer spotted something right in his path. It looked like a body with a brown uniform. He quickly stopped the tractor and jumped down. That's when he found the body of Brenda Wright. Her name was on her badge. With his hands shaking he dialed 9-1-1.

The dispatcher interrupted the conference room meeting, "Sheriff, a farmer about a mile off Highway 175 on County Road 2919 just found Brenda Wright's body in his hay field."

Crystal's stomach fell to her feet. She'd known this was a possibility but was hoping and praying for a different outcome. As King, Masterson and the other Texas Rangers headed out the door, King told the dispatcher, "Keep a tight lid on this one. You understand?

I want no one else to know about this until I investigate." The dispatcher got the message and left.

The officers reached the scene in about fifteen minutes. They found the farmer standing near his tractor, about ten feet from the fallen officer's body. He was puffing on a cigarette. King introduced herself, and they headed to the body. Masterson said, "One bullet to the back of the head. Her service revolver is beside the body. I'd say she's been dead for several days."

King looked perplexed, "Why kill a Mabank detective? This does not fit any pattern that we've been speculating about?"

Masterson said, "I did some digging, but didn't have a chance to fill you in when the car bomb happened. Remember Malaby said he had pictures of a mysterious woman? Well, the dispatcher told me that Lieutenant Wright received a large manila envelope from UPS, and then quickly left the building. The package had to be signed in as standard procedure. It came from Shane Malaby."

King was still puzzled, "Why wouldn't she just turn it over to me?"

Masterson said, "I believe Malaby sent her the pictures because he wanted her to use facial recognition to give him a name. I think he was going to kill the woman just like he killed Van Cleave."

King replied, "So she was going to keep that evidence to herself? Why?"

Masterson said, "Well, I dug around some more and found out Wright and Malaby had been in an ongoing affair for a couple years. They were very careful to keep it a secret. So, she was helping him out without going through official channels."

King was angry, "And I thought she was one of Mabank's best officers. Do you think she knew that Malaby killed Van Cleave and never said anything to us? And trying to help him this time cost her her life. How stupid!"

Masterson nodded, "Love does strange things to people, Crystal."

Sheriff King, back in her office, sent a text to her husband to fill him in on the dead police officer. As he sat in his office, Buddy King went online to check the schedule for Congressman Pete Dicus. He saw the congressman would be in his district office in Athens in two days. He called his assistant and requested lunch with Dicus. The congressman agreed, and the lunch was set for one o'clock. King was hopeful he could convince Dicus to help him track down another Navy SEAL just like he had with Cody Martin.

Fifty-Two

ON CEDAR CREEK Lake, Bobby Phillips was having a difficult morning. His automatic irrigation system, using a pump in the lake, had not worked early today. Unfortunately, Phillips was asleep when the timer turned on the pump and was unaware the pump had run dry and burned up. It was over a $500 loss. Bobby Phillips had lived on the lake for over forty years. He was tall and extremely thin, looking like a strong Texas thunderstorm could blow him away. He wore his usual uniform of tattered bib overalls with a white t-shirt underneath. An ever-present cigarette dangled from his mouth. His teeth were yellow from decades of puffing on unfiltered Camels. His nose bent off to one side. The result of a pool cue in a bar fight a long time ago. His neighbors shunned him because he was the classic grumpy old man.

With a little difficulty due to his hands being wracked with arthritis, Phillips pulled on a pair of waders and headed into the water to see what was going on with the PVC pipe. He slogged his way through the two-foot-deep water along the shoreline, and made it to the end of his dock, where the water was about twice that deep. Recent rains made the water murky, and he was unable to see more than a foot underwater.

With a loud grunt, Phillips bent down to check on the pipe. He immediately recoiled when his hand grabbed a shock of hair.

Curious, he bent over again, and felt all around the area of the pipe. It suddenly struck him that a body wrapped around the PVC, snapping off the connector and causing the dry pump. Phillips turned around, trudged back through the lake water, and headed into the house to call the sheriff.

For the second time in less than an hour, the dispatcher walked up to the sheriff with bad news, "Just got a call from a Mr. Phillips who says there is a body wrapped around the pipe that feeds his irrigation system from the lake."

Crystal asked the dispatcher where Phillips lived, after he told her she said, "It's gotta be Lucinda Sue. This day just sucks." Once again, she admonished the dispatcher to keep the information to himself.

Masterson said, "With all the media still gathered outside, we're going to have to sneak past them." King nodded in agreement.

Sheriff King walked down the hall and found her top SCUBA diver pouring himself a cup of coffee. She filled him in on the situation. They agreed the diver would drive while the sheriff and Masterson huddled out of sight in the back seat. They headed out of the garage, and no one noticed. King asked herself for the hundredth time today, why she ever wanted this job.

They pulled up to Phillips' modest lake home and walked through the side yard to the edge of Cedar Creek Lake. They found him smoking a cigarette while he waited in a rusty metal lawn chair. There were introductions all around, and then the diver entered the water as Phillips pointed out where the body was. Using an air tank, the diver swam to the bottom. He resurfaced after a few minutes.

The diver came over to the sheriff, "It's definitely Lucinda Sue. I remember her from McDuff's. Apparently, the current carried her into the pipe where it sits on a cinder block to keep the foot valve off the bottom. She got entangled in the pipe. Should I bring her ashore?"

King said, "Yes, but please go back and show me the location so I can take some crime scene pictures, then bring her to shore."

While the diver worked on loosening the corpse, King turned to Masterson, "The carnage is piling up. It makes me sick. Four drownings, four people missing, one Mabank deputy shot in the back of the head, and one of my employees blown up. We've got to catch this SOB right now."

The Texas Ranger responded, "Well, I've brought in the cavalry, Crystal. I suggest we have a meeting with everyone first thing in the morning, and put a plan together to stop these killings, and to keep you safe from this psycho."

Romy Moreland sat on the deck of her rented lake home, pondering her next move. She had already decided there would be no more cremations, she felt four drownings were enough, and it was time to concentrate her full attention and skills on killing Crystal King. She mused that another IED was probably out of the question, as they'd be checking the sheriff's car every time before she got in. The killer was not aware it had already been decided the sheriff would switch cars for each of her trips, never using the same one twice.

Despite her protestations, Ranger Masterson also ordered that the sheriff would have a person tracking her wherever she went, keeping their distance, but prepared to jump in to save her against any more attempts on her life. There would also be an undercover officer watching her home day and night, whether she was there or not, in case the killer tried to install a bomb at her residence. Crystal was positive she could defend herself, "I don't need, nor want, any of these protection details, Tolbert. I'm a girl who can handle herself against anyone."

Masterson chuckled, "I know you're tough, Crystal. But I'm now in charge of this investigation, and I have decided you need that level of protection. Now, let's concentrate on catching this sick person before he or she takes any more lives."

While the sheriff's safety was discussed, Buddy King walked into Congressman Pete Dicus' favorite Chinese buffet a few blocks off the downtown square in Athens. He slid into a booth. A few minutes later the congressman joined him. Pete Dicus was a distinguished looking man, with streaks of grey running through his closely cropped black hair. He stood about six-four with the long lean body of a basketball player. He'd been a good one, earning a scholarship to UT-Dallas. He was a sharp shooting guard and still owned a number of records at the college.

Dicus offered a strong handshake. They spent a few minutes catching up on a number of things. After their first trip to the buffet, they ate a few minutes in silence, and then the congressman said, "So, Buddy, I assume we're going to discuss all these unexplained deaths that have occurred recently, especially the death of a well-liked Mabank policewoman, and the attempt to blow up Crystal inside her police cruiser?"

Buddy nodded, "Yes sir. We have reason to believe this is a copy-cat killer following the same M.O. as the Navy SEAL who drowned his victims, and that sick funeral home director who cremated his victims, and then disappeared himself. You've also probably heard that after Shane Malaby disappeared. We found a confession on his computer. He claimed he killed Van Cleave, and he had pictures of a female lurking around the old Van Cleave funeral home. He believed she was using the crematorium just like Van Cleave to dispose of all evidence from her victims."

Dicus interjected, "But you have not found any pictures, right?"

King shook his head from side to side. "No, we haven't. And we believe Malaby sent those pictures to the Mabank policewoman so she could help him identify the mysterious woman using facial rec software. But somehow the killer found out she had the pictures and shot the deputy in the back of the head and dumped her in a hay field. They just found her body."

Dicus had an idea of what was coming next, "And I suppose you need the names of any Navy SEALs in the area, just like you requested when you were sheriff and The Frogman was out creating mayhem?"

King gave him a tight smile, "Yes sir. But in this case, we strongly believe it is a former female Navy SEAL. So, there are very few of them out there."

Dicus nodded, "Yes, that's true but it doesn't make it any easier to pry secret data from the SEALs."

King sighed as he held his fork filled with Kung Pao chicken. "I understand. But the carnage is piling up, and we need to narrow our search as quickly as possible. I'm not involved with law enforcement anymore as you know, but since we know each other well, I'm here on their behalf."

Dicus smiled for the first time, "And I believe you may be married to the current sheriff. And you want to keep her as safe as possible since the killer just targeted her."

King nodded, "Yes sir, we believe the killer is seeking revenge on Crystal, since she was the one who killed Cody Martin in self-defense."

The lunch ended, and the two men shook hands and headed for their vehicles. The congressman had not promised he'd get the names, but he did say he'd quietly look into the possibility and get back to Buddy King. The former sheriff was hopeful Dicus would talk to Senator Bobby Jackson, a former Navy SEAL from Nebraska, who had given names to the congressman when they were chasing Cody Martin.

Fifty-Three

THE OBJECT OF their search glistened with sweat after completing her daily two hundred sit-ups and pushups routine. She also worked with free weights. Romy Moreland wanted to stay in peak form for her final showdown with that blond who killed her man. Once again, she took his picture in her hands and said, "I missed her that time, Cody, but she won't be so fortunate the next time. I will gain vengeance for her murdering you." Her eyes welled up, and some tears rolled down her cheeks. She set the well-worn picture back down, and stared into space, remembering the good times with the love of her life.

She received an alert on her phone that WFAA-TV was broadcasting a news conference live from the Henderson County Sheriff's Office. She quickly found the remote and turned on her television. Sure enough, Texas Ranger Masterson walked toward a bank of microphones.

Masterson took a breath, gazed at the packed conference room, and began. He introduced himself and then said, "Regretfully, I must inform you that we found the body of Mabank Police Detective Brenda Wright. She died by gunshot and was left in a hay field between Eustace and Athens. We offer our condolences to her family, and our prayers for the fallen officer." He ignored the shouted questions, as he thought about mentioning the remains of Lucinda Sue had also been found. The Ranger plunged on, knowing it would be worse if word came from other sources.

He held up his hands for silence, "I also want to let you know that we recovered the body of Lucinda Sue Corvalis who drowned in Cedar Creek Lake. Unfortunately, it appears she became entangled in an irrigation pipe and was unable to free herself. We send our thoughts and prayers to her family and friends as well."

A reporter quickly and loudly shouted, "Who killed both of these women? It seems the body count is getting out of control around here!"

Masterson glared at the reporter, a few veins bulged in his neck as he tersely replied, "If we knew that, sir, we'd have arrested the perps by now. We are working very hard to solve the disappearance and murder of Officer Wright. Lucinda Sue's death appears to be from drowning and, so far, we have found no evidence of foul play."

This time Murphy jumped to his feet, "C'mon, Ranger Masterson, we all know these so-called drownings and disappearances, the death of Officer Wright and the attempt to blow up the sheriff are all the work of the same copycat killer!"

Masterson just shook his head toward Murphy with an incredulous smile on his face. "You, sir, are off in LaLa Land as usual." With that he turned abruptly and strolled purposefully away from the microphones without another word. Shouts from the media circus rained down on him.

The copycat killer smiled as the cameras followed the back of the Texas Ranger as he exited the podium in an angry stroll. His words convinced her that law enforcement, even with the aid of the vaunted Texas Rangers were nowhere when it came to tracking her down. Still, she remained concerned about the pictures of the mysterious woman she kept hearing about. Moreland killed the Mabank officer because she had copies of the pictures. But in the back of her mind, she kept wondering whether Malaby had copies stashed somewhere in his office, and the police search had missed them. She had to be sure. They only thing to do was to break into Malaby's home.

At the Henderson County Sheriff's Office, Tolbert Masterson was leading a large meeting. All the key deputies from the sheriff's department were there, the extra eight Texas Rangers that had been sent to Athens attended, as did the chiefs of police from various towns around Cedar Creek Lake. Masterson gave an impassioned speech about the need to catch the culprit responsible for many deaths in the area, and especially the murder of a Mabank policewoman. Then he turned the meeting over to Sheriff King.

Crystal, using a PowerPoint presentation, recapped the four victims of drownings which were suspicious, but so far, they had found no proof they were murdered. She then went into the history of Cody Martin, The Frogman Of Cedar Creek, and how he had killed many folks making them all appear like they'd drowned. His mistake, she explained was breaking the neck of one of his victims. Then King showed the four people who had vanished, and how there was a suspicion they were cremated in the abandoned funeral home where a guy named Van Cleave had allegedly destroyed evidence of his victims by cremating them, and dumping their ashes in the lake. One of the current missing persons, Shane Malaby, had confessed on video tape that he killed Van Cleave after a jury found the funeral home owner not guilty. Malaby also claimed to have pictures of a mysterious woman at the funeral home, which he had staked out after the new disappearances began.

King pressed a button and a picture of Mabank Police Officer Brenda Wright appeared on the conference room screen. She continued, "We believe that Malaby sent pictures of the mysterious woman to Officer Wright, asking her to try to identify the person without alerting other police officials. Unfortunately, her killer somehow tracked down who Malaby sent the pictures to, followed her out on Highway 175 and murdered her.

The screen went black, and Sheriff King sat down. Tolbert

jumped to his feet, "This is a real mess. Too many people have lost their lives, and we have been unable to develop any solid leads. Job One is to identify this mystery woman. We have a strong suspicion that she, if it is indeed a she, is a former Navy SEAL. Her methods, the drownings, the IED under the sheriff's car, are all skills learned in the SEALs. We believe she may be gaining vengeance for the death of fellow SEAL Cody Martin, who was stabbed to death by Sheriff King after he took her captive."

One of the newly arrived Texas Rangers stood and asked, "Are we thinking of using Sheriff King as bait to draw out this person? We could set up a sting to lure the killer out and then take her down." He sat back down.

Masterson answered, "We have discussed that. I am reluctant to take that risk at this time because this person is a highly trained killer and has proved it over and over in recent weeks. We want to be sure if we put the sheriff in a precarious situation that we can protect her."

The meeting went on for another hour with suggestions offered and rejected. Masterson assigned different tasks to various law enforcement and the meeting broke up. Many grim faces left the conference room, well aware of how difficult finding this killer was going to be.

During the meeting, Romy Moreland was driving past the Malaby Ranch just outside Mabank. The property was guarded by a steel gate, but it was open now and Moreland needed to determine if it stayed like that all night. She'd revisit the ranch late that evening to find out. The killer could see the huge ranch house in the distance. She had no idea if it had a security system. Moreland decided she needed to do more reconnaissance before attempting to search Malaby's office. She was happy to find a diagram of the house on the internet. It was included in a *Dallas Morning News* story about ranches in East Texas.

As Moreland drove back to her rental home, a Henderson

County Sheriff's deputy passed her going in the opposite direction. The officer behind the wheel didn't even glance her way. She took that as a solid sign that they had no idea about her or her vehicle.

While that deputy paid no attention to Moreland as she drove by, she had no idea undercover police officers were deployed around Henderson County keeping an eye out for the copycat killer. One staked out the abandoned funeral home, another sat unobtrusively about a half block down from Sheriff King's home. Others were blending into the crowd at the courthouse and sheriff's department. Other officers were assigned to other locations. Law enforcement was determined to stop these senseless killings.

In Athens, Dwayne Murphy and editor Adler Huxley were actually working together to create a special edition of the newspaper. In all his years at the helm, Huxley could not remember another time when there was so much news to cover, all because of an apparent copycat killer. The bodies were piling up, and Huxley wanted to give each victim a proper spotlight, while also trying to explain the big picture. There was no mention of any conspiracy theories. Though he would never give Murphy the satisfaction of congratulating him for being ahead of the story from the beginning, just the fact that the crusty old editor was working with him side by side on the coverage was extraordinary.

Fifty-Four

THE BLAZING TEXAS sun sunk into the horizon, and a cool breeze made for a pleasant night. But Crystal King was not enjoying the weather. She peered out the window right before dishing up a delicious homemade stew for Buddy and herself. She gave her husband a frustrating look. "They're treating me like some helpless female who can't handle herself." Buddy knew that look well. His wife was determined to be the Henderson County Sheriff, not the Henderson County Female Sheriff. He attempted to drive away her anger, but quickly realized it was a futile effort. They ate in silence.

At ten o'clock Buddy clicked off the table lamp in their bedroom, and they were both quickly asleep. It was about the same time that Murphy and Huxley locked the front door of the newspaper office and headed home. They were exhausted. The articles would be finished tomorrow morning in plenty of time to meet their publication deadline.

Meanwhile, Romy Moreland was watching the local TV newscast. It was filled with information, and misinformation of the mayhem occurring around Cedar Creek Lake. There was some speculation that the killer was a woman, but a so-called expert crime professor from SMU opined that female serial killers were rare. He doubted a woman could drown four people, and cause four others to vanish, kill a policewoman and try to blow up the sheriff. He concluded, "I would be very surprised if these terrible acts are being carried out by a woman." Moreland smiled. *What an idiot,* she thought. They'd find out soon enough who she was because her mission of revenge would press on and if she got caught, they'd never take her alive. Moreland had already decided it was time to join Cody Martin in the afterworld. But first, Crystal King would be dead.

The copycat killer glanced at her watch. The green glow read 11:45. It was time for her reconnaissance mission at the Malaby Ranch. She had to be sure there were no pictures of her stashed in his office or house. Moreland did not want to get caught before she could snuff out Crystal King's life. Dressed all in black from head to toe, Moreland jumped into her car and headed to the ranch just outside Mabank.

As she drove down the rural road to the ranch, Moreland kept a sharp eye out for any police presence. She came to the steel front gate at the Malaby Ranch and was thrilled to see that no one had closed the massive metal gates. Moreland turned off her headlights, and slowly drove down the road. Using night vision binoculars, she slowly scanned the area. No sign of life. She had been unable to determine if the house had a security system but planned on carefully casing the home before getting anywhere in range of cameras.

Inside the Malaby home, Shane's wife, Amanda, was in her usual over-medicated stupor. She was in a particularly melancholy mood tonight and had taken even more sleeping pills than normal. Amanda hadn't attempted an overdose; she had just taken extra pills hoping for some solid sleep, instead of tossing and turning all night thinking about her dead daughter and apparently dead husband.

In that deep coma-like sleep, Amanda Malaby had no idea the copycat killer was lurking outside her rural home. Moreland had no intention of murdering the widow. She'd heard gossip about her pill abuse and was counting on that to allow her to search the place without detection. Moreland circled the house on foot after parking her car about a quarter mile from the home. There did not appear to be any security cameras or security system guarding the sprawling house. In fact, although Moreland didn't know it, Shane Malaby always boasted he didn't need a security system because he'd shoot intruders on sight.

Using burglar tools, Moreland silently unlocked the rear door of the home, and quietly entered. She was pleased to see that the widow had left a number of lights on. She could actually hear Amanda Malaby's snoring coming from down a long hallway. That emboldened her, and she quickly, soundlessly climbed the stairway to the second level where Malaby had his office.

Using a powerful flashlight, Moreland searched every inch of the sprawling office filled with carved oak chairs that were over-stuffed and covered by the finest leather available. Just as the police had experienced before her, the extensive search turned up nothing. The police had confiscated Malaby's computer, but there were plenty of other piles of documents, various reports, and just plain junk.

As Moreland prepared to leave empty-handed, she had a sudden thought. What if Malaby had hidden the pictures in the barn. She knew from her research that he kept a small office in that structure as well. The copycat killer paused and held her breath, straining to hear the sound of Amanda Malaby snoring. There it was. She quickly and silently crept down the stairs, and out the back door.

Aided by the darkness of a cloud-filled sky, and no moon, Moreland quickly walked to the barn which was about a hundred yards from the ranch house. Surprisingly the side door was unlocked, so she walked right in. Her flashlight beam found the office. She went inside and shut the door. Once again, the killer conducted a thorough search. She finished with an angry look. She had found nothing.

Moreland crossed the room, opened the door and started to hurry out of the barn. She was stopped in her tracks by a voice in the darkness, "Get on the ground now and lace your fingers behind your head."

Moreland was startled, "What? Who are you?"

216

Suddenly she was blinded by the beam of a strong flashlight shining in her eyes. "I said get on the ground now and lace your hands behind your head. My name is Orville Richter, and I am an investigator with the Henderson County Sheriff's Office, and you are under arrest for trespassing. Now get on the ground!"

A thousand scenarios ran through Moreland's Navy SEAL-trained brain. They were taught never to be caught, and to take action to get out of the situation. Richter, a veteran detective, knew enough to keep his distance from the suspect. He kept his gun trained on her heart.

Moreland said, "I've got a bad back and can't really lay on the ground. Why are you here anyway?"

The detective gave her a derisive snort, "That's funny. I was about to ask you the same question. And enough stalling, get on the ground now. I don't want to have to shoot you, but I may have to if you don't follow my orders."

Moreland decided to get down on her knees, hoping to wrest control of the situation when the officer tried to place cuffs on her. She knelt on the cool dirt of the barn and raised her wrists, inviting the policeman to cuff her.

Richter fell for her trap and walked up to her still training the gun on her. He stopped a foot away and clicked the first handcuff on Moreland's left wrist. The killer violently punched the officer in the groin, he dropped the cuffs and his gun in pain. Moreland snapped to her feet and was on top of him. She kicked him in the chin and when he recoiled, Moreland grabbed his right wrist, and with a loud snap broke it as he once again cried out in pain. The gun tumbled to the ground, and Moreland pounced on it. Her motions were a blur. Her SEAL training had totally taken over.

With Richter on the ground moaning in pain, she heard another sound a siren in the distance obviously heading toward them. Moreland smashed her coiled fist twice into Richter's chin in rapid succession, and he fell to the ground. He was out. While Moreland would have preferred to kill him, to eliminate him as a witness, she knew her escape window was rapidly closing.

217

She grabbed his police revolver, since her fingerprints were on it, sprinted out of the barn as fast as her legs would carry her, and jumped into her car. She spun a 180 degree turn spewing gravel in all directions, and sped out the gate, turning right, to lead her away from the nearing police cars. She could see their pulsating lights in the dark night but she was too far away for them to see her. Moreland mashed the accelerator and screeched ahead on the blacktop road, driving as rapidly as possible while avoiding potholes.

Fifty-Five

THE POLICE CARS roared onto the Malaby Ranch. Two officers entered the home, and two other officers headed to the barn.
They found Richter out cold lying on the dirt floor. They felt for
a pulse and were relieved to find he was alive. They called for an
ambulance, and radioed the other officers to tell them the deputy
had been found and he was still breathing, although he had taken a
terrible beating.

The rest of the police team noticed the open rear door at the
Malaby home and went in, calling Amanda Malaby's name. No response. They walked through the large home, until they stumbled
onto her bedroom. At first, they thought she may be dead, but then
she moaned and they approached her. Everyone knew about Amanda's pill problem. They shook her and called her name quite loudly.

Finally, she opened her eyes and screamed at the sight of two
strange men in her bedroom. Her eyes focused, and she noticed the
police uniforms. She slurred her words. In a fog, she had difficulty
following what they were saying. Finally, she mumbled, "I've been
sleeping. I never heard anything."

The paramedics arrived, and after patching up Richter and
using a gurney to place him in the ambulance, they checked out
Amanda Malaby. She was unhurt and apparently had not been

touched. Malaby kept dozing off while officers tried to interview her. But it quickly became clear she had no recollection of an intruder in her home.

⁂

Romy Moreland finally slowed down after traveling about five miles down the rural farm-to-market road. She was still breathing a bit rapidly. That had been a close call. All she could figure was the police must have had the Malaby Ranch as part of a stake out, most likely looking for her. She was angry with herself for not thinking of that. And now, while her mission had been to get potentially troublesome pictures of her before the police found then, there was a detective out there who could give a sketch artist enough to identify her. She banged on the steering wheel in anger. Her first thought was to quickly find him and kill him. She kicked herself for not simply shooting him with his own police-issued pistol. She'd panicked for the first time in her life. Did the deputy get a good look at her during their battle?

⁂

The doctor finished stitching up Orville Richter's chin. They wanted to keep an eye on him overnight in case he had any signs of a concussion from his violent encounter. With two IV's streaming into his right arm, detective Richter fell asleep.

Sheriff King and Ranger Masterson sipped on some decidedly tasteless black coffee in the waiting room of the hospital. They were anxious to speak with Richter as soon as he woke up. For the first time since the murder spree began, he may be able to give them a description of the attacker. At this point, they didn't know if he'd scuffled with a man or a woman.

After a two-hour wait, the doctor came out and said that officer Richter was alert and awake and it appeared he'd make a full recovery. The doctor turned to King, "I can give you five minutes, Sheriff. But then he needs to get more rest. After you talk with him, we'll give him some stronger medication that will put him out for the night to allow his body to heal."

King and Masterson pulled back the curtain. Detective Richter was indeed awake, although he looked like he'd been in the ring with Ali during his prime. His right eye was purple and blue and swollen shut. A large bandage covered the stitches in his chin. The doctors thought he might have a broken arm, but x-rays proved negative. It was just badly bruised. He had a cast on his broken wrist.

King said, "How ya feeling, buddy? It looks like you wrestled a very aggressive black bear."

Richter replied through swollen lips, "I've never been hit and kicked that hard during my career. That woman was strong as an ox."

King and Masterson exchanged looks, as Crystal said, "Are you sure it was a woman, Orville?"

He nodded, "Oh yeah. The toughest female I've ever tangled with. She is obviously well-trained in martial arts and knows how to deliver the strongest blows."

Sheriff King motioned a sketch artist into the room, she was running out of time. Crystal said, "Detective, do you believe you can give Dick a good description of your attacker? It will be our first lead in this case." Richter slowly nodded; it was clear he was still groggy from the heavy medication. But he was a longtime veteran and was able to give the artist a clear description of the woman, and to help him make some changes to get it just right.

The sketch artist finished the drawing in the nick of time, as the doctor came into the room and shooed them all away. The sheriff thanked Richter for his great description and wished him well in his recovery. They left the hospital room as King was already dialing the sheriff's office, "I want everyone in the conference room in one hour. Everyone. No excuses. Also invite the area chiefs of police to the meeting. We have our first lead."

Fifty-Six

THE HENDERSON COUNTY Sheriff's Office conference room was packed. All the chairs had been taken, and other officers lined the walls as Sheriff King strolled into the room. She pushed a button, and the sketch of the female suspect flashed on the big screen TV at the front of the room. There was a murmur from the crowd.

King began, "Yes. A woman is our prime suspect for the attack on Detective Richter. She was confronted in the Malaby's barn. Unfortunately, she put a good beating on Orville. He says she was definitely well-trained in martial arts, was very strong, and clever as she wrested his gun away."

An officer spoke up, "Sheriff, do you believe this woman is also responsible for the murder of officer Wright, and all those other victims?"

King said, "At this point, we can only arrest her for the assault on a police officer and trespassing. That much we know for certain. We believe she was at the ranch to try and find the pictures Malaby says he took of her while she was at the funeral home. So job one is to find her and arrest her for the assault so we can hold her for forty-eight hours and try to find a link to the murders."

From near the back of the room, a voice said, "Sheriff, I arrested that woman for speeding a few weeks ago." King craned her neck

222

until she found Texas State Trooper Jaden Jackson. Jackson was an extremely handsome African American trooper, a dead ringer for a younger Denzel Washington. Jackson was tall, muscular, and had a reputation for having a freaky photographic memory. His voice was deep as it boomed from the rear of the conference room, "Give me a minute to get my ticket book and I can give you a name to go along with that sketch.

Jackson was back in a few minutes. He was looking at his ticket book. That woman's name, I believe is Romy Moreland. Her license is from South Carolina. I stopped her for going eighteen miles an hour over the speed limit. The fine was $309. As I recall, she was definitely not an attractive woman. I don't say that to be sexiest, but honestly, she looked like and was built like more of a man than a woman. Although she was very polite. Said she was visiting, and really liked Texas."

Even before his finished his description, King had used the department computer to call up the name of Romy Moreland. The picture popped onto the screen. She was a dead ringer look alike to the sketch. King smiled for the first time in weeks, "Thanks, Trooper Jackson. You're amazing memory just gave us a person of interest. The license plate is South Carolina. She is driving a 2021 Chevy Trailblazer LS. It is white in color. Moreland has a clean driving record."

The sheriff turned to her computer expert, "I need all the information you can find on this woman. Employment history, home address, any relatives who live around the lake etc. And I want it in one hour! The rest of you head out and find that vehicle. The meeting is over." With a renewed purpose, the officers left the conference room.

Masterson was stunned, "How in the hell did Jackson remember he gave her a speeding ticket? He's written many tickets over the past few weeks."

King grinned, "He has this amazing photographic memory. He remembers everyone and everything. Thank God!" They headed to the sheriff's office to further discuss a new plan of attack for finding the perp.

As everyone searched for her, Romy Moreland decided that it was prudent to stay out of sight for the next few days. She parked her car in the garage of the rental house, closed all the blinds, and sat sipping on a cup of coffee with a myriad of ideas racing through her mind. Moreland knew that officer would have met with a sketch artist by now, and her likeness could be everywhere. Of course, she had no idea that law enforcement already had her name, license plate and description of her car.

Sheriff King called her husband, Buddy, "Hi, honey. Have you heard back from Congressman Dicus yet?"

Buddy replied, "Not yet." Crystal filled him in on the person of interest who was from South Carolina. She texted him the driver's license photo and explained they were thoroughly searching through her life." Buddy said, "Okay. This is excellent new information. Let me run the name past Dicus and see if he'll be able to break the Navy SEAL cone of silence."

Forty minutes later, the computer expert rushed into King's office. The sheriff asked, "What have you found out?" Wesley Vandenberg was the classic computer nerd. He was short and slight, had the perquisite coke-bottle glasses, his hair was a disheveled mess, and to top it off his squeaky voice was more irritating than the proverbial nails on a blackboard. But he was a top-notch researcher.

Vandenberg settled into a chair at the small conference table and flipped open his laptop. The squeaky voice said, "This is very strange, Sheriff. Romy Moreland has absolutely no social media presence, no job history, no banking information, no school history. Nothing!" The first thought that flashed into the brains of King and Masterson was the government had scrubbed all her information. That only happens for CIA agents and Navy SEALs.

Vandenberg said, "Despite the fact she has a South Carolina driver's license that says she lives in Charlotte. There is no paper trail or paperwork of any kind that lists an address or anything." Vandenberg snapped his laptop shut. He was clearly frustrated, and not used to coming up empty handed in her searches. King thanked him for his work so far and told him to get back to his desk and keep digging.

Buddy King, after being on hold for nearly fifteen minutes, finally heard the upbeat voice of Congressman Pete Dicus, "Hello Buddy. Still looking for information on potential Naval SEALs around Cedar Creek Lake?"

Buddy said, "Yes sir. And I believe we have our first solid lead on a person of interest. It's a woman who beat the hell out of one of the sheriff's deputies. We've searched information on her online, but everything has been scrubbed. Now we really believe it is a Navy SEAL behind these attacks, and it is a woman."

Dicus cleared his throat, "I really want to help, Buddy. But so far, my only SEAL contact, Senator Bobby Jackson is not cooperating. He helped us last time, and I've gently broached the subject with him to help us again, but he had no interest."

Buddy was frustrated, "Congressman, is he aware that this person most likely shot and killed a local policewoman, and just beat up a sheriff's deputy? We desperately need his help." Dicus replied, "I've got to run to a finance committee meeting on Capitol Hill Buddy. Let me see what I can do." Buddy thanked him and the phone went dead.

Fifty-Seven

MEANWHILE, AT THE hospital in Athens, doctors were becoming concerned about Officer Richter. A brain scan showed some swelling. He also seemed to be in a bit of a fog. The lead doctor said, "I'm worried that our patient might have a pretty serious concussion. He took quite a beating. Now he's showing some signs of memory loss." They moved Richter into the Intensive Care Unit for closer observation and tests.

As lunchtime approached Romy Moreland pulled into the parking lot of the hot new restaurant between Caney City and Malakoff called The Pier. It had only opened a few weeks ago but was already very popular with reservations sold out on the weekends. Moreland had heard it was much easier to get a seat at lunch so that's why she ventured that way today. Of course, she had no idea that every law enforcement organization in Texas was on the lookout for her license plate.

After the lunch hour, Sheriff King and Ranger Masterson paid a visit to the hospital. They were intercepted by Richter's doctor. They noticed the concerned look on his face. Crystal said, "Good after-

226

noon, Doc. How is Orville doing today? We're hoping to show him a picture of who we believe is the woman who attacked him."

The doctor shook his head, "Sorry, Sheriff, but we just moved Mr. Richter into the ICU. We have discovered some swelling of his brain and fear he may have a serious head injury from the fight. At this point he is drifting in and out of consciousness, and I'm not allowing any visitors." The doctor promised to give them an update and hopefully an opportunity to show him the picture later that day.

As they drove back to police headquarters, Crystal stared out the windshield, deep in thought. Masterson was thinking the same thing. He turned to her and said, "If Richter has lost his memory that pretty much throws out the case. He is our only witness."

King grimly replied, "Yup. This could be a disaster."

As the sheriff went through paperwork at her desk, she had a phone call from Jo Ann Strom, president of the Cedar Creek Lake Area Chamber of Commerce. After a short exchange, Jo Ann got to the point, "Crystal, my members are getting very concerned about all the bad publicity from the murders of a policewoman, a number of other local residents, and now the severe beating of Officer Richter. I've heard from several hotels who are receiving cancellations because of fear something might happen to them or their family if they visit the lake area. Restaurant sales are down, and some retail stores are also feeling the pinch. We need you to do something about this right now."

King let out a long sigh, "I understand, Jo Ann. We've known each other a long time, and you know that I'm doing everything I can to catch this person. We've brought in a dozen Texas Rangers, and confidentially, we finally have a suspect."

Jo Ann said, "Well that's good news. Maybe you should let the public know that it might tamp down some fears."

King replied, "We can't do that right now, Jo Ann. We have no intention of tipping off the suspect. We have her license number and now we just need to find her and arrest her."

Begrudgingly Strom agreed, "I understand Crystal. But please make that arrest happen as quickly as possible. Our local businesses are hurting and it's only going to get worse." The sheriff had no idea that Dwayne Murphy was penning a detailed story on the murders and the missing for the Sunday edition of the *Athens Courier*. It was going to shine a bright unwanted spotlight on the fear and concern of the local populace.

At The Pier Restaurant, Romy Moreland finished a tasty bowl of tortilla soup, paid her bill in cash, and emerged into the bright afternoon sun beating down in hot fingers of heat with little breeze. She slid behind the wheel of her car, and slowly backed out of the parking lot, turning right on Highway 198 heading back toward Gun Barrel City. As soon as she hit the highway, a Henderson County Police Cruiser zoomed by in the opposite direction. She checked the rearview and saw that the police cruiser was making a U-turn and heading her way. Blue and red lights suddenly flashed on as he neared her car.

Moreland pulled the car off to the side of the road, and the police car parked right behind her. The officer sat in his car for a few minutes, apparently checking his computer, and calling someone on his police radio. Moreland's mind was racing. Should she speed away and try to lose him? It seemed impossible on the narrow, curving road that always had a lot of traffic. She felt the gun under the front seat and wondered if she just shoot him as he approached the car. But with car after car zipping by in both directions that seemed like suicide.

So, she sat and waited. He couldn't be arresting her for speeding. She'd just left the parking lot. Her license and registration were up to date. Then she remembered her fight with the county officer. *Maybe he'd given them a description?* She glanced in her rearview mirror just as the officer opened his driver's door and emerged holding his revolver in his right hand.

Suddenly three more squad cars converged on the scene with lights flashing. They surrounded her car as the officer reached the driver's window. There was no way to escape. The officer motioned her to roll down the window. "Miss Moreland, I need you to exit the car, lay flat on the ground, and lace your hands behind your head." He motioned the gun at her in a silent gesture to get out of the car, now.

Fifty-Eight

THE COPYCAT KILLER laid on the hot pavement, and the officer quickly clicked the handcuffs on her wrists. He then helped her to her feet and led her to the rear seat of the squad car. The other officer surrounded her with guns drawn pointing at her. Moreland asked, "What is going on? What do you think I did?" The officer stayed silent as she slid into the rear seat, surrounded by a mesh cage. He slammed the door shut and joined his fellow officers.

In a few minutes, Sheriff King and Ranger Masterson arrived in her car. They quickly took charge of the scene, as three Texas Rangers also pulled up in their cruisers. Two officers directed the growing traffic jam as onlookers craned their necks to see what was going on. They kept all the gawker's cars moving.

King and Masterson peered into the back seat and glanced at the print they carried with Moreland's picture. Satisfied it was her, the caravan headed to the Henderson County Sheriff's Office in Athens. Once at the police station, the cruiser carrying the suspect drove directly into the garage and out of sight. They led Moreland out of the squad car, took her into a dinghy conference room, and handcuffed her to a steel bar screwed into the table. Then they let her sit for nearly an hour.

Finally, with a plan in place to question the suspect, King and

Masterson entered the room, pulled up two battered wooden chairs and faced the suspect. King said, "Miss Moreland my name is Crystal King and I'm the sheriff of this county." She acknowledged Masterson, "and this is Texas Ranger Tolbert Masterson. We have a few questions for you."

Moreland stared at her with the most hateful eyes King had ever seen, her jaw was set, as she leaned forward, "I've got nothing to say. You haven't even told me why I was arrested."

King nodded, "Well, let me fill you in. You are under arrest for assaulting one of my police officers. He identified you as the assailant. That's what we want to talk to you about."

Moreland snorted, and said in an evil voice, "I've got nothing to say." Both officers couldn't help but be impressed by the bulging biceps on the former Navy SEAL.

Moreland had a smirk on her rather homely face when she said, "I want a lawyer. Now."

King replied, "We'll assign a public defender as soon as we ask you a few questions."

Moreland's smirk grew meaner. "First off, I am not saying another word without my lawyer present. And there's no way in hell I want some rookie public defender." Leaning forward to reach her shirt pocket, she handed the sheriff a fancy, embossed business card, "I want you to call my lawyer and get him down here." Her defiant demeanor grew darker.

King and Masterson glanced at the business card. King let out a small sigh, which didn't escape Moreland. The sheriff and Masterson were well aware of her lawyer. He was a Dallas legend, and in fact he was the lawyer who got a not guilty verdict for the man they believed to be a serial killer, Thaddeus Van Cleave. The funeral director who cremated his victims. Moreland had followed the same M.O. with the disappearance of four people, including Shane Malaby. The rancher who had confessed to killing Van Cleave. This was going to complicate their case.

The legendary Harold "Double Down" Haines was the most expensive, most flamboyant, and most successful defense lawyer in the Dallas Metroplex and probably all of Texas. At seventy-four, and six-five, with large strong hands, and a shock of flowing silvery hair, Haines still had the slim, athletic build that served him well as star quarterback at Texas Tech a half century ago. He injured his right knee playing Pickle Ball, and was using a cane these days.

Haines favored custom-tailored three-piece Italian suits made of the finest materials. His vest always sported his ever-present antique gold-chained pocket watch. Custom-made pocket silks complemented his custom-made, expensive silk ties from Hong Kong.

Haines steely-blue, piercing eyes were known to bore into the very soul of the hapless witnesses he was cross-examining in search of justice for his rich clients. He never asked his clients if they were guilty. Haines only mission was to defend them and get them acquitted.

He earned the nickname 'Double Down' by frequenting casinos from Shreveport to Oklahoma to Las Vegas. He was famous for doubling down when he held fifteen, no matter how many chips were at risk, one of the supposedly stupidest bets in blackjack. Invariably he would win those bets to the delight of fellow players and the chagrin of casino bosses. Dealers loved him, because Haines was a big tipper.

The legendary lawyer rarely lost a case. During the local trial for Thaddeus Van Cleave the jury was charmed by his gentlemanly southern demeanor and the suspected killer was acquitted. If this case went to trial, young, but crafty Henderson County District Attorney Blair Brooke would get a second chance to beat Haines.

In the few years since losing to Haines, Brooke, now thirty-five years-old had won some big cases and gained the reputation of a strong prosecution lawyer. The woman, who graduated at the top of her class at Yale, had become even more adept at shredding the testimony of the defendant's witnesses. She was a strictly by-the-book lawyer, cocky and self-assured. Brooke had evolved her clothing choices from severe, almost school teacher-like tailored suits to a more modern wardrobe that enhanced her attractive looks and well-toned body. It served her well with male jurists.

Sheriff King was surprised to hear that a stranger from South Carolina would know about Harold Haines and would already have him on retainer. The fact is Moreland found an article about how Haines had earned an acquittal for Thaddeus Van Cleave. When she arrived in North Texas, she drove straight to Haines'office. He was curious why she wanted him on retainer but had learned long ago not to ask questions when he didn't want to know the answers. To test her resolve, he said his retainer fee was $50,000 which would make him available to her day or night. She never blinked at the fee, and the retainer papers were signed.

Sheriff King and Ranger Masterson headed to the Athens Hospital, hoping that Officer Richter was awake and available to make a positive ID of Romy Moreland from her driver's license picture. After a quick discussion with the doctor in charge of the ICU unit, they stepped into Richter's room. They were shocked to see how Richter's health had deteriorated in just a day. There were two IVs pumping fluids into him, his right eye was a deep purple and blue and was swollen shut. He was on oxygen.

Richter slowly turned his head toward his visitor's. He seemed in a bit of a fog, and at first didn't appear to recognize the sheriff or Masterson. In a quiet voice King said, "How are you feeling Orville?"

With some difficulty he replied, "I'm OK. You're Sheriff King, right?" Crystal slowly nodded. She had known Richter for over ten years and now he had trouble recognizing her. She could feel their case slipping away.

The sheriff pulled out the picture of their suspect and held it up in front of Richter, "Orville, do you recognize this person?"

He peered at the photo a few minutes, then slowly said, "Yes. That is the woman who attacked me." King let out a sigh. Masterson motioned her to join him outside.

The Texas Ranger had a troubled look on his face, "Crystal, I'm afraid that your officer is not going to be a very reliable witness. I believe he is suffering some memory loss. Haines will tear him apart on the witness stand. That is if he recovers enough to even make it to court."

King grimly agreed, "How about if we record his testimony now before his condition gets worse?"

Masterson shook his head, "That'd be a good idea except for the fact that opposing counsel is allowed to ask questions as well. Not only will Haines most likely confuse Richter with his questions, but he'll also realize just how weak our case is because it relies on the recollection of a witness who has lost, or is losing, his memory."

King agreed, "We need to have a conference with the district attorney to decide the best way to proceed."

At the Henderson County Jail, Romy Moreland used her one phone call to dial up Harold Haines. He never asked why she was in jail. "Okay, Miss Moreland. I'll be there in less than two hours. In the meantime, as we discussed in my office, you talk to no one, including any cell mates. I'll do all the talking when I get there." He hung up.

Fifty-Nine

MEANWHILE, COMPUTER experts at the Sheriff's Office, and at the Texas Rangers office in Dallas, were scouring the internet trying to piece together information on the suspect. It proved to be a futile effort. Any information about a Romy Moreland had been scrubbed clean. She was a ghost, which meant only one thing. The suspect had been, or currently was, in the CIA or Navy SEALs. That level of security was reserved for those secret operatives.

They did find some information on a Rear Admiral Griffin Moreland. It was a short bio. Moreland was a former decorated Navy SEAL who moved up in the ranks until he was the top dog on three different destroyers before retiring a couple years ago. The brief blurb made no mention of a wife or family. It did list his age as sixty-four. That was it. They had no idea if he was any relation to the suspect currently being held for the assault on the policeman.

Suddenly a burst of energy flew through the front door of the Henderson County Sheriff's Office. It was Harold Haines, decked out in an uber expensive pinstripe suit with a red prep tie accented by a large gold tie pin. His perfectly pressed light blue dress shirt was topped off with large gold cufflinks. His wrist was adorned with a large Rolex Oyster watch. Despite using a cane, Haines quickly approached the front desk. His long, wavy silver hair was perfectly coiffed.

Always seeking to be the center of attention, the lawyer announced in a booming southern drawl, "Harold Haines, esquire, here to see my client one Romy Moreland." He was led into a small conference room. A few minutes later Romy Moreland, wearing cuffs on her wrists and ankles shuffled into the room clad in an orange jumpsuit. The county officer closed the conference room door, locked it, and sat down on a chair just outside the door in case the suspect tried to escape.

Moreland flopped into a wooden chair. Haines looked at his client and was struck by how unattractive she was. Moreland certainly did not have the innocent face that could help sway a jury. The lawyer spent a few minutes scanning through the arrest documents, and her charges which included assault of a peace officer, attempting to flee from a policeman, and the big one, attempted murder.

Haines set down the paperwork, tugged on his cuffs, and gazed at his client, "So, Romy, you want to tell me what happened?"

Moreland shrugged, "That cop attacked me. It was self-defense on my part." She leaned back in the chair, crossed her arms in front of her chest and gave him a defiant look. Haines was struck by the size of her biceps.

The famous lawyer leaned forward and said in a quiet voice, "Miss Moreland, there is just one thing wrong with that alibi. You were intercepted after breaking into the Malaby ranch house. How do you explain that?" It was his turn to lean back in the chair, arms folded waiting for her reply.

The copycat killer gazed at one of the brick walls, deep in thought. Then came her reply, "I guess that's why I'm paying you all the money, counselor. To figure that out, and to get me acquitted just like you did Thaddeus Van Cleave, when we both know he killed all those people."

Haines replied, "Yes. I'll work on your defense of these charges, but I fear we have a bigger issue. My police sources tell me they plan on holding you on these charges, and take it to trial, so they have more time to investigate you in connection to the recent spate of drownings, disappearances, and most importantly the murder of the Mabank police officer."

Moreland was unflinching, "I had nothing to do with those."

Haines looked at her, "I sure hope that's the case because they're convinced you did."

The sheriff's deputy knocked on the door, "Time's up." He unlocked and opened the door. The deputy handed Haines a document. The lawyer turned to his client and said, "Your initial court appearance is tomorrow afternoon. I'll have my assistant get you some new clothes for the arraignment."

While that meeting was occurring, King and Masterson sat down with District Attorney Blair Brooke. The county's top lawyer was wearing a black pencil skirt, white blouse and a tailored black blazer and a pair of Rochelle heels. She had a pixie haircut with frosted streaks. Her skin was soft and clear. King outlined a potential problem with the attack on Orville Richter. He was the only eyewitness to the assault, but a severe concussion made his memory a bit shaky. In addition, the doctors didn't expect it to improve in the near future. In fact, they feared he might lose his memory completely.

A scowl crossed Brooke's face. Not only did she have to face one of the top lawyers in all of Texas, but her only witness was most likely unreliable. Masterson had another curveball to throw at the D.A. He said, "We are also nearly certain that Moreland is a copycat killer responsible for our recent string of murders, including Brenda Wright. But we need more time to develop our case."

Brooke looked at both of them, "So you're saying you want me to drag out this trial to give you more time?" They nodded. The district attorney said, "You know I can't be a party to that. I go strictly by the book. And that book says a defendant is entitled to a speedy trial. So that's a hard no!"

The sheriff began to protest but Brooke quickly raised her hand in a motion to stop, "Crystal, it is not going to happen. My advice is to work harder to find the evidence you need. Now if you'll excuse me." She started shuffling through some papers. King and Masterson left her office. They were not pleased.

Sixty

DARKNESS CLOSED IN on Cedar Creek Lake, a few stars twinkled in a dark sky mostly shrouded in clouds. The quarter moon appeared and disappeared as clouds moved across the Texas landscape. On the east side of Cedar Creek Lake, a small, battered sixteen-foot aluminum Lund fishing boat drifted along in the light night breeze, passing within a few yards of boat docks. Samuel Green cast a purple spinner bait under the nearest dock, and slowly retrieved the lure through the muddy water.

Green, a retired auto mechanic, looked like a fisherman right out of central casting. The sixty-seven-year-old sported a patchy gray beard that partially covered his pock-marked face, the remnants of a bad bout with acne in high school. Grey hair sprouted out from under his ripped and stained fishing cap. He needed to drop about forty pounds. He opened a small can of Copenhagen Wintergreen Long Cut and tucked it between his teeth and gums. His gnarled fingers were stained from the tobacco as were his yellowed teeth. There was a gap where three teeth were missing. The result of a bar fight from years ago.

He reeled in the shiny lure. There were no takers. The aluminum boat drifted past another dock. Green made a perfect cast far under the middle of the dock. Suddenly there was a loud splash and the old fisherman yanked the line, driving the razor-sharp hook deep into the largemouth bass' lip. He began to reel in the monster as it leapt out of the water again desperately trying to shake the hook.

As Green concentrated on the fight, he never noticed the dark figure covered in a black wet suit that surfaced a foot away from the boat. The fisherman finally felt the presence of someone in the water, and jerked his body around to see what was happening. He was startled when two very muscular arms lifted him out of the boat in one quick movement and dragged him under the water.

Green thrashed in the water but was unable to free himself from the steel-like arms that held him in a death grip. The retired mechanic was way out of shape and ran out of energy within seconds. He gasped for air but all he swallowed instead was mouthful after mouthful of the murky water. Soon he went limp and the killer let go watching as he floated to the bottom in about twenty feet of water. Silence returned to the lake.

In the Henderson County Jail, Romy Moreland tossed and turned on the terribly uncomfortable bed in her small cell. The bed had a small, thin mattress spread across worn out steel springs. Sleep was impossible.

Back at Cedar Creek Lake, Minerva Lee was at her usual post, sitting on a high bar stool on the deck of her lakeside home, peering through her powerful telescope. The eighty-two-year-old widow had lived on the lake for over forty years. She loved scanning the vast Texas sky for planets and stars. Her neighbors would also privately tell you that Minerva was a big snoop. Her telescope was known to scan the lake and nearby homes. It did not sit well with most of her neighbors.

On this night, the elderly star gazer was searching for her favorite constellation when the silence was interrupted by a loud splash.

She spun the telescope toward the sound and was surprised to see two people in the water, splashing around near a small boat. The expensive telescope was equipped with night vision. She quickly flipped it on while peering into the lens. She caught a glimpse of more thrashing in the water, and then clearly could see that one of the combatants was wearing a black hood, black wet suit, and mask. A few seconds later both people disappeared into the turbid water of Cedar Creek Lake.

The killer in the black wet suit had a firm grip on Green's shirt collar as he slowly dragged the body farther out into the deeper water of the lake. Meanwhile Lee dialed the emergency number for the Henderson County Sheriff's Office. The dispatcher answered on the second ring, and quickly recognized the voice on the other end.

He said into the phone, "Good evening, Miss Lee. What can I do for you tonight." Minerva Lee was well known in the department. At least once a week she'd call with information about something happening in her neighborhood. Lee replied, "I was just on my deck gazing at the stars when I heard a loud splash. I quickly moved my telescope in the direction of the noise and saw two bodies thrashing in the lake. It looked like they were fighting."

The dispatcher was paying attention now. "Can you describe the people involved Miss Lee? Were they your neighbors?"

Lee said, "I'm afraid not. I only saw them for a few seconds, but it looked like the person in the black wet suit was trying to drown the other guy. Then they disappeared into the water. I watched for fifteen or twenty minutes but neither guy came back to the surface."

The police officer thanked her for the information. After he hung up the phone, the dispatcher pondered his next move. Everyone in the department knew Minerva Lee. Most of her tips turned out to be worthless, but she seemed quite certain about this one. He glanced at the clock on the wall, it was nearing 11 p.m. The dispatcher wrote up the information from the call and put it on the sheriff's desk. It was too late to bother her tonight, but she'd get the info when she walked into the office in the morning.

Just after eight o'clock the next morning, Harold Haines was back in the small conference room at the Henderson County Jail preparing his client for her initial court appearance. The fabled Dallas lawyer was resplendent in a dark blue three-piece suit. His shirt was a vivid white, topped off with solid gold cufflinks that were in the shape of an H. His tie was a darker blue with small silver stripes. He opened a box and gave his client a sharp-looking outfit for her court stint. The dark blue jacket matched the skirt. A crisp white blouse rounded out the look.

Romy Moreland reluctantly went into a nearby restroom, with a jail matron waiting outside the door as she changed clothes. As she re-entered the conference room, Haines was again concerned about her unpleasant facial features. He decided to bring in a stylist before she faced a jury. Haines wanted her to be liked by the people deciding her fate.

A half-hour later Sheriff King walked into her office, poured herself a cup of coffee, and started thumbing through the reports and documents cluttering her desk. The report right on top stopped her in her tracks. She set down the coffee cup, gripped the document with both hands and wondered how this could be possible.

Tolbert Masterson entered the sheriff's office. Once he saw King's demeanor, he knew something was wrong. He asked, "What's going on, Crystal? You look like somebody kicked your dog." King motioned him to close the door of her office. Without a word, she handed Masterson the report outlining the phone call from Minerva Green.

Masterson scanned the document, and his morning smile was instantly replaced by a puzzled look. He looked at King, "How is this possible, Crystal? We've got the killer locked in a jail cell. Are there two of them? Is Moreland not the copycat killer? What the hell is going on?"

King shrugged, "I have no idea, Tolbert, but we definitely have work to do today."

Sixty-One

AS THE TWO police officials pondered their next moves, Moreland was being instructed by Haines how to behave at her arraignment, "I need you to have the look of an innocent victim. Just keep your eyes on the judge. Say nothing other than "not guilty" when asked by the judge how you plea." Haines continued, "I believe we can easily win this case. My sources tell me that the police officer has a nasty concussion, and his memory seems to be fading more each day. If he can't positively ID you as the person who attacked him. We win!" Moreland just nodded.

As the suspect prepped for her arraignment, Sheriff King was in a deep funk. She was sure they'd captured the copycat killer. The problem now is her only witness may soon be unreliable. She dialed up her husband. Buddy was in the midst of an embezzlement investigation for a client in Wills Point. He'd been on the case day and night, so they'd hardly seen each other for a couple weeks. Crystal said, "Buddy, is there any way we can meet somewhere for lunch, I need some advice." They decided to meet at one o'clock in Canton at a restaurant just off the town square that served the best pies in Texas.

As soon as she hung up the phone, Sheriff King gathered her

water search and rescue team and dispatched them to the section of Cedar Creek Lake where the fisherman was reported to have been wrestling in the water with a shadowy figure in a black wet suit. The team hooked up the rescue boat, hopped into their SUV and headed to the location.

As the clock struck nine, the bailiff brought Romy Moreland into court. Despite the fact that her lawyer had purchased an expensive outfit for her court appearance, she looked disheveled with her hair uncombed and stringy. Moreland had no sense of style and cared little about her looks.

District Attorney Blair Brooke read the charges against Moreland. The judge looked at the suspect, "And how do you plead, Miss Moreland."

The suspect jumped to her feet, "I plead not guilty to all charges, Your Honor." She slumped back in her chair.

The judge entered the plea and asked Brooke, "What is your recommendation on bond for Miss Moreland?"

The district attorney replied, "Due to the serious nature of these charges, and the serious injuries inflicted on the police officer, the state requests that there be no bond offered in this case."

Haines jumped to his feet, scoffed at the district attorney, and turned to the judge, "Your Honor, this case does not rise to the level of denying bond. My client is charged with simple assault, not murder."

Brooke mumbled half under her breath, "Not yet."

Haines took a step toward her, "What did you say?" Brooke just shook her head from side to side and said nothing. She vowed not to let the celebrated attorney get the better of her this time around.

The judge pounded her gavel, "That's enough I will have no grandstanding or outbursts in my courtroom. As to the bond, it is set at $100,000."

Haines again jumped to his feet, "Your Honor, that seems a bit excessive in this case."

The judge replied, "No sir it is not excessive. Your client is accused of attacking a policeman who remains in the hospital." Haines said nothing. The judge went on, "This case is set to be heard two weeks from now."

Moreland leaned toward Haines and said in a low voice, "So once you post bond how soon can I get out of here?" The famed lawyer replied, "That depends. You need to post ten percent of the bond, so I'll need $10,000 to post bail."

Moreland had a puzzled look on her homely face, "Me? You're my lawyer. It's your job to post bond."

Haines shook his head, "That's not true. Your representation agreement clearly states that you must post your own bond, so you need $10,000."

Moreland pounded on the table, startling everyone in the courtroom, "What are you talking about? I already advanced you $50,000. Take it out of there." Haines stood up, shoved some documents into his briefcase and said, "That payment is for my retainer. You need to come up with the bail money not me."

Moreland jumped to her feet, viciously grabbed Haines' right arm, spinning him around. Her face was an angry red mask, "You get that bond money right now or I'll…" She suddenly noticed how quiet the courtroom had become. Many spectators were shocked by her anger.

Haines said through gritted teeth, "You are causing a scene that is not helping your case at all. Now, settle down. I'll be back in two days to plan our trial strategy." Moreland calmed down as the bailiff handcuffed her and led her back to her cell. District Attorney Brooke was elated to see how quickly the suspect went ballistic. Now, if she could only get her on the stand and bring out that wrath in front of the jury.

A few hours later, Sheriff King walked into the Beasley Cattle Company restaurant. She was happy to see the handsome face of her husband, sitting in a booth near the rear of the establishment. Buddy King stood up, gave his wife a warm hug, and a peck on the cheek. He was struck by the dark rings under her eyes. His beautiful bride was definitely having a difficult time.

Buddy King knew how chasing a serial killer can drive you crazy. He was Henderson County Sheriff while The Frogman Of Cedar Creek was wreaking havoc on the area. He gently took his wife's hand, "Honey, I know what you're going through. Chasing a serial killer can drive you over the edge."

Crystal squeezed his strong hand, "It's just so frustrating. And now there's apparently been another drowning, while my suspect sits in a jail cell. Are there two serial killers? Is Moreland innocent? She was in the Malaby home, I strongly believe, looking for pictures taken of her at the funeral home. It's just one hot mess."

King gave her a sympathetic nod, "I really wish that Billy Richardson was here. I know he'd have some ideas for us." Richardson, Buddy's best buddy, had followed him as sheriff and had worked to solve the missing young women they all believed Thaddeus Van Cleave had kidnapped and cremated. When Richardson retired, Crystal became the first female sheriff in Henderson County.

Crystal agreed, "Unfortunately, he is so wrapped up taking care of his ailing parents in McKinney, we can't bother him." Buddy nodded, "Yeah, I'm afraid so. Poor guy was planning a quiet retirement fishing and then both of his parents fall ill at the same time. I feel sorry for him."

About fifteen miles away, the Sheriff's Department Rescue Team was slowly chugging along, searching for the missing fisherman and his boat. One of the officers peering through powerful binoculars cried out, "Head due east. It looks like a boat is floating next to that dock over there." They increased their speed, and quickly arrived at the beat-up aluminum boat. One of the deputies keyed his radio, I need to know who is registered to this boat. The TX number is KXL-756."

A few minutes later, the dispatcher said, "That boat is registered to one Samuel Green. He lives in Gun Barrel City at 145 Driftwood Lane." The dive team tied a long rope to the bow of the aluminum fishing boat and slowly worked their way to the nearest boat launch. They told the dispatcher to have an officer from Gun Barrel City conduct a welfare check at Green's home.

Sheriff King's phone rang. A concerned look swept across her face. "Okay. Let me know what they find." She glanced around and then whispered to Buddy, "They just found the missing boat. It belongs to a Samuel Green from Gun Barrel City. Buddy thought for a minute, "I know who that is, Crystal. He used to own his own little garage and was a darn good mechanic. He's a pretty well-known fisherman. He's out there almost every day."

Sixty-Two

THE GUN BARREL CITY police officer knocked on the door at 145 Driftwood Lane. There was no answer. The small home was badly in need of a fresh coat of paint, and there was a blue tarp on the roof apparently to fix a leak. The officer looked in the window. There were a couple pizza boxes sitting on an old weather-beaten coffee table. Several empty beer bottles littered the thread bare rug. There was no sign of Samuel Green.

The officer went around to the back of the house. It was a jungle with tall grass and weeds everywhere. He tried the back door. It was unlocked. The officer swept through the grimy home, then called his dispatcher to inform there was no sign of the missing fisherman.

Back at the restaurant, Crystal gave Buddy a hug goodbye, just as her phone buzzed again. It was Dwayne Murphy, "Hi, Sheriff. I understand you have another drowning victim. I'd like to talk to you about that and the woman who's charged with assaulting one of your officers."

Crystal blew him off, "I have no time for you today, Murphy. The reports are available at the front desk. And at this point we don't have a drowning victim. We have a missing fisherman." She hung up, bringing a smile to Buddy's face.

He said, "I guess some things never change huh?"

Crystal's engaging smile soon turned to a deep frown, "Buddy, what if Green was drowned by another killer? That means Moreland, who was sitting in a jail cell at the time of the disappearance, couldn't have done it."

Buddy gently took both her hands, looked deeply into her gorgeous blue eyes and sighed, "I was thinking the same thing, honey, but didn't want to bring it up right now. You were so happy to finally have a solid suspect."

Crystal gave her husband a weak smile, "I appreciate that, but I have to deal in the real world, and this could mean that Moreland is not our culprit. Now, that would really suck because there are a number of possibilities. It could be an accomplice of Moreland. It could be a third copycat killer. Or it could mean that we have the wrong prime suspect."

At the same time, a tall, muscular man in his sixties sat out of sight in a run-down motel on the west side of the lake, just outside Tool. It was midweek, and only one other customer was staying at the dilapidated establishment. There were only eight units. All of them were in desperate need of paint. The weathered boards on the outside of the units were cracked, peeling and badly faded. The clerk/owner was a man with a huge beer gut, unshaven face, and a bad limp. The motel was down a short, pothole-filled dirt road just off Highway 274. It was the perfect hideout.

The man in Unit 3 was about six-feet tall with silver-grey hair in an old-school crewcut. His lantern jaw was meticulously clean-shaven. His right cheek was marred by an L-shaped scar, the result of a knife fight in a Korean bar decades ago. His eyes were steely blue and it was said they could pierce right through your soul. You could tell that he had worked hard to achieve a chiseled body. The taut muscles were beginning to sag slightly as age began to catch up with him.

Retired Rear Admiral Griffin Moreland, peeled a large blood orange as he sat in a lumpy chair with the TV droning on in the background. He had read about his daughter's arrest. Griffin had also been following the missing persons and drowning victims around Cedar Creek Lake. When he lost contact with her months ago, he feared his only daughter might be planning to avenge the death of Cody Martin.

Griffin, a former decorated Navy SEAL, drove from his home in Savannah, Georgia, to Cedar Creek Lake. He believed if he could drown a couple victims while his daughter was behind bars it would remove the cop's suspicion of her as the copycat killer. He was surprised by his ability to just drown a man he did not know, but the love of his daughter, even though he had never showed it, was strong. He was also living with a dark secret regarding Cody Martin.

While her father munched on the orange, Romy Moreland sat in a tiny conference room with her lawyer Harold Haines. His attire was quite a contrast from her orange jail jumpsuit. Haines, always a meticulous dresser, was resplendent in a tailored Brunico virgin wool two-piece suit. The suit from Bergdorf Goodman cost nearly $7,000. The handmade Italian suit was black. His hundred percent silk tie from Stefano Ricci cost another $1250. His $1400 alligator shoes from Paolo Scafora gleamed under the fluorescent lights.

Moreland gave him a pained look, "You know, if you just sell that suit, you could post my bond and get me out of this hell hole."

Haines smiled, "My dear Romy, as I said before, my clients are responsible for their own bail. It's just the way I run my business. If you don't have the money, how about asking your parents?"

Moreland snorted, "I haven't been in touch with them for three or four years. They're totally out of the picture."

Haines shrugged, "Okay, we'll figure that out, but let's talk about your case in the limited time we have today."

At the Henderson County District Attorney's office, Blair Brooke was prepping for the Moreland case. She was still upset about losing the Van Cleave case to that flashy lawyer from Dallas. This time she'd beat the great Harold Haines. Her investigators had been scouring cameras in the streets around the sheriff's office, hoping to tie Moreland to the bombing of the sheriff's patrol car. She was also searching for video to place Moreland at the scene of the attack on Investigator Orville Richter. So far the search had been fruitless.

At the Athens Hospital, doctors were becoming more concerned about the health of Richter. His brain continued to swell after being severely injured in the fight with Moreland. His breathing was getting weaker, and his memory foggier by the hour. They returned the policeman to the intensive care unit.

Sixty-Three

MORELAND POUNDED ON the steel table in the conference room, making her handcuff chains clang against the bar holding her shackles. Haines was startled at her sudden burst of anger, as she said, "I need you to get me the hell out of here on bail, right now."

It was the second time Haines had witnessed her trigger temper, and sudden bursts of anger. He regained his composure, shot his fancy French cuffs with the gold cufflinks out of his suit jacket, cleared his throat and said, "Miss Moreland, we cannot have you show this scary, angry side of you in the courtroom. We need the jury to sympathize with us, not be afraid of you."

Romy leaned in with a mask of anger on her face, "I'm not in front of the jury right now, hotshot. I just want you to get me out of here!"

Haines said in a calm voice, "There must be funds you can tap to get the $10,000 bail money. Do you have an investment broker?"

Moreland shook her head from side to side. "Nope. I do have a bank account in Maryland. But it'll be tricky to access it with me in jail."

Haines replied, "Just give me the account information and I'll be able to get the money as your lawyer. We can compose a letter with your signature."

Exasperated, she asked, "How many days will that take?"

Haines, in a calming voice said, "It's the best we can do, Miss Moreland. It'll only be a few days at most."

Again, a dark, angry cloud crossed the copycat killer's face as she stood up and yelled, "Guard!" She turned to her attorney, "Just hurry it up!" The guard arrived and Moreland left without another word to Haines. After she left the veteran lawyer just shook his head. She was definitely a loose cannon and would most likely not listen to any strategy he'd devise. This was going to be a tough case.

Meanwhile her father was driving around Cedar Creek Lake looking for another victim. The admiral had decided that a second victim would really throw off the scent of the police. He wanted to strike as quickly as possible. But it had to be a higher profile victim to assure as much publicity on the drowning by the local media.

His neighbors in the ritzy gated Marsh Harbor community in Savannah would be shocked to hear the retired Navy SEAL had killed someone. He lived alone in a nine thousand square foot home on an acre lot along the banks of Turner's Creek, a deep-water passage to the ocean. He kept to himself but usually was in the club house before dinner enjoying a dirty martini. Of course, they had no idea he was a retired Navy SEAL and that he'd killed many an enemy on missions over the years.

As he grew older, Moreland felt ashamed at the way he'd treated his daughter. His entire focus was on his career, moving from base to base with his wife and Romy in tow. He was extremely proud of her work as a SEAL and was dismayed to suspect she was a serial killer in Texas. When she was arrested, he'd hurried to Gun Barrel City ready to do anything to help free her. If that meant killing innocent civilians, so be it, his motto was always mission over people. After one more drowning, he'd bail her out of jail, and they'd reunite for the first time in a decade.

The *Cedar Creek Treats* pontoon boat was a floating ice cream shop. Launched last year, it motored around the lake selling delicious frozen goodies to eager boaters and lakefront owners. The boat was operated by Alvin "Sugar" Duckstein. For years the overweight man with the bald head and bushy beard had run a small ice cream stand in Eustace. Business was okay, but then a customer suggested he go mobile, selling his wonderful treats around the lake to overheated boaters and fishermen.

His ruddy face with the fat jowls was well-known all around the Cedar Creek Lake area. He had a great sense of humor, and was always ready with a friendly smile, and a joke or two. As he plied his wares around the lake today, Sugar had no idea he was being watched by a man who wanted to end his life.

❦

While the killer was stalking Sugar, Sheriff King was huddled with District Attorney Brooke in her office. King said, "I'm becoming increasingly concerned about the health of our only witness in the Moreland case. His health, and more importantly his memory, seem to be fading rather quickly. Even if he lives, he is most likely not going to be an effective witness for us."

Brooke frowned, "Crystal, this could blow the entire case."

King nodded in agreement, "Absolutely, and we still have her as our suspect in the copycat killings. We just can't let her walk. Any ideas?"

Brooke steepled her fingers as she appeared lost in thought. She came out of her mini-trance and turned to the sheriff, "We have no evidence, Crystal. I can't hold her on other charges when we have no proof. I believe she attempted to kill you by blowing up your cruiser, but my investigators, and yours, can't find anything to tie her to the explosion. Not one surveillance camera caught her anywhere near your car." They talked for another hour but could not come up with anything to help make their case against Romy Moreland.

❦

The hot Texas sun was rapidly disappearing in a spectacular red ball along the west shoreline of Cedar Creek Lake, and darkness soon enveloped everything. Sugar Duckstein slowly drove his boat to a rented lift at a gas station located next to the bridge connecting Gun Barrel City and Seven Points. Using the remote control, he raised the ice cream boat out of the lake. He spent the next ten minutes unloading his product, tossing the heavy coolers filled with ice cream treats onto the back of his pickup truck. He had no idea that a pair of steely eyes were watching his every move.

Sixty-Four

IN THE HENDERSON County Jail, Romy Moreland prepared to spend another restless night. She was a free spirit, and being locked in a small, smelly cell with a loud snorer in the adjacent cell caused her to feel trapped and miserable. Every night her hatred of Crystal King grew stronger. She was comforted only by the knowledge that someday soon the sheriff would be dead. Her picture of Cody Martin was her only refuge. She talked to him nightly.

Meanwhile, her father was sitting in the dingy motel with a cold Miller Lite in his hand. He'd decided that tomorrow he'd kill the ice cream man. Then he'd bail his daughter out of jail with police wondering who the real serial killer is, since two more drownings occurred while she was in a cell. She'd no longer be a suspect. He'd be able to reunite with her, bring her back to his mansion in Savannah, and make up for lost time. The father would show his daughter he was a changed man.

The morning sun beamed brightly onto Cedar Creek Lake with the reflection looking like thousands of tiny sparkling diamonds. Sugar loaded his pontoon boat, preparing for a busy Friday as all the weekenders flooded the lake. Dollar signs danced in front of his eyes.

The admiral finished his morning jog, a ritual every morning just after dawn. His early start would beat the oppressive Texas heat and get his day started the right way. He had only one item on his agenda today, taking the life of that ice cream purveyor. He'd seen on Facebook that Sugar would be working the westside of Cedar Creek Lake near the Key Ranch Estates. This would be a tricky mission. He'd have to snatch Sugar off the boat and into the water without anyone seeing the murder. It would take every ounce of his SEAL training to pull off this very tricky mission.

Business was brisk for the ice cream guy on a day when the temperature would touch one hundred degrees on the lake. He loved the smiles on the kid's faces, and their parents, too, as they enjoyed his frozen treats. He was oblivious to the small, rented speedboat that seemed to be off in the distance, watching his every move.

The sun was beginning to disappear into the horizon. Normally, Sugar would be heading to the dock to assure he arrived before darkness, but he was having his best sales day ever. He spotted three children waving at him from their dock and chugged on over. They shouted with glee as he pulled up. Ten more children came spilling onto the dock. An adult joined them, pulling out his credit card and telling Sugar they were having a birthday party.

Three hundred yards away, fading into the growing darkness was the boat piloted by the admiral. He was gleeful too. Sugar had never worked this late while he'd been staking him out. Now, his greediness would allow the killer to drown him under the cover of darkness. He put the boat in neutral and waited for the pontoon boat to leave the dock.

Sugar used the Square app on his phone to accept the credit card. The sale had been for over $75 with the tip. An awesome way to end the day. He thanked the father, waved goodbye to the kids and headed home. He turned on his running lights because the lake was now totally under the cover of darkness. There was only a sliver of moon shining on to the lake.

A few minutes later, near the middle of the lake, he saw a small speedboat with a man on board waving his arms. Sugar thought maybe the man was having engine issues, so he headed that way to help him out. He was humming to himself after a very profitable day on the water.

The admiral made a 360-degree sweep of the lake. There was not another boat in sight as Sugar's brightly painted pontoon pulled next to his speedboat. Sugar smiled, "What's up buddy are you having engine issues?"

The admiral nodded, "Yes sir. I can't get the dang motor to fire. Do you know anything about outboard motors?"

Sugar, with a rope in his hand, maneuvered next to the speedboat, and tossed the rope to the admiral so he could tie the boats together. The admiral smiled, "Oh. You're the ice cream man."

Sugar grinned broadly, "Yes sir. That's me. Let me take a look at that motor." He opened the side gate on the twenty-five-foot pontoon boat and jumped onto the rented speedboat.

The killer sized up his quarry. He was a bit surprised how strong and burly the ice cream guy was close up. They shook hands, and again the admiral was surprised by the strength of the grip. It was clear it would be a difficult struggle to wrestle the dude to the ground. He'd have to surprise him, also being sure not to cause any bruises or other marks that the police could focus on to make the case it was not an accidental drowning.

The admiral's mind was racing, remembering moves he'd been taught years ago during Navy SEAL training. To the admiral's advantage, Sugar climbed onto the rear of the boat, leaning over to remove the outboard cowl. That was his mistake. The killer delivered a strong kick to his back, knocking the surprised man off the boat as he hit the water with a loud splash.

Moreland was on top of him in a split second, pinning his arms behind his back. Sugar was strong, but the former Navy SEAL had him in a death grip. Unknown to the killer, Sugar also did not know how to swim, putting him at a further disadvantage. The admiral gulped a deep breath of air and using his own powerful legs drove both of them deep into the dark waters.

Sugar fought mightily to free his arms, but the killer's honed technique made it impossible to break the grip. The ice cream man was also a chain smoker, so he could only hold his breath a few seconds. The average SEAL can hold their breath two-to-three minutes during underwater training. The admiral was one of the few who could hold his breath for nearly five minutes. Sugar never had a chance.

As the killer continued to use his strong legs to go deeper and deeper, Sugar quickly ran out of air and stopped struggling. The admiral stayed underwater for nearly five minutes before releasing the inert body on the lake bottom, about thirty-five feet down. Using strong arm and leg strokes he drove his body back to the surface, gasping for air as he surfaced.

The admiral wiped down both boats, assuring he'd left no fingerprints, untied the rope, and slowly motored away. He left Sugar's pontoon boat floating gently on the water as a slight breeze came out of the south. Once he was a hundred yards away, the killer pushed the throttle control forward and roared away into the darkness.

The next morning, Sheriff King was engaged in a brisk Pickle Ball game with Buddy, and another couple. The woman on the other team, Paula Duxbury, was a top-notch player, while her companion was just learning the game. Paula used a backhand punch to win the set. This cool little shot always catches your opponent off guard. The backhand punch shot is typically used at the net that literally involves you punching at the ball. The shot is designed to turn a high dink that your opponent made to a shot that shoots straight at them.

Both teams shook hands, and King grabbed a towel. Although it was early in the morning, the outdoor court was already hot in the steamy Texas heat. She was interrupted by the ringtone on her iPhone. It was the dispatcher. King said, "Hello. This is Crystal King. What's up, Patsy?" Buddy saw his wife's face become very serious and upset as she listened to the call. The sheriff said, "Alright, Patsy. Give me an hour to shower and meet the dive team over at Key Ranch."

She gave Buddy a look that said don't ask right now. Paula was sitting right next to her, gulping water, filled with electrolytes. Crystal smiled, said her goodbyes, and headed to Buddy's truck. She hopped in and slammed the door. Buddy crawled into the driver's seat, "What was that call about, babe? You don't look happy."

Crystal was already on the phone with Tolbert Masterson, "Tolbert, this is Crystal. It appears we may have another drowning. This time it's a very popular guy who sells ice cream from a pontoon boat on the lake."

Buddy quietly said, "Oh, no. Not Sugar?" Crystal nodded. She told Masterson to meet her at Key Ranch in an hour.

She ended the call and turned to Buddy, "I'm afraid so. A number of boaters just found the pontoon boat floating near the middle of the lake. There's no sign of Sugar. Buddy, that could be the second mysterious drowning since Moreland has been stuck in jail. That pretty much proves she's not the killer." She gazed out the window. Buddy said nothing. This was very bad news.

Admiral Moreland had finished his brisk walk about an hour ago. Now, he sat in the tiny, rundown motel sipping on a cup of black coffee from the Gun Barrel City Starbucks. So far, there'd been nothing on the local TV stations about the drowning of the ice cream guy. He was hoping for a big splash.

Dwayne Murphy was finishing breakfast at the Berry Laurel Café in Athens. Today he had his usual coffee with three sugars, and a southern egg casserole. His phone buzzed. It was one of his fishing guide informants. "Hey, Dwayne. I'm over at Key Ranch and the Sheriff's Office dive team is here. So is that ice cream dude's pontoon boat. I believe it was empty." Murphy thanked his source, grabbed two more bites of breakfast and stormed out the door.

Sixty-Five

KING AND MASTERSON were aboard one of the dive boats, watching as a detective tried to retrieve fingerprints from Sugar's pontoon. After a half hour of scouring the boat, he joined Crystal on the dive boat. He was not happy, "I'm afraid this is a pretty worthless effort, Sheriff. We had a brief rain shower overnight that washed a lot of fingerprints and any other evidence. Plus, and I can't be sure, but I believe this boat was carefully wiped down to get rid of any fingerprints." King thanked him for his work and turned her attention to the SCUBA divers searching for Sugar Duckstein.

A number of boats were keeping a respectful distance, as they watched the search. One of the boats kept coming and drove right next to the Sheriff's dive boat. King was fuming, it was Dwayne Murphy. She snapped at him, "Murphy, this is a potential crime scene, so get the hell back with the other gawkers before I haul you into a jail cell."

Undaunted, the pesky reporter replied, "C'mon, Sheriff. This is a big story. Sugar is one of the most well-known guys around the lake. He had that little ice cream shop for a decade before he hit on the pontoon idea. This is a big story."

King was unmoved, "You're going to be part of the story if you don't get the hell out of here right now, Murphy. Now scoot!"

She turned her back to the reporter. Murphy quickly snapped a few pictures, received another nasty look from King, and moved away from the search perimeter. The sheriff turned her attention back to the search.

The admiral flipped on the fuzzy television in his motel room. It was five o'clock. Time for the local news. The lead story on this day was the search for the beloved ice cream man who disappeared overnight from his pontoon. The reporter did a live report from a boat outside the search area. She spoke glowingly about what a wonderful man Sugar was. She described him as an institution on Cedar Creek Lake. Moreland smiled; this was exactly the high-profile coverage he was hoping for when he snuffed out Duckstein's life.

The sun was almost out of sight and Sheriff King was about to call off the search for Sugar until tomorrow as darkness settled in across Cedar Creek Lake. They couldn't drag the bottom with their big hooks because the water was so deep, so SCUBA divers had been searching in thirty-five feet of water. The fact that the wind had been dormant for a couple days led them to believe neither his body, nor the pontoon boat, had drifted far from the spot he apparently fell into the water.

Suddenly there was a shout from a diver about a hundred yards from Crystal's boat, "I've got 'em." Another diver joined him, and soon the water-logged body of Sugar Duckstein surfaced in their arms. Crystal's hope that he had simply abandoned the boat on the lake was crushed. Sugar had joined five other victims in recent mysterious drownings.

Duckstein's body was carefully laid on the bottom of the sheriff's boat. A quick check of the body found no bruising, no gunshot or other injuries. It became clear that Sugar had drowned. A deputy said to King, "What a shame. Such a great guy. I told him many times that he needed to take swim lessons."

Crystal turned her attention to the deputy, "Sugar couldn't swim?"

The deputy shook his head from side to side, "Not a lick, Sheriff. He could have fallen overboard and drowned because he couldn't swim."

The sheriff nodded grimly, "But he also could have been tossed overboard and held underwater like we believe happened to the other victims."

Tolbert Masterson, who'd been meeting with some of his Texas Ranger contingent, drove up to the shore just as the boat with Sugar's body reached the dock. He and King huddled off to the side. Masterson said, "So this is our sixth victim, Crystal. Two of the drownings occurred while we've had Romy Moreland in a jail cell. What the hell is going on?"

King shrugged. "There seem to be two options, Tolbert. The first is he fell overboard and drown. I'm told he couldn't swim. Option two is very disturbing. Either we've been focusing on the wrong suspect, or there is now a second copycat killer out here continuing whatever mission Moreland is on. It's a mess."

Their conversation was cut short as a contingent of reporters descended on them, led by Dwayne Murphy. He shouted, "Sheriff, this is drowning number six. Do you have any suspects?" The reporters were now right next to her, some shoving microphones and cell phones at her to capture her reply. Sheriff King took a deep breath and said, "We have just recovered the body of a beloved icon around the lake. Our thoughts and prayers go out to Mr. Duckstein's family. We have just begun our investigation, but I'm told by one of my deputies that Sugar did not know how to swim. That could have been a factor in this drowning death."

A cacophony of voices shouted at the sheriff, but once again Murphy was louder than the rest as he asked, "So let me get this straight, Sheriff. You're saying Sugar fell overboard and drowned because he couldn't swim? How about the other five unsolved drowning deaths? Did they also not know how to swim?"

An exasperated King snapped, "I'm not sayin' that, Murphy,

and you know it. We'll have more information as we continue our investigation. Goodnight everyone." With questions raining down on her, Sheriff King briskly walked to her police cruiser and drove away without so much as a glance back at the media horde.

Sixty-Six

THE ADMIRAL WAITED two days and then had his Savannah lawyer post bail money for his daughter. He wanted to remain anonymous. The lawyer sent a cryptic note to Romy as well.

Room 3. Lakeside Motel. 9 p.m. today.

The note was in a sealed envelope.

To be opened by Romy Moreland only.

Moreland was doing her usual two hundred daily sit-ups in her cell, when a guard approached, "Grab your stuff, Moreland, you've been bailed out." Romy was shocked, "What? Who posted my bond? Haines?" The guard shrugged indifferently, "No idea. Let's go!"

Moreland signed some papers, was given a bag with her wallet, watch, and phone, and stepped into the bright Texas sunshine for the first time in days. Her mind was racing. *Who is the person in room three of that seedy motel? Why did they post bail?* She didn't know anyone around the lake. Her car was brought from the impound lot, and Moreland had enough cash to pay the storage bill. She jumped in her car and drove to her rented home.

The copycat killer munched on a fast food burger she'd grabbed on the way to her house, as the sun set in East Texas. Her curiosity was off the charts, wondering who the mystery person was who posted her bond. She aimlessly watched an old *"Cheers"* episode on the TV set, waiting for 9 p.m.

It would take about twenty minutes to reach the motel just outside of Tool. At 8:40, Romy grabbed her pistol, checked the clip, and headed out the door. She wanted to be sure to protect herself from this mystery person.

In Unit 3, Admiral Moreland sipped on a diet coke, glancing at his watch every few minutes, trying to will the time to go faster. He was anxious to see his only daughter and help her plan strategic moves to get her out of this mess. Her father had already taken the lives of two innocent people in an effort to keep Romy from being charged with murder. It went against his personal code to kill non-combatants, but he was determined to save his only child.

At 9:05, Romy Moreland drove into the dirt parking lot of the dilapidated motel. As she exited her car, Moreland tucked her 9mm Magnum 9 pistol with built-in silencer into the rear waistband of her blue jeans. She had no idea who was on the other side of the door of Unit 3.

The admiral heard the knock on his door, unlocked it, and opened it, ready to greet his daughter. As the door swung open, Romy was shocked to see her father. It had been years since they'd even talked on the phone. The admiral reached out to give her a hug, but Romy recoiled, pushed him away and said, "What are you doing here?"

As her father stood uncomfortably, Romy asked him again. "Seriously it's been years. How did you find me?"

Her father managed a small grin, "It's good to see you too, Romy."

She was having none of it. "Good to see me? I said what the hell are you doing here?" She defiantly crossed her arms, staring at him. This was not how the admiral pictured this reunion going.

He said, "Romy, I'm here to get you out of this mess. That's why I bailed you out of jail, so we could work together on this."

His daughter snorted, "Work together. Why do you care? You've never cared about me. To you, I was always your ugly daughter when you really wanted a boy to follow in your Navy footsteps.

Even when I did the exact same thing, you never even gave me a hug and told me you were proud of me. You were too busy being the stern father-figure."

The admiral sighed, and slumped down, sitting on the lumpy bed. "I admit I have made mistakes in the past, but when I read about the copycat killings around this God-forsaken place, I figured it had to be you avenging Cody's death."

Romy finally sat down on an old wooden desk chair, "So what, you suddenly loved me and wanted to help for the first time in your life?"

Her father nodded, "Exactly."

Romy snorted derisively, "Really? You're a new man? Not the guy who drove my mother to alcohol because you ignored her for years until she drank herself to death? Not the guy who has never in his life given me a loving hug, or told me you love me?" She shook her head in disgust.

The elder Moreland replied, "I have killed two people for you, Romy. I figured if two more drownings occurred while you were locked up that the police would stop suspecting you. I am here to help you." The man who was used to men saluting him and obeying his every command was exasperated and frustrated. He clearly was not getting through to his daughter.

Romy just stared at him in stony silence. The admiral said, "I am right, Romy. You are the copycat killer, right? I assume you are going after the sheriff because she was the one who stabbed Cody to death?" His daughter was confused. Her father had mentioned Cody Martin twice. How did he know that Cody was the love of her life? Hell, how did he even know Martin existed?

Romy asked, "How do you know Cody Martin? Did he serve under you on some Navy SEAL missions? He was the only person in my life who loved me. Cody always watched out for me in the SEALs. He saved my life on two missions. Then he disappeared and the next time I hear his name they're calling him the Frogman Of Cedar Creek. He was on a killing spree here to get back at all the people who had picked on him unmercifully during his school years, He was a wimp who was turned into a killing machine by the SEALs and it eventually cost him his life. I lost the only person in the world who loved me for who I am?"

The admiral took a deep breath, "Romy, I'm afraid Cody Martin had a secret he never told you." Her father stopped, stared into space, with his mind racing. Should he tell Romy the terrible secret about Cody? After all this time she deserved to know. He looked back to Romy who was intently watching him with a look of curiosity on her homely face.

Romy said, "Secret? What are you talking about? Cody and I had a special relationship, and I loved him. Yes, I'm here to scare the locals and ultimately to take the life of that woman who killed Cody. I will gain vengeance for his murder!" The admiral looked at his daughter with a sad expression. Romy prompted him again, in a raised voice this time, "What is the big secret?"

The admiral took a deep breath. He was about to spill a secret that he'd kept for nearly thirty years. He asked Romy, "When you say Cody loved you, where you intimate with him?"

The daughter was taken aback by the very personal question, "And how is that any of your damn business?" Again, the admiral paused this was a much more difficult discussion than he'd imagined.

Romy was growing impatient, "You have sent men into battle to be killed. You've taken the lives of how many people? How can this be so difficult? Spill the beans, I need to be on my way and don't have any more time for this." The admiral nodded. It was time.

He gazed into his daughter's angry and apprehensive eyes, "Romy, nearly three decades ago I had an affair with a woman I'd met in a bar in Annapolis. We had a son together. Her name was Barbara Martin. She named our son Cody. He was your half-brother."

Romy was furious. She balled her fists, pounded on the desk filled with cigarette burns, and shouted almost in a primal scream, "What are you saying? Cody was my brother? And you never told me? Did he know? Tell me right now, did Cody know I was his sister?"

The admiral nodded, "Yes. I told him when he was a teenager."

Sixty-Seven

ROMY'S FURY WAS boiling over, as she said through clenched teeth, "And you didn't think to tell me?" She angrily stood up, "I loved him, not as a brother, but as the only person in the world who really seemed to care about me. He took me under his wing. Now, I find out he was just trying to protect his sister. He really didn't love me in the way I loved him. Now, I find out the only person I have ever loved was not my boyfriend, but my damn brother instead!" She paced the room, shaking in her anger.

Her father tried to appease her, "I am so sorry, Romy. I was just trying to protect you. I had Cody assigned to your SEAL unit so he could look after you. I was just trying to keep you safe."

Romy exploded, "Keep me safe! I'm sure you and Cody had a good laugh about this ugly woman, who was really his sister, falling in love with him. Thanks for making a fool out of me!" She was clearly ready to erupt in a blind rage.

The admiral took a step toward his daughter, he wanted to do something he'd never done before, give her a warm hug and tell her he'd always loved her, and wanted the best for her. He stopped in his tracks when Romy reached behind her, and suddenly aimed her silenced pistol at him.

He stammered, "Romy, what are you doing? I'm your father. I

just killed two people to help you go free. I'm so sorry I never told you about Cody."

Romy was literally shaking. She'd never been angrier in her life. They'd made her the fool. She was sure they shared a number of laughs about her professing her love for a guy she had no idea was her brother. This was the most embarrassing moment of a life filled with embarrassing episodes. She always felt that Cody never even kissed her because he was shy. Now, she knew it was because he knew she was his sister.

Her father was talking in a quiet voice, attempting to tamp down her anger. It was a futile effort. Romy waved the gun at her father as she said in a menacing voice, "Let's go. Get into my car." The admiral raised his hand to protest but then he noticed Romy flipped off the safety on the pistol. He decided it would be best to comply, and then keep trying to calm her down and to understand why he'd kept the secret from her for so long.

With the pistol trained on his back, the elder Moreland slid into the passenger seat, while Romy got behind the wheel. She was aware that her father had been highly trained in combat tactics in the Navy. Romy did not want to give him a chance to disarm her, "Put both hands on the dashboard, palms down, and keep them there, or I will shoot you in the head."

The admiral was running possible escape scenarios in his head, but he also was aware that Romy was highly trained as well and was apparently angry enough to shoot him if provoked. He decided the best option was to comply with her orders and continue to calmly talk to her. Romy started the engine, checked her surroundings, there was no one in sight, and slowly drove out of the parking lot of the motel.

It was a dark night with clouds obscuring the moon and stars as she flipped on her GPS and dialed in a location. They traveled in silence with the admiral intently watching his daughter. She seemed to be calming down as they navigated a number of back roads heading deeper and deeper into tree-lined woods.

After about thirty-five minutes a dirt road led them to the

edge of a pond. The admiral spoke for the first time, "Where are we, Romy?" His daughter didn't answer. She put the car in park, shut off the engine, and told him to get out of the car. He opened the passenger door and ran quick escape calculations through his head. It appeared futile. If he tried to run away, Romy could simply shoot him. *Would she be able to kill her own father?* Sadly, as an angry former Navy SEAL, he was sure the answer could be yes.

The admiral asked again, "Romy, where are we?" The clouds had disappeared, and in the light of the moon he could see a pond a few yards away. His daughter said, "This is where Crystal King killed Cody. Stabbed him to death with his own knife. Despite what you have told me, I will remain on my mission to gain vengeance for his death. But I'm afraid there will be no more missions for you." She gave him an ominous look.

Griffin Moreland was desperate to come up with an escape plan. He was now sure that she was going to kill him. That became clear when Romy said, "You are no different than all those people who shunned me all these years because of my looks. They laughed at me too."

The father protested, "Romy, Cody and I never laughed at you. We were just trying to keep you safe." For the first time ever he said, "I love you!"

That brought a belly laugh from Romy, "It's a little late to tell me that, Admiral. I don't believe you. You're just trying to keep me from shooting you dead."

The father tried another approach, "Not at all, Romy. I really care about you. Why else would I kill two people to get the spotlight off of you, and I bailed you out of jail."

Romy snorted, "Too little. Too late, old man."

The admiral had run out of options. He was sure she was going to shoot him out of anger. His only chance was to surprise her, wrestle the gun away, and point it at her. Then he'd decide his next steps. Deep in thought, he was aware of how closely Romy was watching him. She was sure he'd bull rush her at any moment, and she was ready.

The elder Moreland suddenly made his move. He was too slow. Romy aimed the pistol and fired a bullet right between his eyes. He fell to the ground in a heap, unmoving. In her sick, angry mind Romy had decided back at the motel to bring her father to the pond where Cody was killed, and to drag his body to the hidden cave at the end of the pond. It was where The Frogman had kept Crystal King before her husband helped her escape and she killed Cody.

Romy went into her car, shed her clothes, except for bra and panties, pulled out a pair of swim fins, snorkel and mask and headed back to her dead father. She dragged his lifeless body to the edge of the pond, slipped on the swim fins, grabbed him by the back of the shirt collar, and breathing through the snorkel swam the few hundred yards to the other end of the pond.

Once there, she dragged the body underwater, and onto the dirt floor of the hidden cave. She dropped it there and swam back toward her car. When she reached shore, Romy slipped off the fins, carried them to the car, grabbed a towel and dried herself off.

She then sat behind the steering wheel and pulled the battered picture of Cody Martin out of her purse.

Tears rolled down her cheeks as she held the picture and thought of how much she loved the man who turned out to be her brother. How could Cody and her father mislead her for so long. No wonder Cody never wanted to hold her, kiss her or truly be her boyfriend. She could not get the thought out of her troubled mind that her father and Cody had been laughing at her clumsy efforts to be his girlfriend.

Her anger again reached the boiling point, as she suddenly ripped the picture of Cody to shreds and tossed the pieces out the window. He was a liar. He misled her. He probably made fun of her behind her back, but despite all that she had to admit to herself that she still loved him. She was also determined to avenge his death at the hand of Crystal King. After all, Cody might not have been the love of her life, but he was still her brother. She wiped the tears from her eyes and drove home. She had to be in court in the morning.

Sixty-Eight

ROMY MORELAND'S TRIAL was scheduled to start at 10 a.m. at the Henderson County Courthouse. She arrived at 9:30 to find her attorney pacing back and forth outside the courtroom. Harold Haines spotted his client and hurried over, "Where have you been? I was surprised when you weren't at the jail."

Romy replied, "An old friend of mine heard about my situation and sent bail money. I spent last night in my own bed, no thanks to you."

Haines shook his head, "Always the antagonistic one! Put on your friendly face, I need the jury to like you. I really think we can beat this charge either today or tomorrow. They have no case."

Haines, as usual, was dressed to the nines. He meant to impress. His suit, a Brioni grey and black checked wool New Plume suit set him back over $6,000. He was also wearing an Ice Grey velvet $300 bow tie from Brioni. His shoes were black with an incredible shine. Even Romy had to concede he looked like a million bucks.

The judge gaveled the proceedings to order and a jury was quickly seated. Then Henderson County District Attorney Blair Brooke took center stage to begin the trial. Addressing the jury with her opening argument, Brooke noted, "The defendant is charged with assault on a peace officer, a third-degree felony, as well as burglary." She pointed at Moreland, "This woman was surprised while burglarizing a home, and then severely beat the police officer who responded to the call. He remains in the hospital with severe head injuries. This is a cut and dried case. She got caught and she attacked an officer of the law to escape." Brooke sat down.

Harold Haines jumped to his feet, immediately commanding the attention of every set of eyes in the nearly empty courtroom. There were a few media in the gallery, including Dwayne Murphy. Haines got right to it, "Ladies and gentlemen, these are trumped up charges against my client. The only supposed witness is the police officer who was so severely beaten the doctors tell me his memory is very foggy and deteriorating more every day. I certainly don't condone anyone attacking a law enforcement official, but I also don't want to see my innocent client convicted of something she did not do."

He approached the jury box, placed both hands on the front rail, and leaned toward the jurors looking them in the eye one after another as he said, "Studies have shown that mistaken eyewitness testimony accounts for about half of the wrongful convictions in this country. That same study found that it is not uncommon for people to remember false information and details of a supposed crime when they are scared, nervous or afraid. Now, I know the policemen who was beaten is a trained professional, but I have subpoenaed his doctor, who will testify that not only has the officer never identified his supposed attacker in person in a lineup which is common practice, but he has little memory of what happened on the night in question. In short, he is an unreliable witness who has never met my client. The state has no case. They are grasping at those proverbial straws trying to convict someone, even if it is an innocent person like the defendant." He strolled back and forth in front of the jury box. The man was an amazing actor. He looked like someone had just kicked his puppy. Brooke noticed some of the jurors nodding in agreement with Haines' opening comments.

The District Attorney knew her case was weak. They had found no evidence that Moreland was actually in the house, outside of the fight with Officer Orville Richter. Since he was still in the hospital ICU, he was unable to come to court and testify. And, he was in such bad shape, that they could not even do video testimony. Haines was right, due to Richter's injuries, they never were able to follow usual procedures and have him pick Moreland out of a lineup.

The judge's voice interrupted her thoughts, "Miss Brooke call your first witness, please." Brooke nodded and brought another police officer to the stand. He'd been the investigator on the case. The detective explained that someone had broken into the Malaby ranch house, had been confronted by Officer Richter and he had been beaten so badly he remained in the Intensive Care Unit at the Athens Hospital. He droned on. The detective was not at all confident. It was the first time he'd testified in a trial. His presentation, in a word, was boring.

Brooke thanked the detective for his testimony, and reluctantly turned the witness over to Haines. This time the defense attorney's demeanor was much like a concerned parent, feeling sorry for the inept detective. As expected, Haines sliced his testimony to ribbons. Brooke watched the jury and knew instantly she'd lost them to both Haines' charm and her lack of solid evidence.

The judge asked, "Rebuttal questions for your witness, Miss Brooke?"

The district attorney had learned in law school that when your witness clearly is not having the desired effect on the jury to hustle them out the door as quickly as possible. Brooke stood up, "I have no further questions, Your Honor." She sat down with a glum look on her face. Brooke had tried to project confidence, but the effort fell as flat as her witness. Unfortunately, for Brooke many jurors took note of her sullen expression.

Haines, who knew victory was soon to be his, rested his case without calling any witnesses. The judge banged her gavel, "We'll break for lunch. Closing arguments begin at one o'clock sharp." Brooke hurriedly left the courtroom. She had about ninety minutes to craft a closing argument that would dig her out of a deep hole. Haines took Romy Moreland to a leisurely lunch. He already knew what he was going to say to achieve his not guilty verdict.

While the district attorney wrestled with her case, Sheriff King was also about to receive some bad news. Tolbert Masterson walked into her office just before lunch, "Crystal, do you have a minute?" He settled into a chair in front of her desk, "I'm afraid I have bad news. Our entire contingent of Texas Rangers has been called to the Rio Grande. They are being overwhelmed by migrants right now. I'm sorry to leave you high and dry, Crystal."

The sheriff smiled, "I understand, Tolbert. I'm grateful for your help. You be safe down there." With that they shook hands, and Masterson headed out.

Sixty-Nine

AT ONE O'CLOCK on the dot, the judge gaveled the court case back into session. District Attorney Brooke tried mightily to get the jury back on her side. She focused on the victim, "Defense counsel is making a big deal out of the fact that the defendant is unable to face her accuser. There's a simple explanation for that. Officer Richter is still hospitalized with severe injuries from the defendant beating him almost to death. Immediately after the assault, Officer Richter helped our sketch artist craft a spot-on drawing of his attacker. He also identified her later from the picture on her driver's license. So, while Mr. Haines is trying to make it seem like his client is not guilty simply because Officer Richter is too injured to be here in person is a Trojan Horse. His client is guilty and he knows it!" She sat down, trying to get a read on the jury.

Haines was already strolling toward the jury box. His approach for his final argument was a combination of preacher, and doting grandfather. He was masterful as usual. His voice was barely above a whisper, which caused the jury to listen intently to hear him. Haines looked from juror to juror as he began, "Ladies and gentlemen, I don't want to be too technical here, but the sixth amendment to the constitution is an important tenet of this great country that protects all of us. The so-called 'Confrontation Clause' found in the sixth amendment clearly states that in a criminal case the accused shall enjoy the right to be confronted with witnesses against her."

Haines paused for dramatic effect, then continued, "The clause is intended to prevent the conviction of a defendant upon written evidence without the defendant having the opportunity to face his or her accusers and to put their honesty and truthfulness to test before the jury." He stopped, his expression changed to one of deep concern, "Now, I know we all feel sorry for Officer Richter and wish him a speedy recovery. But, without the opportunity for me to ask him some questions, well, it violates my client's sixth amendment right. That makes your decision easy. To be fair, to follow the law, you must find Romy Moreland not guilty." He thanked them for their unselfish service and sat down.

The jury was out for less than an hour before finding Romy Moreland not guilty of assaulting Officer Richter. It was another victory for the hot shot Dallas lawyer, and a bitter defeat for Blair Brooke. Paperwork was signed, and Moreland walked into the bright afternoon Texas sunlight. She shook hands with Haines, thanked him for his work, and turned and walked away. Moreland was anxious to end the life of Crystal King. She'd run numerous scenarios through her head while sitting in the jail cell. It was time to get to work.

Seventy

WHEN MORELAND GOT back to her rented house, she built a second IED. She and the sheriff were going to go out in a big explosion. Moreland's many solitary hours in the tiny cell had helped her reach the decision to end her life along with King's. She was devastated to learn the love of her life was actually her half-brother, and her father had kept it a secret from her. Moreland was convinced there was nothing more to live for. But first she had to lure King to a meeting, alone. The copycat killer smiled to herself. She knew just the person to set up the meeting.

Using a voice synthesizer, to disguise her own voice, Moreland dialed the number for Dwayne Murphy. When he answered, Murphy heard a voice that sounded like Darth Vader's, "Mr. Murphy. I am the copycat killer you've been writing about. I need you to call Sheriff King and have her meet me tomorrow at 6 p.m. at Tom Finley Park so I can turn myself in. She is to come alone. If she's not I will disappear forever and she'll never find me. Is that clear?"

Murphy's heart was racing. What a scoop. He had to ask, "I will do that but in return I want an exclusive interview with you." Moreland did not answer. The phone line went dead.

Murphy was excited. It was going to make a great exclusive story when he wrote how he helped capture the copycat killer. He dialed Sheriff King. Crystal answered, "What's up Murphy? More conspiracy theories?"

Murphy was undeterred as he responded with a sarcastic voice, "Well, for your information, Sheriff my theory was just proven to be true!"

He had King's attention now, "And what do you mean by that Dwayne?"

Murphy paused for effect, then said, "Because I just got a call from the killer!"

King sat up straight, "What? What are you talking about."

Murphy recounted the phone call from the copycat killer and passed on the message to meet tomorrow. He emphasized, "The killer said if you didn't come alone, he would disappear and you'd never find him."

King asked, "You said the voice was synthesized and sounded like Darth Vader, how could you tell if the call was from a man or a woman?"

Murphy thought about that, "Hmmmm. That's a good question, Sheriff."

King's mind was racing. It could be dangerous to meet alone with the person who tried to kill her by blowing up her squad car. But, at the same time, if the killer was serious about turning themself in, she could prevent another senseless loss of life. Then she turned her attention back to Murphy, "Dwayne, thanks for this. But here are the ground rules. First, you keep this meeting strictly between you and me. Nothing gets printed or posted about the meeting until it's over. You stay the hell away from the park, I don't need you spooking the killer. Finally, because of your cooperation, I will give you an exclusive interview after the person is in custody, and you can take a picture of us heading into the jail. You understand?" Murphy said he did. King thanked him again for being the messenger and hung up the phone.

For the rest of the day, Sheriff King mulled over the best way to handle this situation. She finally decided that the best thing to do was to meet the killer alone, and not to tell anyone, even her husband, about the meeting. So far, this person had drowned six innocent people, made four others disappear, had killed a Mabank officer, and badly beaten one of her men. She had to take a risk to stop the carnage. King did not really buy the fact that if she didn't come alone the killer would simply disappear. The sheriff was sure that if she botched this more law-abiding citizens would be killed.

The next day, the minutes seemed to drag by. King was constantly checking her watch. Finally, it was 5:30. The sheriff had worn her uniform today. She strapped a small ankle holster to her right leg and checked to be sure her Glock 43 was ready to fire if needed. She also strapped on her utility belt with handcuffs, night stick, and a holster containing her larger Glock 22 with its potent .40 caliber Smith & Wesson cartridge that held fifteen rounds. The sheriff grabbed her hat to complete her uniform and headed to her car.

Before she got in, one of her officers used a mirror to check for any IEDs under the vehicle, and then searched inside the cruiser. He finally gave her a thumbs up, and the sheriff headed to Tom Finley Park.

Meanwhile, despite being warned, Dwayne Murphy pulled into the parking lot at the park. He was driving a Ram pickup truck and towing his 2013 twenty-four-foot Pantera cigarette boat. The boat looked brand new as Murphy gave it a great deal of TLC. It was powered by a 425-horsepower inboard engine giving it a top speed of seventy miles an hour. There were three other vehicles parked in the lot, with their empty trailers giving him some cover. He hunkered down in the driver's seat and waited, trying to stay out of sight.

Seventy-One

AT EXACTLY SIX O'CLOCK, Sheriff King drove into the gravel parking lot. Her eyes swept the scene. She saw four parked vehicles. Three of them had empty boat trailers, and one had some fancy boat on it. Outside of that, there wasn't a soul around. The killer obviously knew there were two waves of boat launches. The fisherman who come early in the morning and leave by mid-afternoon, and the second wave when fisherman get out of work at five o'clock. That made six o'clock the perfect time to meet with no witnesses around the park. It was also the middle of the week, a slow time at the park. On the weekend there would be boaters, swimmers and picnickers everywhere.

Sheriff King pulled the police cruiser into a shaded spot at the far end of the parking lot, away from the bridge traffic. As she shut off the engine, King noticed a lone figure with her back to the sheriff, sitting on a picnic table. The person had on blue jeans, and a hoodie pulled over their head. That was certainly out of place since the temperature was eighty-three degrees on this sun-bathed day.

King slowly walked toward the hooded person, her hand at the ready on her pistol. When she was about ten feet away the hooded person said, "Stop right there, Sheriff."

King halted in her tracks. Her brain was on high alert for anything. Before she'd left the office King had pulled on her Kevlar body armor as a safety precaution. She replied, "OK. You asked to meet with me here to turn yourself in, so I want you to raise your arms above your head, slowly turn around and lay flat on the ground."

Her order was met with a hearty laugh. Without turning around the suspect said, "That's a good one, Sheriff, but you're not the one in charge here. I am. So, I want you to drop your utility belt and walk slowly toward me."

King quickly replied, "I was told you wanted to meet to surrender to me. That doesn't put you in charge."

The hooded figure kept their back to the sheriff, "I will. But under my terms. And the first one is for you to drop your utility belt and slowly walk toward me so we can talk."

By this time, King knew she was talking to another woman. She decided to change the game a bit, "I know who you are. You are Romy Moreland. But I don't understand why you are killing people who did nothing to you and trying to kill me."

Still with her back to the sheriff, Moreland said, "Good guess, Sheriff. Now drop your damn utility belt right now."

King's retorted, "And if I don't?"

The hooded one said, "I will turn around and shoot you in the head before you have time to unholster your weapon. Now, drop the belt."

King finally complied with the killer's request, partially comforted by the fact she had the small Glock in her ankle holster, and aware that she did not want to antagonize her. It was important to keep the suspect calm in these situations. Moreland heard the belt hit the ground, and simultaneously she spun around pointing a .357 magnum at King's head. She said, "That's better, Sheriff. Now, we're going to walk to my boat and go for a little ride."

King demurred, "No. Let's just have our talk and then we'll get the cuffs from my utility belt, and you'll surrender like you promised. You want this over, and so do I. And the fact that you voluntarily turned yourself in will benefit you with the district attorney."

Moreland smiled. "You really are a rookie sheriff. Did you think you'd come here, and I'd follow your directions like a little puppy?" She snorted, "You've got a lot to learn, if you live long enough."

King tried the soft approach, "Romy, I'd really like to know why you are killing all these people? I'm sorry that I had to kill Cody Martin, but it was a case of him or me. I had no choice. Was he your boyfriend in the Navy SEALs?"

King had no idea that her comment would get the reaction it did. She didn't know, of course, about Moreland loving Martin, and then finding out he was really her half-brother. In an instant, a dark cloud passed over Moreland's face as it turned into a grotesque mask of pain. She said gruffly, "That's none of your damn business. Now, get into my boat or I swear to God I'll put a bullet between your eyes. Move!" The killer picked up King's utility belt and threw it over her shoulder.

Murphy was sneaking a peek at the two women, being very careful not to let them know he was watching. He was concerned when he saw the person in the hood holding a pistol on the sheriff. That concern grew as he saw them walking to the dock.

King did as Moreland asked and walked slowly toward a twenty-foot runabout tied to the dock. Her mind was working hard to come up with ideas to disarm the killer. At the same time, King knew she had to be wary of Moreland's combat skills learned in the SEALs. The sheriff knew it was probably a bit foolish to have dropped her holstered weapon, but she was hopeful to be able to diffuse the situation through a calm approach. It was a risky move at best.

They reached the boat and Moreland waved the gun toward the bow seats, "Sit down up there. And don't try anything."

King was still trying to figure out why her question about Cody Martin had set off the killer. She said, "I'm complying with your wishes. We can go for a boat ride, talk about whatever you want to discuss, and then return here so you can surrender."

Moreland threw the dock rope into the boat and looked at King as you would a young child, "Sheriff, do you really think I'm going to surrender to you? That's not going to happen. We're going out together in a blaze of glory."

That comment sent chills down the sheriff's back. Crystal had hoped by being calm and cooperative she could gain Moreland's trust. But she had misread the situation. The killer was going to commit suicide and take her down as well. She'd been in what seemed like an impossible situation when Martin held her captive in the underground cove. She'd escaped death that day. Could she do it again?

Dwayne Murphy watched the boat move farther away from the park and into the middle of the lake. He had to do something because he saw the suspect holding a gun on the sheriff, after he saw King drop her pistol along with her utility belt. Murphy made his decision. He backed his speedy boat down the launch ramp and into the lake. He tied the boat to the small dock next to the ramp and parked his truck and now empty trailer.

The cigarette boat roared to life, and Murphy zoomed onto the lake. He was about a half mile behind the killer's boat. He watched it pass by the nearly hidden island in the lake. He figured it was traveling at about twenty-five miles an hour. It would be easy to catch up to the boat. The question was, once he got there, what should he do to keep King from being shot by the woman holding the gun on her?

Seventy-Two

KING CONTINUED HER so far futile efforts to calm down the suspect. But she figured as long as she could keep her talking, she probably wouldn't shoot her. The sheriff said, "Romy, what can I do to help you get out of this mess. If you turn yourself in, I can work out a deal with the district attorney."

Moreland's eyes narrowed as she looked at the sheriff, "First of all, I don't believe you. You're still trying to gain my confidence like it tells you to do in the police manual. Give it up. That won't happen." She briefly gazed into the distance, then turned sad eyes toward King, "I have been picked on, laughed at and called ugly my entire life. Then I met what I thought was a wonderful man during my time in the Navy SEALs. For the first time in my life, I found a man who looked after me, and I stupidly believed loved me as much as I loved him, even though we never got physical." She pointed the pistol menacingly at King, "Then you killed him! Yeah, I came here to avenge his death, and eventually to draw you into a situation where I could kill you."

King started to respond but Moreland wasn't finished. "Stop talking! Then while I'm in jail my father comes here and drowns two people because he believes that will get you off my back for the other murders. It would convince you I wasn't the copycat killer."

Tears were now rolling down her cheeks. She wiped her nose and continued, "And then my father tells me that Cody was actually my half-brother and my father had him assigned to my SEAL unit to look after me. Cody never had any interest in me. I'm sure he and my father had many a laugh about how the poor ugly sister fell in love with her own brother." She stopped talking but continued to sob as tears flowed.

King asked, "And where is your father now, Romy?"

Moreland gave her a small smile. "I shot him in the head and dragged him to the same cave where Cody kept you captive. It seemed like a fitting resting place for the old bastard." All the pieces were falling into place for King. She now knew what happened, but that knowledge would be useless if she was dead. It was very clear to the sheriff that Romy Moreland was mentally unstable, and perfectly capable of killing her any moment.

Murphy shadowed the runabout, staying about a quarter mile behind. So far, the suspect didn't seem to notice him following them down the lake. He was wrestling with the best way to swoop in and save the sheriff without getting her, or himself, killed. He stayed the course for now.

Seventy-Three

CRYSTAL'S HEART BEAT faster as Moreland set the IED on the boat floor between both of them. She watched as the copycat killer flipped a switch, and a big red digital display ticked down from three minutes.

Moreland gave her a big grin, "It'll all be over soon, Sheriff. This bomb will kill both of us and destroy this boat in a big fireball. You will be showered with nails and die instantly, just like me. Then my nightmare life will be over."

Crystal tried again to penetrate the killer's mind to talk her out of this crazy ending. "Romy, killing both of us won't solve a thing. You have a lot of life left. Don't do this!"

Moreland snorted, "I told you to give it up, King. You're wrong. This is the perfect ending. I kill the woman who killed Cody, and I leave this miserable world at the same time." She seemed to savor the moment.

King was terrified but alert. The timer was at 1:34 and counting. She had to do something fast!

Murphy made up his mind. He would roar up behind Moreland's boat to distract her, which might allow the sheriff to gain control, or dive out of the boat and escape. The downside is Moreland might shoot him at the same time. He had no idea there was a bomb on board the boat.

King glanced at the timer...:28. Suddenly she and Moreland heard the roar of a powerful speedboat closing fast. Moreland kept the gun pointed at the sheriff and looked over her shoulder at the intruder.

Murphy was within twenty yards of the boat.

The timer ticked down.

...:12...:11...:10

Murphy was now within a few feet of the other boat.

Moreland fired a shot at him.

Murphy ducked as the bullet ripped into his console just a few inches from his heart.

King started to make a move, but Moreland leveled the gun at her head. She stopped.

...:07...:06...:05

Murphy shoved his throttle all the way forward and rammed the front of his boat into the speedboat with a glancing blow.

The impact knocked Moreland onto her back. Her gun flew out of her hand into the lake.

...:04...:03...:02

Crystal was thrown from the boat by the collision. She landed about six feet from the boat and dove underwater as deep as she could.

At the same time, Murphy made a sharp turn to the left and zipped away from Moreland's boat. The fiberglass on the right front of his expensive boat was cracked but remained intact.

...:01...:00

The IED detonated in a huge explosion, sending the small runabout four feet into the air and snapping its fiberglass hull in two.

Moreland took the brunt of the blast, her body ripped to shreds from the force of the explosion and the hundreds of nails that peppered her body. She was killed instantly.

Murphy was knocked to the floor of his boat by the concussion from the powerful homemade bomb. He scrambled to his feet and regained control of his boat. Seeing the other boat engulfed in flames, split in half, and beginning to sink, Murphy frantically scanned the water for Sheriff King.

The sheriff broke the surface and gulped a big gasp of air. She waved at Murphy. He spotted her and slowly chugged her way. Murphy helped the sheriff into his boat and handed her a towel. He looked at her, "Are you okay, Crystal?"

The sheriff smiled at him, "I'm fine, Dwayne. Thank you so much. You saved my life!"

Murphy grinned at the sheriff, "And I guess that means you owe me that exclusive interview, right?"

King, laughing for the first time in weeks, threw a life preserver at Murphy and said, "Maybe. I guess you earned it." The sheriff used Murphy's mobile phone to call headquarters and explain the situation. Already six boats had sped to the scene after witnessing the explosion.

King ignored the nosy boaters, sank deeply into the special bucket seats on Murphy's boat and relaxed a bit for the first time since the killing spree began. Then using Murphy's phone one more time, she dialed her husband and explained what happened. She was truly glad to be alive and had to admit to herself that Dwayne Murphy was more than a pest. This time he was a hero.

About the Author

This is Gun Barrel City resident Jim Willi's fourth book in the past four years. All four mix real facts about the Cedar Creek Lake area with fictional arsonists and serial killers. They tell the history of local towns, festivals, and area volunteer fire departments.

The books have garnered quite a following with positive comments.

"I couldn't put it down"
"It was a real page turner"
"I love guessing the local places described in the books"
"When is the next book coming out"

Jim enjoys meeting his readers at various events around the lake, as well as speaking to groups like the Cedar Creek Lake Woman's Club, the Cedar Creek Literary Society, the Henderson County Literary Society, The Bookworms in Mabank, the AARP chapter in Dallas, and other local book clubs and libraries.

Before beginning his writing career in his 70s, Jim was a well-known media consultant, and a partner/owner of Audience Research & Development in Fort Worth. During his career, Jim offered strategic advice to CNN, MSNBC, ESPN, The Golf Channel and over a hundred television stations across the country.

Before becoming a consultant, Jim was a radio and TV reporter, anchor, news director and general manager for TV stations in Green Bay, Buffalo, Phoenix and Columbus, Ohio. He won two EMMYs for directing coverage of an explosion in Phoenix. He was selected to be in the *Who's Who of America*.

Jim has owned property on Cedar Creek Lake for over thirty years and moved to the lake full-time when he retired. He believes in giving back to the community. Jim has been a Meals on Wheels driver, president of the Spanish Shores POA, is currently a member of the Rotary Club of Cedar Creek, and president of the board of directors for the East Cedar Creek Freshwater Supply District.

When he's not writing, Jim enjoys traveling, fishing, meeting the folks who buy his books, and hanging out with his two wonderful grandchildren.

www.ingramcontent.com/pod-product-compliance
Lightning Source LLC
Chambersburg PA
CBHW070443030726
47503CB00004B/869